THE OZARK GUARDIAN

WHERE SECRETS SLEEP BENEATH THE PINES

RICHARD J. STEPHENS JR., MA

OZARK PUBLISHING

Contents

FOR MY GIRL'S

Throughout life, each person faces the decision to disregard the legends they hear about, bypassing the possible evidence and laughing them off or to hold on tight to the possibility of their truth. We face the choice of either embracing each thought as a fond fantasy of our imagination, simply disregarding their existence. For this legend, explored throughout this literary offering, I dedicate it to my two youngest daughters, Lilli and Riyann. Within both of you I have found the motivation to look beyond the routine into a world of hope, joy, and anticipation. The fun we have had imagining the beasts hidden deep in the woods have added immensely to my joy as we traverse this journey of life together. Keep looking through the distractions my ladies, for in the distance true revelations can be had.

1

WHISPERS IN THE WOODS

Truly found comfort in the Ozark Mountains, where the dense forests and mist-shrouded peaks offered her refuge. A place where she could be herself, communing with nature and the things others could not see. Unlike her outgoing peers and well-meaning family, she often felt misunderstood and burdened by the expectations of others. Her peers, with their boisterous laughter and ability to easily make friends saw her as an outcast of sorts, a puzzle they couldn't quite figure out and had no interest in solving or even getting to know her. She was simply too different than they were, weird according to many. Her family, though they loved her deeply, often seemed to look through her, never truly understanding the brilliance the child possessed inside. Their expectations were a weight she could never quite stand up under.

It was in the heart of this wilderness that Truly found joy and a willingness to live outside herself. She knew the paths less traveled, the ones that twisted and turned like forgotten memories, leading to hidden hollers where sunlight sprinkled the forest floor and moss-covered rocks seemed to hum with ancient secrets. The rustling of leaves was her symphony, the chattering of squirrels, her conversation, and the singing of the wind through the trees, her lullaby. She added to these solitary hours with imagined friends, companions spun from the threads of her own solitude, their playful whispers a comfort to her lonely soul. These weren't simply the creations of a child's overactive imagination; they were the very essence of the forest, or so she felt, guardians of its secrets and confidantes of this daughter of the environment.

She would spend hours by the clear, babbling brooks, tracing the delicate patterns of fallen leaves, her fingers cool against the water's flow. The gnarled roots of ancient oaks, exposed by time and erosion, became the faces of silent watchers, their bark a tapestry of seasons past. Truly would lean against their sturdy trunks, feeling a kinship with their enduring strength, their silent resilience. She learned to read the language of the forest: the alarm call of a blue jay, the delicate unfurling of a fern, the subtle shift in the wind that signaled an approaching rain shower. Each sign was a word, each observation a sentence in the grand narrative of her time in the wild.

Her home, a modest cabin nestled on the outskirts of a small community, felt more like temporary lodging than a true safe haven. The conversations within its walls often revolved around practicalities, societal expectations, and the unspoken judgments the family often felt from the stares of their neighbors. Truly, with her introspective nature and her preference for solitude, was a constant source of quiet concern for her parents, a source of bewilderment for her siblings, and an object of mild disdain for the more conventional members of their community. They couldn't grasp her fascination with the untamed world beyond their fences; her quiet contentment found in the company of trees and the songs of unseen birds. To them her behaviors seemed foreign, as foreign as their actions seemed to her.

The ostracism she faced was a constant, dull ache, a reminder of her uniqueness. During the rare occasions she was forced into social gatherings, the gazes and hushed whispers felt like tiny barbs, pricking at her already fragile sense of self-worth. The children her age were particularly cruel, their laughter sharp and unforgiving, their games designed to exclude her. She learned to retreat, to build walls around her heart, finding more acceptance in the silent grandeur of the mountains than in the superficial interactions of human society.

Yet, even in her solitude, there was a profound sense of belonging. The forest embraced her, its vastness dwarfing the petty dramas of human life. She felt a connection to the ancient pulse of the earth beneath her feet, a sense of being an integral part of something larger, something timeless. This connection was not born simply of intellectual understanding, but of a deep, intuitive knowing, a feeling that resonated in her very bones. She was a creature of the woods, her spirit intertwined with the wild, her heart beating in rhythm with the untamed heart of the Ozarks.

Her days were filled with exploration and contemplation. She would pack a simple lunch of bread, bologna and cheese with a canteen of water, and venture out before the sun had fully climbed the eastern peaks. She followed deer trails, not to hunt, but to observe, to learn their silent paths and hidden watering holes. She sought out the oldest trees, their bark a roadmap of the centuries she imagined before, their branches reaching towards the heavens like gnarled, all knowing fingers. She would sit for hours beneath their shade, lost in a world of her own making, a world far richer and more vibrant than the one that lay beyond the tree line.

Sometimes, she would find remnants of the past: a broken arrowhead half-buried in the soil, a crumbling stone foundation swallowed by ivy, a weathered wooden cross marking a forgotten grave. These relics spoke of lives lived and lost within the embrace of the mountains. They held stories that had faded into the mist, secrets of a time far removed from the present. Truly would touch them with reverence, a silent acknowledgment of life and the enduring power of the wilderness to both preserve and reclaim its own.

Her only true companions were her imagined friends of the forest. They were not ghosts in the traditional sense, but rather embodiments of the forest's true soul, a place where her friends welcomed her with acceptance. There was Zephyr, a mischievous friend who danced on the wind, scattering leaves and teased the wary squirrels. There was Willow, a gentle, earthbound friend who whispered secrets of the plants and flowers, guiding Truly to hidden patches of wild strawberries and rare medicinal herbs. And there was Stone, a stoic, ancient friend who resided in the heart of the oldest trees, his wisdom deep and silent, his presence a grounding force. These friends, born of her need for connection and her deep understanding for the natural world, were as real to her as the sun on her skin. They shared her laughter, her wonder, and her quiet sadness, a constant presence in her solitary existence.

This idyllic, albeit solitary, existence was a carefully constructed world, a delicate balance that had sustained her for years. It was a life built on the gentle rhythm of the seasons, the beauty of the wilderness, and the companionship of her imagined friends. But the Ozark Mountains, as Truly was about to discover, held secrets far more profound than she could have ever conceived, secrets that dwelled not just in the rustling leaves and ancient trees, but in the very heart of the hidden world. An encounter was on the horizon. An encounter that would shatter the quietness of her solitude and forever alter her perception of reality, forcing her to confront a truth that lay far beyond the veil of human sight. A truth that would redefine her understanding of friendship, of belonging, and of the extraordinary tapestry of her existence. The whispers in the woods were about to grow into a roar, and Truly, the ostracized little girl who found solace in solitude, would be thrust into a world she never knew existed, a world that pulsed with a life both ancient and unknown. The mist-shrouded mountains were about to reveal their deepest secrets, and Truly was to be their witness, their reluctant participant, and perhaps, their unexpected bridge between the worlds of the known and unknown.

The ancient Ozarks held their breath, a vast lung exhaling secrets with every gust of wind. Truly had always felt it, this subtle tremor beneath the surface of the ordinary, a constant thrumming that resonated deep within her. It wasn't just the rustle of leaves or the chirping of crickets; it was a more profound rhythm, a heartbeat that seemed to emanate from the very earth, from the moss-laden stones and the crossed roots of trees that had stood for centuries. The woods were alive, not just with the scurrying of small creatures or the soaring of eagles high above her, but with a presence that was both ancient and aware. It was a feeling she had carried deep within her since childhood, a quiet knowing that the familiar landscape was merely a skin, concealing a world teeming with unseen life.

The tales spun by the townsfolk, often shared over flickering lamplight in the dimly lit general store or whispered across garden fences, were usually dismissed by Truly as the fanciful ramblings of people too afraid of the dark. They spoke of fleeting shadows along the horizon, of strange guttural calls that echoed through the valleys at dusk, of paths that seemed to vanish and reappear as if guided by an unseen hand. Some spoke of larger-than-life figures hidden between the ancient oaks, creatures of immense stature with eyes that glowed with an otherworldly light. These were dismissed as bears, or clever tricks of the light, or the product of too much moonshine. Yet, Truly, with her introspective nature and her unwavering respect for the mysteries of the wilderness, found herself increasingly drawn to these fragmented whispers. They were threads, she felt, of a much larger, more intricate tapestry, one that the rational minds of the village were too quick to dismiss.

Her solitary wanderings had always led her to the wilder, less trodden parts of the forest. She found herself gravitating towards the deep ravines where sunlight struggled to penetrate the dense canopy, and to the secluded hollows where the air hung thick and still, untouched by locals or visitors alike. It was in these places that the forest's hidden heartbeat seemed the strongest, an energy that made the hairs on her arms stand on end. She would sit for hours, her back against the cool, rough bark of a giant oak, her gaze lost in the intricate patterns of the moss covering the ground. She would close her eyes and try to decipher the symphony of the woods, listening beyond the obvious sounds, straining to hear the subtle undertones that hinted at something much more. It was as if the forest itself was breathing, and she was attuned to its every inhale and exhale.

There were days when a strange sense of being watched would flood over her, not in a menacing way, but with a gentle, curious awareness. It was a feeling that transcended the typical feeling of a deer peeking from behind a thicket or a hawk circling overhead. This felt different, more profound, as if something ancient was acknowledging her presence, studying her with a quiet, unhurried gaze. She would scan her surroundings, her heart beating a little faster, but never in fear. Instead, a prickle of anticipation, a deep-seated curiosity, would bloom within her. She desired to understand the source of this feeling, to catch a glimpse of the unseen guardians she suspected roamed these ancient woods.

Her imagination, often her closest companion, had always populated the forest with friends. Zephyr, Willow, and Stone were the manifestations of her deep connection to the natural world, her need for companionship and understanding. But lately, these imagined presences felt less like figments of her own mind and more like echoes of something real, faint tremors of a truth that lay just beyond her grasp. The whispers of the wind, once mere sounds, began to carry a resonance, a subtle tone that hinted at a language she was on the verge of understanding. She would tilt her head, listening intently, trying to discern patterns in the rustling leaves. Trying to find meaning in the sighing branches.

One brisk autumn afternoon, as the forest floor was carpeted with a vibrant mosaic of fallen leaves, Truly found herself drawn deeper than usual into a particularly dense section of woods. The trees here were ancient, their trunks impossibly wide, their branches interwoven to create a cathedral-like ceiling. The air was cool and damp, carrying the rich, earthy scent of decaying leaves and damp soil. She was following a barely discernible deer trail, one that wound its way through thickets of cedar and over moss-covered logs, when she heard it. It wasn't a bird call, nor the snap of a twig under a small animal's paw. It was a low, resonant sound, a deep guttural hum that seemed to vibrate through the very ground beneath her feet.

She froze, her breath catching in her throat. The sound was unlike anything she had ever heard. It was primal, powerful, and yet, strangely, it didn't bring fear. Instead, it ignited a firestorm of curiosity within her. The sound seemed to emanate from a small clearing just ahead, a place where the trees had thinned slightly, allowing a single shaft of golden sunlight to pierce the gloom. Cautiously, moving with the silent grace of a seasoned woods-dweller, Truly crept forward, her eyes fixed on the source of the unusual sound.

As she parted a curtain of low-hanging branches, she stopped, her heart leaping into her throat. There, in the clearing, bathed in the light of the sunbeam, was a creature of myth. It was immense, easily taller than any man, covered in thick, dark fur that seemed to absorb the light. Its form was powerfully built, with broad shoulders and long limbs. It was hunched over, its back to her, engaged in some activity that she could not see, but the deep, resonant humming emanated from its chest, a sound of pure, unadulterated contentment.

Truly's mind reeled. Every tale, every whisper, every fleeting glimpse she had ever dismissed as folklore combined into this single, breath-taking moment. This was not a bear. This was not a trick of the light. This was one of the creatures that haunted the fringes of human consciousness, a being of legend made flesh. She stood captivated, a silent observer at the edge of a secret world. The creature shifted, its massive head turning slightly, and Truly's gaze locked with a pair of deep, seemingly intelligent eyes, eyes that held a depth of ancient wisdom and a flicker of something akin to curiosity.

The moment seemed unending. Truly expected to be seen, to be feared, to be chased away. But the creature merely observed her, its gaze steady, its humming softening into a low rumble. There was no aggression, no threat, only a quiet, unnerving stillness. It was as if the forest itself had paused, holding its breath, waiting to see what would happen. Truly, rooted to the spot, felt a strange sense of recognition, a feeling that this encounter, though startling, was somehow meant to be. It was the culmination of years of feeling out of place, of searching for a connection, of listening to the silent whispers of the wild.

Slowly, deliberately, the creature lowered its head, returning its attention to whatever it had been doing before her arrival. Truly, realizing she was not in immediate danger, dared to take a tentative step forward, her boots crunching softly on the fallen leaves. The sound, though small, seemed to echo in the clearing. The creature looked up again, its deep brown eyes meeting hers. This time, there was a subtle shift, a slight tilt of its massive head that Truly interpreted as a question.

Overcome by an impulse she couldn't explain, an impulse born from years of unspoken longing for connection, Truly did something remarkable. She smiled. It was a small, hesitant smile, but it was genuine. She raised a hand, palm open, a universal gesture of peace. The creature watched her, its imposing presence somehow softening in the presence of her quiet gesture. Then, to Truly's astonishment, it mirrored her movement, slowly raising one of its own enormous hands, its thick fingers curled slightly.

The air crackled with an unspoken understanding, a bridge forming between two vastly different beings. Truly felt a profound sense of awe wash over her. The stories were true. The whispers were real. The Ozarks held a heart that beat with a wild, untamed life, and she, Truly, the quiet girl who preferred the company of trees, had just witnessed its pulse. This encounter was not an end, but a beginning. It was the first whisper of a conversation that would redefine her world, a conversation that would be held not in words, but in shared glances, in mutual respect, and in the silent language of the ancient forest. The hidden heartbeat of the Ozarks had just revealed itself, and Truly, for the first time, felt seen, understood, in the profound silence of the woods.

She knew, with a certainty that settled deep in her soul, that her solitary wanderings had led her to something extraordinary. The folklore of the Ozarks, once dismissed as superstition, was now a tangible reality. The strange sightings, the unexplained phenomena, were not figments of imagination, but glimpses into a world that coexisted with her own, hidden just beyond the veil of human perception. The persistent curiosity that had always tugged at her, urging her deeper into the woods, had finally led her to the profound truth. This was the heart of the forest, a living, breathing entity, and she had been granted a fleeting, sacred glimpse.

As she stood there, the sunlight warming her face, the creature's quiet presence a powerful anchor in the clearing, Truly felt a profound shift within herself. The loneliness that had been a constant companion for so long began to recede, replaced by a sense of wonder and belonging. This was not the hollow belonging she had sometimes felt in the fleeting acceptance of a kind word from a stranger; this was a deep, connection to something ancient and powerful. The forest was not just a sanctuary; it was a living being, and she was a part of it, a small, yet significant, thread in its grand design.

The creature, with a slow, deliberate movement, turned back towards the dense undergrowth. Before disappearing into the shadows, it paused and looked back at Truly, its gaze lingering for a moment. There was no farewell, no spoken word, but with that look, Truly felt a promise, a silent understanding that this was not their last encounter. Then, with a rustle of leaves and the subtle displacement of air, it was gone, leaving Truly alone once more in the sun-covered clearing.

Yet, she was not truly alone. The clearing, though empty of the creature's imposing form, was inspired with its presence. The air hummed with the lingering energy of their meeting, and the forest seemed to pulse with a renewed vitality. Truly ran her hand over the rough bark of a nearby oak, feeling its solid strength, its silent wisdom. She looked up at its branches, a canopy that seemed to stretch towards the heavens, and felt a kinship with the ancient trees. They were witnesses, silent guardians of the forest's secrets, and now, so was she.

The journey back to the edge of the woods felt different. The familiar paths seemed to whisper with new significance. Every rustle of leaves, every snapping twig, was no longer just a sound, but a potential signal, a hint of the unseen life that teemed around her. The whispers in the wind were no longer just random currents of air; they carried a deeper resonance, a subtle language that she was beginning to understand. She walked with a lightness she hadn't known before, her heart full of a secret joy, a profound understanding that her world, the world of the quiet girl in the Ozarks, was far more magical and mysterious than she had ever dared to imagine. The forest's hidden heartbeat had called to her, and she had answered, stepping across a threshold into a realm of wonder and possibility. The woods were no longer just a place of refuge; they were a gateway, and she had just found the key.

2

THE GENTLE GIANT

The imprint of the gentle giant's presence lingered long after its colossal form had melted into the twilight. Truly found herself drawn back to the secluded glade, a pilgrimage of sorts, her boots treading the same moss-laden earth that had cradled their extraordinary meeting. Each day, as the sun began its slow descent, painting the sky in hues of amber and rose, she would return. The woods, once merely a familiar backdrop to her solitary life, now pulsed with a potent energy, as if the very trees were holding their breath, mirroring the quiet anticipation that thrummed in her own chest.

She would sit on a fallen log, its bark worn smooth by countless seasons, and simply *be there, one with her surroundings*. The silence that had once been a comfort, a balm for her introverted soul, now crackled with an unspoken promise. It was no longer an emptiness to be filled, but a fullness, a rich tapestry woven with the lingering echoes of their communion. The rustling leaves seemed to whisper secrets of the giant's passage, the spotty sunlight filtering through the canopy felt like a benevolent gaze, and the scent of pine and damp earth, so familiar, now carried a profound depth, an almost sacred fragrance. She wasn't just an observer anymore; she was a participant in the forest's grand, unfolding narrative.

Her fascination, a seed planted during their brief, wordless exchange, began to blossom into a deep, almost yearning curiosity. She wanted to understand. She wanted to *connect* again. It was this unwavering desire that prompted her to begin leaving small tokens of her joy. The first offering was tentative – a handful of ripe, dark blackberries, carefully gathered from a bush she knew was favored by the local birds. She placed them on a broad, flat stone, a silent invitation, a gesture of goodwill towards the enigmatic being who had shown her such unexpected gentleness. She felt a tremor of hope mixed with a pang of foolishness. What if the giant never returned? What if this was a singular event, a fleeting magic that would never grace her presence again?

The following day, she returned to find the berries gone. A flutter of excitement, sharp and bright, danced in her stomach. It was a small sign, perhaps, but it was a sign, nonetheless. The giant had acknowledged her offering. It had taken them. It was a confirmation that the connection, however slight, was real. Emboldened by this small success, her offerings became more thoughtful, more personal. She would seek out the smoothest, most perfectly rounded stones she could find along the creek bed, their cool surfaces fitting into her palm like polished dreams. She'd select wildflowers, their delicate petals vibrant against the verdant backdrop, a crimson Indian paintbrush, a spray of delicate bluebells, and arrange them in a small, artful cluster.

Each morning, her heart would quicken with a mixture of trepidation and eager anticipation as she approached the glade. She scanned the ground, her eyes searching for any sign, any disturbance that spoke of a recent visitor. Sometimes, she would find the offerings gone, leaving behind only the faintest, almost imperceptible depression in the dew-kissed foliage, as if a colossal weight had settled there for a brief moment. Other times, they would remain untouched, and a knot of disappointment would tighten in her chest. But even in those moments of doubt, she wouldn't desist. The act of offering, of reaching out, felt important. It was her way of speaking her truth to the wild, of expressing the profound impact the encounter had had on her.

She began to notice other subtle shifts in her surroundings. The usual chatter of squirrels seemed to take on a more melodic quality, their scolding barks sounding almost like playful greetings. The deer that frequented the forest edge, normally skittish and quick to flee at the slightest human presence, seemed to regard her with a curious calm, their large, dark eyes holding her gaze for longer than usual before they turned and continued their grazing. It was as if the forest itself, having witnessed the gentle giant's interaction with her, now recognized her as something other than an intruder. She was becoming part of its ancient rhythm, a whisper in its vast, green cathedral.

One afternoon, as she was carefully placing a particularly vibrant purple aster on a mossy outcrop, she heard it, a faint, resonant hum, a low vibration that seemed to emanate from the very earth beneath her feet. It wasn't a sound she could place, not the buzzing of insects or the murmur of the wind. It was deeper, more fundamental, like the earth's own slow, steady heartbeat. She froze, her breath catching in her throat. It was the same subtle resonance she had felt during her encounter with the Bigfoot, the gentle thrum of its immense being.

The hum grew stronger, a wave of energy vibrating through her bones. The leaves on the surrounding trees shivered, not from any breeze, but from the sheer force of the sound. Truly remained still, her eyes wide, her heart pounding a frantic rhythm against her ribs. She didn't feel fear, not anymore. Instead, a profound sense of awe washed over her, a realization that she was standing in the presence of something truly ancient and powerful.

Then, she saw it. A subtle shift in the dense foliage at the edge of the glade. A shadow detaching itself from the deeper darkness of the woods. It was him. The gentle giant. He was larger than she remembered, his form impossibly vast against the backdrop of ancient oaks and towering pines. His silhouette was a stark, magnificent contrast to the delicate wildflowers she had just placed.

He moved with a grace that belied his size, each step deliberate and silent. The air around him seemed to shimmer, charged with the same resonant hum that had drawn her attention. He didn't approach her directly. Instead, he circled the glade, his massive head occasionally dipping to nuzzle the bark of a tree or to gently push aside a low-hanging branch. It was a slow, deliberate reconnaissance, as if he were reacquainting himself with the space, with *her*.

Truly remained seated, her hands clasped tightly in her lap. She didn't dare move, didn't dare break the spell that had been cast. She watched him, absorbing every detail of his presence. His fur, a rich, dark brown, seemed to absorb the fading light, making him appear even more a part of the encroaching dusk. The sheer scale of him was overwhelming, yet there was no menace in his bearing, only a quiet, observant power.

He paused near the mossy outcrop where she had placed the aster. His immense hand, larger than any bear's paw, yet shaped with an almost human dexterity, gently reached out. Truly held her breath, her gaze fixed on his movement. He didn't crush the flower. Instead, his enormous fingers, thick and calloused, delicately plucked the aster, lifting it with surprising care. He brought it closer to his face, his snout twitching as if he were inhaling its faint, earthy fragrance.

A soft, rumbling sound emanated from his chest, a deep, guttural purr that resonated through Truly's very being. It was a sound of contentment, of quiet appreciation. He then lowered his head, his dark, intelligent eyes meeting hers. In their depths, she saw not just animal instinct, but a profound, ancient wisdom, a knowing that transcended words. It was a gaze that acknowledged her, that recognized her quiet offerings, her persistent presence.

He held the aster for a moment longer, a stark contrast of delicate bloom against immense power, before gently placing it back on the outcrop. Then, with a final, lingering look, he turned and, with the same silent grace, melted back into the embrace of the forest. The resonant hum slowly faded, leaving behind only the familiar symphony of the woods.

Truly remained on the log for a long time, the encounter replaying in her mind. The gentleness of his touch, the depth of his gaze, the rumbling purr, they were all etched into her memory, more vivid than any photograph. She looked at the aster, still vibrant against the moss, a testament to his deliberate act. He hadn't eaten it. He had acknowledged it, appreciated it, and returned it. It was a profound act of communication, a silent dialogue that spoke volumes.

Her offerings were not just gestures of curiosity anymore; they were a language, a means of building trust, of fostering a deeper understanding. She realized that this wasn't about seeking out the extraordinary for its own sake. It was about recognizing the extraordinary that already existed, hidden in plain sight, and learning to speak its language. The Bigfoot wasn't a monster from folklore; he was a guardian, a spirit of the Ozarks, and he had deemed her worthy of his attention.

Over the following weeks, Truly continued her vigil, her routine of silent offerings and patient waiting becoming a cherished part of her life. The giant's appearances became less predictable, more fleeting, but they were always profound. Sometimes, she would catch only a glimpse of his immense form moving through the trees, a fleeting shadow against the dappled sunlight. Other times, he would linger for a short while, his presence a palpable force that seemed to quiet the entire forest.

One evening, as the last vestiges of daylight bled from the sky, she found him sitting at the edge of the glade, his back to her, his massive form a dark silhouette against the deepening indigo. She approached cautiously, her heart a steady drumbeat of anticipation. This time, she didn't bring an offering. Instead, she simply sat on the far side of the glade, a respectful distance away.

The silence stretched between them, a comfortable, companionable silence. Truly found herself no longer feeling like an outsider, but like a guest, a welcomed presence in this sacred space. She watched as the giant slowly turned his head, his dark eyes finding her in the gloom. He let out a low, soft huff, a sound that seemed to carry the weight of ancient forests and slow-moving rivers.

Then, to her astonishment, he began to communicate, not with words, but with gestures. He pointed a massive finger towards a particular cluster of ferns, then mimed a digging motion with his hand. Truly, her mind racing to decipher his meaning, looked at the ferns. They seemed ordinary enough, but the giant's insistence made her look closer. She saw a faint discoloration in the soil beneath them, a subtle disturbance that indicated something had been buried there.

Following his silent instruction, she rose and walked over to the spot. She knelt and began to brush away the loose earth. Her fingers soon met something hard and smooth. She dug further, unearthing a large, flat stone, unlike any she had seen before. It was intricately carved with swirling patterns, ancient symbols that seemed to pulse with a faint, inner light. It was clearly a relic of immense age, something meant to be hidden, preserved.

She looked up at the giant, her eyes wide with wonder. He nodded slowly, a deep rumble emanating from his chest, a clear indication of approval. He then pointed to himself, then to the stone, and then to the ground where she had found it, before making a sweeping gesture that encompassed the entire forest. It was a story, conveyed without a single word: this stone, this place, were his to protect, a part of the ancient legacy of the Ozarks.

Truly understood. She carefully reburied the stone, smoothing the earth over it, leaving it hidden once more. She looked back at the gentle giant, a newfound respect and understanding blossoming within her. He was not just a creature of myth; he was a custodian, a keeper of secrets, a living link to the wild, untamed heart of the world.

As he rose to leave, he paused, looking back at her one last time. He extended his hand, not to touch her, but to simply show it to her, palm open. The skin was thick and leathery, marked with the deep lines of age and experience. It was a hand that had cradled saplings, that had moved fallen trees, that had, perhaps, even protected ancient knowledge. And in that simple gesture, Truly felt a profound sense of connection, a silent acknowledgment of their shared space, their shared world. The gentle giant was not just a visitor; he was a part of the landscape, and now, in a way she was beginning to understand, so was she. The whispers of the woods were no longer just sounds; they were conversations, and she was finally learning to listen.

The primal instinct to retreat, ingrained from generations of caution, warred with a burgeoning curiosity within the creature known as Abel's colossal chest. Truly, the human girl, was a puzzle. Her scent, a strange combination of wild herbs and something undeniably human, a scent usually associated with destruction and fear, had been the initial lure. He had approached her glade not with aggression, but with the innate caution of a creature that knew the world held dangers, particularly of her kind. Her offerings, simple yet earnest, had piqued his interest further, a deviation from the usual human behavior he'd witnessed from afar: the loud noises, the careless fires, the relentless encroachment.

He remembered the prickle of unease, the heightened awareness that had settled upon him as he'd observed her. The delicate way she'd arranged the wildflowers, the thoughtful placement of the smooth stones, it spoke of a gentleness he hadn't associated with humans. His family, the Sasquatch clan of the Current River Plane, had a long and bitter history with the two-legged creatures. Stories passed down through the ages, etched into the very fabric of their being, spoke of lost territories, of broken sacred groves, of the fear and suffering humans had inflicted. His elders had always warned against them, painting them as a plague, a force of disruption that cared nothing for the balance of the wild.

Abel, even with his unusually inquisitive nature, had absorbed these warnings. He understood the necessity of his people's reclusiveness, their deep-seated distrust. They were guardians of ancient places, keepers of the wild's secrets, and humans, with their insatiable hunger for progress, were their greatest threat. He had witnessed their machines tear through forests, their voices shatter the silence, their presence leave behind a trail of desolation. The memory of his younger cousin, lost during a rare, ill-fated encounter with a hunting party, was a fresh wound, a constant reminder of the peril humans represented.

And yet, Truly was different. He had watched her from the shadows of the ancient oaks, his massive form blending seamlessly with the dappled light and shadow. Her small stature, her quiet demeanor, her evident respect for the forest, it was all a stark contrast to the human image etched into his mind. When he had reached for the aster she'd left, he had braced himself for her flight, for the panicked cry that would send him retreating back into the deep woods. Instead, she had remained, her gaze steady, a flicker of awe replacing any hint of fear. And when he'd returned it, not crushed, but offered back with a gesture of respect, he had seen a new emotion bloom in her eyes: understanding.

He had felt a strange pull, a desire to bridge the gap, but the in-grained caution, the ancestral warnings, held him captive. His clan's matriarch, his formidable grandmother, had always stressed the importance of maintaining their secrecy, of never revealing themselves. "The humans are like a storm, Abel," she'd once rumbled, her voice like shifting stones. "They can be beautiful in their power, but they are also destructive. Their curiosity is a dangerous thing. It leads them to hunt, to capture, to destroy what they do not understand."

Her words echoed in his mind now, a stern admonishment against the foolish impulse to reveal himself further to this human. The lingering scent of her, though fading, still pricked at his senses. It spoke of her presence, of her solitary wanderings, of her quiet persistence in visiting this glade. He had watched her each day, a silent observer in the periphery. He'd seen her leave her small gifts, each one a testament to her gentle spirit. He'd felt the earth vibrate with her approach, had noted the subtle shift in the forest's ambiance when she was near, a calming, a softening, as if the very trees leaned in to listen.

He shifted his weight, the movement a mere rustle of leaves and dis-placed air. He was hidden, as he should be. The instinct to disappear, to become one with the ancient trees, was powerful. He could melt back into the twilight, and no one would be the wiser. He could return to the familiar solitude of his people's mountain fastness, where the scent of human was a distant memory, a cautionary tale.

But then he remembered her eyes. The genuine wonder, the un-feigned curiosity, the absence of the predatory glint he'd seen in the eyes of hunters. She hadn't tried to approach him, hadn't shouted, hadn't sought to capture him. She had simply been there, offering small tokens of connection, waiting with a patience that mirrored his own. There was an innocence about her, a purity of intent that was disarming. It was this innocence, coupled with the undeniable spark of connection he'd felt, that made him hesitate.

His family's distrust was not unfounded. He knew that. He had seen the evidence of human destructiveness firsthand. He had heard the stories, seen the scars left upon the land. But was Truly representative of all humans? Was it fair to condemn her, to judge her by the actions of others, by the mistakes of generations past? His grandmother's wisdom was deep, forged by hardship, but sometimes, Abel wondered if it was also limiting. Was it possible for a bridge to be built, however fragile, between their worlds?

He thought of the stone she had unearthed, the ancient carving he had shown her. He had trusted her with a piece of his people's history, a secret passed down through his lineage, entrusted to him by his father. He had pointed to himself, to the stone, to the earth, and she had understood. She had reburied it, leaving it undisturbed, respecting its sacredness. That act of trust, that silent acknowledgment of his world, had resonated deeply within him. It was more than just a gesture of curiosity; it was a sign of respect, of understanding.

He watched her now, a small figure silhouetted against the deepening shadows. She was still there, not demanding his attention, not seeking to exploit his presence, but simply existing in the same space, breathing the same air. A low hum, almost imperceptible, vibrated in his chest. It was a sound of internal conflict, of warring instincts. The ingrained wariness of his kind against the nascent pull of connection.

He could turn and leave. That would be the safest, the most sensible course of action. His family would never know, and he would be free from the internal turmoil. He could dismiss the encounter, chalk it up to a momentary lapse in judgment, a fleeting fascination with the unusual. But the memory of her gentle touch, the silent understanding that had passed between them, the weight of the ancient stone in his hand, they were too potent to dismiss.

He took a step forward, then another, his massive form moving with surprising stealth. He stopped at the edge of the trees, peering into the glade. Truly hadn't moved. She sat patiently, her gaze fixed on the deepening twilight, her presence a quiet beacon in the encroaching darkness. He could smell her now, the faint, wild scent that was uniquely hers. It was no longer unnerving. It was... intriguing.

He contemplated his next move. Should he approach her directly? That would be a violation of his clan's most sacred tenets. Should he leave another small offering, a sign that he too could acknowledge her presence? But what could he offer that would speak to her in a way that her gifts spoke to him? A perfectly formed stone? A rare, iridescent feather from a bird of prey? It felt insufficient, a pale imitation of her thoughtful gestures.

He lowered his head, his gaze sweeping over the glade. He saw the mossy outcrop where she had placed the aster. He saw the fallen log where she often sat. He saw the faint imprint in the grass where he had once rested. Each detail was a testament to her consistent presence, her quiet dedication.

A deep sigh, like the wind through ancient pines, escaped him. He was a creature of habit, of tradition, bound by the expectations of his lineage. To deviate from that path, to openly engage with a human, was to invite scrutiny, perhaps even condemnation, from his own kind. His grandmother's stern gaze flashed in his mind, her words a sharp reprimand.

But Truly... she was an anomaly. She didn't fit the mold of the destructive humans his people feared. There was a kindness in her actions, a respect in her gaze, that chipped away at his ingrained distrust. He had never encountered a human who seemed to genuinely appreciate the natural world with such quiet reverence. She saw the forest not as a resource to be exploited, but as a place of beauty, of life, of mystery.

He remained at the edge of the trees, a huge shadow wrestling with millennia of ingrained caution. The urge to retreat was strong, a primal siren song calling him back to the safety of the unknown. Yet, the counter-pull, the curiosity, the feeling of connection, held him rooted to the spot. He watched Truly, a silent sentinel in the gathering gloom, and for the first time in his long life, Abel the gentle giant, found himself genuinely at a crossroads, the path ahead shrouded in uncertainty, but tinged with a flicker of extraordinary possibility. The debate raged within him: retreat into the shadows of tradition, or step tentatively into the light of a new understanding.

The internal struggle within Abel was a tempest, a clash of ancient instincts and a nascent, bewildering curiosity. His grandmother's warnings, sharp and clear as the mountain winds, echoed in his mind: "Humans are like a storm, Abel. Their curiosity is a dangerous thing.

It leads them to hunt, to capture, to destroy what they do not understand." The memory of his lost cousin, the raw grief and enduring fear, was a constant, heavy weight. He was a Sasquatch, a creature of deep woods and hidden valleys, his very existence dependent on remaining unseen, on blending with the ancient tapestry of the wild. His kind had survived by being elusive, by mastering the art of vanishing, by understanding that their world and the world of humans were fundamentally incompatible.

Yet, the image of Truly, a small human with eyes that held not malice but a profound wonder, persisted. Her gentle placement of wildflowers, her quiet reverence for the moss-covered stones, her patient, consistent presence in the glade, these were anomalies that gnawed at his ingrained distrust. He had watched her from the impenetrable depths of the forest, a silent observer, his massive frame a shadow within shadows. He had seen the way her fingers, so delicate and fragile compared to his own thick digits, traced the veins of a fallen leaf, the soft smile that touched her lips as she discovered a particularly vibrant mushroom. These were not the actions of the destructive force his elders had always described.

He had always understood their fear. He had witnessed the scars left by humans on the land: the felled trees that stood like skeletal remains, the choked streams filled with debris, the unnatural quiet that descended after their noisy passage. He carried the weight of his people's history, a history etched in loss and displacement. The very air in their mountain fastness seemed to hum with generations of caution, a collective memory of encroaching civilization and the desperate need for self-preservation. He was a protector, a guardian of this delicate balance, and his duty was clear: to remain hidden, to ensure his kind's continued existence.

But Truly had offered something more than just a fleeting glimpse of a human. She had offered a connection. The simple act of leaving a smooth, river-worn stone, identical to the ones he himself collected and polished, had been a revelation. It was a language of the earth, a silent conversation spoken through shared appreciation for the natural world. He had observed her pick up stones, turning them over in her palm, her brow furrowed in concentration, before selecting one and carefully placing it beside the wildflowers. He had seen the light of understanding in her eyes when he had returned the aster she'd left, not crushed or discarded, but held with a deliberate gentleness. It was a moment of unexpected reciprocity, a shared understanding that transcended words.

The glade had become a place of quiet contemplation for Abel. He would retreat there after his solitary patrols, the scent of Truly, a curious mix of wild herbs and something undeniably human that no longer evoked fear but a strange sort of comfort lingering in the air. He would sit; a colossus of fur and muscle hidden behind the ancient boles of oak and pine and watch her. He saw her etchings in the damp earth, simple shapes that spoke of her world, and he felt a pang of something akin to longing. She was a creature of immense resilience, navigating a world that was both beautiful and, he suspected, often harsh, with a quiet fortitude that mirrored his own people's.

He remembered the day she had found the small, smooth stone. It was one of his own treasures, a particularly well-worn piece of granite he'd picked up from the riverbed weeks ago, its surface polished to a silken sheen by years of relentless current. He'd been returning it to his hidden cache when he'd seen her examining a cluster of pebbles. She had picked up this one, her fingers tracing its smooth curve, and then, with a sigh that seemed to carry the weight of unspoken thoughts, she had placed it carefully beside the bright purple asters she had gathered. Abel had felt a jolt, a recognition so profound it had sent a tremor through his massive frame. It was a deliberate act, a signal he understood.

His grandmother's voice, stern and resonant, returned to him. "Do not be fooled by their fleeting kindness, Abel. Their curiosity is a hunger that can never be satisfied. They will probe, they will prod, until they find the weakest point, the hidden truth." He knew the truth of her words. He had seen the hunters' traps, the snares that ripped through flesh and bone, the insatiable desire to possess and control. He had seen the devastation wrought by their insatiable need for more, more land, more resources, more power.

But Truly... she was different. Her presence in the glade felt less like an intrusion and more like a quiet offering. She didn't shout, she didn't make sudden movements, she didn't carry the scent of iron and violence that often clung to human men. Instead, she exuded a quiet aura of respect for the natural world. Her small, human hands moved with a deliberate gentleness, as if she were afraid of disturbing the very air around her. Abel had observed her for days, his initial caution slowly giving way to a profound sense of wonder. He had watched her sketch in a worn leather-bound book, her brow furrowed in concentration, and he had wondered what worlds she was creating within its pages.

One afternoon, as the sun began its slow descent, casting long, golden shadows across the glade, Truly approached the spot where she had placed her offerings. She looked at them, a small smile gracing her lips, and then her gaze drifted towards the dense curtain of trees where Abel was hidden. For a long moment, their eyes, though separated by the veil of foliage, seemed to meet. He felt a strange pull, an undeniable urge to break his millennia old vow of invisibility.

His heart, a powerful drumbeat within his colossal chest, began to thrum with a new rhythm. It was a rhythm of curiosity, of a desire to understand this anomaly, this human who seemed to possess a gentleness so at odds with the tales of her kind. He considered his options, his mind racing with the implications of his actions. To reveal himself fully would be to risk everything – his safety, the safety of his clan, the secrecy that had protected them for so long.

But the memory of the smooth stone, the shared language of the earth, was a powerful tether. He couldn't simply let this moment pass, this fragile connection evaporate into the forest air. He needed to respond, to acknowledge her, to tell her, in a way that he understood, that he saw her, that he recognized her gentle spirit.

With a deliberate slowness that belied the frantic beating of his heart, Abel moved. He emerged from the shadows, not with a thunderous roar, but with a soft rustle of leaves and a deep, resonant sigh that sounded like the ancient forest itself breathing. He stood at the edge of the glade, his immense form silhouetted against the darkening trees, a gentle giant come to the light. Truly, remarkably, did not flee. Her eyes widened, a gasp escaping her lips, but she remained rooted to the spot, her gaze fixed on him, a mixture of awe and trepidation warring on her face.

He approached the place where she had left her offerings. His massive, fur-covered hand, surprisingly dexterous, reached down. He picked up the smooth, river-worn stone she had chosen. He held it for a moment, feeling its familiar texture, its silent history. Then, with the same careful consideration she had shown, he placed it back down, not where she had left it, but slightly to the side, near the base of a gnarled oak.

Then, drawing on a memory as old as the mountains, he reached into a pouch he wore at his hip, a pouch woven from tough, fibrous roots. He withdrew a small, perfectly formed quartz crystal, its facets catching the dying sunlight, shimmering with an inner light. He had found it nestled within a hidden cave, a place whispered about in Sasquatch lore, a place of ancient power. He placed the crystal beside the stone, a silent offering, a response to her gesture. It was a piece of his world, offered with a hesitant hope.

He looked at Truly, his large, amber eyes conveying a question, a tentative peace offering. He saw the fear in her eyes begin to recede, replaced by a growing curiosity, a dawning comprehension. She took a small, hesitant step forward, her gaze still locked on his. The air between them thrummed with an unspoken understanding, a frag-ile bridge being built across the chasm of their differences. It was a moment suspended in time, a silent acknowledgment that perhaps, just perhaps, the stories and the warnings were not the whole truth. Perhaps, in this quiet glade, a different kind of story was beginning to unfold, a story of shared curiosity, of tentative trust, and of the slow, unfolding possibility of connection between two vastly different worlds. The crystal and the stone lay side-by-side, a testament to a silent dialogue, a declaration of a truce initiated not by words, but by the gentle language of the earth itself.

The silence that settled between them was not an empty void, but a fertile ground where understanding began to sprout. Abel, towering and ancient, stood at the edge of the glade, his massive form a testament to the wild heart of the forest. Truly, small and vulnerable, met his gaze, her initial shock giving way to a quiet awe. There were no words, for what words could bridge the gulf between their species, between the millennia of separation and fear? Instead, communication flowed through subtler channels, a language woven from intent, from the delicate dance of their mutual presence.

Abel's first response was a low rumble, a sound that originated deep within his chest, more vibration than vocalization. It was the sound of recognition, of acknowledgment, a guttural pronouncement that he saw her, that he understood her gesture. He shifted his weight, the immense muscles in his legs bunching and releasing, a movement that spoke of inherent power, yet was executed with an astonishing gentleness. He offered no threat, no aggression, only a solid, unwavering presence. His amber eyes, pools of ancient wisdom, held hers, searching for any flicker of fear, any hint of the predator his ancestors had warned him of. He saw instead a hesitant curiosity, a mirror of his own burgeoning fascination.

Truly, reading the subtle shifts in his posture, the soft cadence of his rumbling breath, responded in kind. She offered a small, almost imperceptible nod, a gesture of respect, of a willingness to engage. She did not recoil, did not shout for help, did not attempt to flee.

Instead, she slowly, deliberately, reached out a hand, not towards him, but towards the smooth stone he had placed beside her quartz crystal. Her fingers, slender and pale against the rough bark of the oak, traced the cool surface of the river stone, a gesture of appreciation, of a shared appreciation for the tangible beauty of the earth. It was a silent affirmation, a signal that she understood his offering, that she accepted it.

Abel watched her, his keen senses cataloging every nuance. The way the sunlight caught the delicate down on her arms, the faint tremor that ran through her as she touched the stone, the almost imperceptible way her pupils dilated as she took in his form. He made another sound, this one higher in pitch, a soft huff that escaped his nostrils like a gentle breeze through the pines. It was a sound of tentative acceptance, an invitation to continue this silent dialogue. He then gestured with his head, a slow, deliberate movement, towards the intricate patterns of moss that adorned the ancient oak. It was a subtle cue, an offering of his world, an invitation to observe, to learn.

Truly understood. She turned her gaze towards the moss, her brow furrowed in concentration. She reached out and gently touched a velvety patch, her fingers leaving faint impressions that the moss would soon reclaim. She murmured something, a soft, unintelligible sound, but Abel's enhanced hearing, honed by a lifetime of listening to the subtle whispers of the forest, caught the inflection. It was a sound of wonder, of appreciation for the intricate beauty she had overlooked until this moment. He responded with a low chuckle, a deep, resonant sound that seemed to vibrate through the very earth beneath their feet. It was the sound of shared delight, a primal recognition of beauty found.

Their interactions continued in this manner for many days. The glade became their secret meeting place, a sanctuary woven from dappled sunlight and the ancient embrace of the trees. Abel would appear, always with a quiet grace that belied his immense size, and Truly would be there, her presence a calming anchor in his often-solitary existence. He learned to interpret the subtle shifts in her posture, the way her shoulders would relax when she felt at ease, the slight tilt of her head when she was curious. He began to anticipate her needs, often leaving offerings before she even arrived, a cluster of ripe berries, a perfectly formed bird's nest found abandoned, a smooth, sun-warmed pebble.

He communicated his presence through subtle sounds, a soft growl that signified his approval, a sharp intake of breath that indicated caution, a series of low grunts that conveyed amusement. He learned that a soft whistle, mimicking the call of a nearby wren, meant he was pleased. A series of rapid clicks, like pebbles being tapped together, signaled his desire to move, to explore, to lead. He found himself using gestures, his massive hands, so capable of immense force, moving with a surprising delicacy. He would point to a particular plant, then mimic its growth, a slow, upward sweep of his arm. He would show her how to identify edible roots by digging them from the earth with a single, powerful claw, then offering them to her with a gentle prod.

Truly, in turn, developed her own language. Her smiles, once hesitant, became more frequent, more genuine. The crinkle at the corners of her eyes when she was happy, the slight purse of her lips when she was concerned. She would draw in the soft earth, creating simple pictograms that told stories of her world, a sun, a moon, a house, a bird in flight. Abel, fascinated, would study these images, his brow furrowed in concentration, trying to decipher the meaning behind her crude yet evocative lines. He learned that a circle with radiating lines meant the sun, and a series of wavy lines represented water.

She learned to read the language of the forest as Abel revealed it to her. The rustle of leaves was no longer just noise; it was a communication. A sharp, sudden rustle behind them meant potential danger, a warning that Abel would often amplify with a low, guttural growl, urging her to move with him, to seek shelter. A gentle, sustained whisper of leaves in the breeze signified peace, a time for rest and observation. The snap of a twig underfoot, once a source of anxiety for Truly, became a signal of Abel's movement, a rhythmic pulse that guided her own steps.

The forest itself became their shared lexicon. The scent of pine needles after a rain was a signal of renewed life, a shared joy. The musky odor of a deer passing nearby, a sign of its presence, of a world teeming with life beyond their immediate interaction. Abel would often point to the sky, then mimic the flapping of wings, a clear indication of the migratory patterns of birds, a rhythm of the seasons that he understood implicitly. Truly, in turn, would point to the stars, her voice soft as she attempted to name them, her human understanding of the cosmos a fascinating counterpoint to his intuitive connection to the celestial bodies.

He discovered the power of touch, though it was a hesitant exploration. One afternoon, while showing Truly how to identify different types of fungi, her hand brushed against his. It was a fleeting contact, but it sent a jolt through him, a warmth that spread from his fingertips to his heart. He hesitated, then, with a deliberate slowness, reached out and gently tapped her hand with the back of his own massive digit. It was a question, a tentative seeking of connection. Truly, understanding, didn't pull away. Instead, she turned her hand palm up, a silent invitation. Abel, with an almost reverent care, placed his fingertips on her palm, the contrast of their textures, his coarse fur against her smooth skin, a stark and beautiful reminder of their differences, yet somehow, it felt profoundly right.

The forest floor, usually a blanket of decaying leaves and vibrant moss, became a canvas for their shared experiences. Truly would collect fallen feathers, their delicate structure a source of endless wonder. Abel, seeing her fascination, would guide her to ancient trees where ravens nested, his silent presence a reassurance that she was safe to observe. He would show her the tracks of various animals, tracing their paths through the undergrowth with a single, deliberate finger, explaining through gestures the habits of the creatures that called this place home. He'd puff out his chest and mimic the lumbering gait of a bear, then point to the berries it favored, a silent lesson in the delicate balance of the ecosystem.

He learned that Truly's laughter was a sound of pure joy, a melody that echoed through the trees and made his own chest vibrate with a strange, pleasant resonance. He would often make a soft, chuffing sound when she laughed, a way of acknowledging and sharing in her happiness. He even found himself mimicking her expressions, a subtle lift of his brow when she seemed puzzled, a slight widening of his eyes when she expressed surprise. These were not conscious imitations, but rather the natural responses of a being slowly, cautiously, opening himself to another.

Their bond deepened not through grand pronouncements, but through a thousand tiny interactions, a continuous exchange of gestures, sounds, and shared moments of quiet observation. The forest, once a place of concealment and survival for Abel was transforming into a shared space, a neutral ground where two vastly different souls could meet and, in their own unique way, begin to understand one another. The language of the forest, the subtle whispers of wind and leaf, the silent stories etched in bark and stone, was becoming their shared tongue, a testament to the extraordinary power of connection that could bloom even in the most unlikely of circumstances. The towering trees bore silent witness to their burgeoning understanding, the dappled sunlight a soft benediction on their unconventional friendship. This was a dialogue of the heart, spoken in the ancient, enduring language of the wild.

The glade, once a sanctuary for Truly's solitude, now buzzed with a shared energy. The clandestine meetings, initially tinged with the caution of two wary beings, had unfurled over the past few weeks into a rhythm of comfortable companionship. Abel, with a grace that belied his colossal frame, would emerge from the ancient woods, his presence announced not by a thunderous tread, but by the subtle parting of branches, the hushed deference of the smaller creatures in his wake. Truly, no longer the apprehensive girl who had stumbled upon his domain, would be waiting, a small figure silhouetted against the dappled sunlight filtering through the dense canopy. The initial awe had settled into a quiet understanding, a recognition that in this wild heart of the Ozarks, they had found something akin to a haven, a place where the boundaries of their disparate worlds blurred into a shared existence.

Their days were now an exploration, a slow unfolding of each other's realities. Abel had become her silent guide, a gentle behemoth leading her through paths unseen by human eyes. He would move with a profound knowledge of the terrain, his massive form navigating the tangled undergrowth with an almost ethereal lightness. Truly, her usually hesitant steps now confidently following his lead, found herself traversing trails that wound deeper into the verdant embrace of the forest. He showed her the secrets held within the emerald depths: clusters of rare medicinal plants, their leaves unfurling with the promise of healing, their identification conveyed through patient gestures and the softest of rumbling explanations. He would point to a particular moss, its velvety texture a stark contrast to the rough bark of the ancient trees and then mimic the action of crushing it between his fingers, a silent lesson in its poultice making properties. He would lead her to hidden springs, their waters so clear they seemed to capture the very essence of the sky, and then mime the act of drinking, his amber eyes conveying a deep respect for the life-giving sustenance.

He revealed the secret nesting places of forest creatures, not to disturb, but to observe. Truly would watch, mesmerized, as Abel indicated a hollow in an ancient oak, his massive finger gently pointing to a flicker of movement within. It might be a family of squirrels, their tiny forms a flurry of activity, or a rare bird, its plumage a splash of vibrant color against the muted greens and browns of the forest. He taught her the art of observation, of recognizing the subtle signs of life, a disturbed patch of leaves, a fallen feather, the faint scent of a passing deer. He would point to a dewdrop clinging to a spiderweb, its delicate strands shimmering with a hundred tiny rainbows, and then, with a soft exhalation, create a gust of air that sent the droplet tumbling, a fleeting moment of ephemeral beauty captured and then released.

These were not just lessons in nature; they were offerings of trust, glimpses into Abel's world, a world steeped in the ancient rhythms of the earth. He would often pause, his massive head tilting as if listening to a distant melody, then gesture for Truly to remain still. In those moments of profound silence, she began to understand the forest not as a collection of trees and plants, but as a living, breathing entity, its every rustle, its every whisper, a form of communication. Abel, in his quiet way, was teaching her to listen, to attune herself to the subtler frequencies of existence, a skill that Truly, in her human experience, had largely forgotten.

In return, Truly offered him her world, a realm that, for Abel, was as alien as the stars. She spoke of her life, her voice, at first, a hesitant murmur, then growing stronger, more confident, as she navigated the uncharted territory of sharing her innermost thoughts. She spoke of the small cottage she called home, of the loneliness that had been her constant companion for so long. She described the quiet ache of her childhood, the absence of a family that had left a void within her, a yearning for connection that she had never truly known how to fill. Abel would sit, his immense frame a comforting presence, his amber eyes fixed on her, absorbing her words, the subtle nuances of her tone, the emotions that flickered across her face. He didn't always understand the specifics of her human world, the concept of "school," the intricacies of "jobs," the fleeting nature of human friendships, but he understood the underlying currents of longing, of a spirit searching for belonging.

She spoke of her dreams, those fantasy driven visions that danced in the quiet hours of the night. Dreams of belonging, of finding a place where she was not an outsider, where her gentle nature was not seen as a weakness. She dreamt of laughter, of shared moments of joy, of a warmth that could chase away the persistent chill of isolation. Abel would often respond to these narratives with a low rumble, a sound that Truly had come to interpret as empathy, a deep, resonant acknowledgment of her feelings. He would sometimes extend a massive hand, not to touch, but to hover near her, a silent offering of his presence, a tangible symbol that she was not alone.

He learned the rhythm of her human speech, the way certain words could evoke a cascade of emotions, the way her eyes would brighten when she spoke of something she cherished, and dim when she recalled a painful memory. He was a keen observer, his understanding of her growing not from explicit instruction, but from the cumulative effect of countless shared moments. He saw the way her brow furrowed in concentration when she tried to explain a complex idea, the way her lips would curve into a gentle smile when she felt understood. He began to anticipate her needs, to offer a steadying hand when she stumbled on a loose stone, to shield her from the sudden downpour with his colossal body, his mossy hide offering a surprisingly effective, if somewhat earthy, shelter.

Their friendship, this improbable alliance forged in the wild heart of the Ozarks, was a beacon of hope. It was a testament to the extraordinary possibility of connection that could bloom between beings who, by all societal accounts, were destined to remain separate, forever divided by the chasm of their inherent differences. Abel, the gentle giant of the ancient woods, and Truly, the solitary girl from the fringes of human civilization, had found common ground in the shared language of the wilderness. Their clandestine meetings were no longer acts of defiance against unspoken rules, but essential anchors in their lives, rituals that nourished their spirits and defied the expected order of their worlds.

The forest, once a place of solitude for Truly and a realm of deep solitude for Abel was transforming. It was becoming a shared space, a sanctuary where the rigid boundaries of their origins softened, where the whispers of the wind carried not tales of separation, but echoes of understanding. Abel would often find himself seeking Truly's presence, a quiet anticipation building within him as the appointed hour approached. He would observe her, her small form a vibrant counterpoint to the ancient majesty of the trees, and a profound sense of contentment would wash over him. He had learned that her presence brought a unique kind of peace, a quiet joy that settled deep within his ancient heart.

One afternoon, as they sat by a babbling brook, Truly was sketching in a worn notebook, her brow furrowed in concentration. Abel watched her, his gaze soft, curious. She was drawing a particular fern, its fronds unfurling in a delicate, intricate pattern. When she finished, she turned the notebook towards him, her eyes questioning. Abel leaned closer, his massive head dwarfing the small book. He recognized the fern, not by its name, but by its essence, its place in the forest's tapestry. He pointed to a specific detail in her drawing, a slight asymmetry in one of the fronds, and then, with a single, powerful finger, mimicked the gentle curve of a naturally growing fern, demonstrating how the wind, over time, had shaped its form. Truly's eyes widened in understanding, a small gasp of delight escaping her lips. She quickly corrected her drawing, her movements quick and eager, her appreciation for his silent correction evident in the renewed vigor of her pencil strokes.

This exchange, seemingly insignificant, represented a profound shift. It was no longer just Truly learning from Abel; it was a true dialogue, a shared creation. He, in turn, was learning to articulate his understanding of the world in ways she could comprehend, and she was learning to translate his intuitive knowledge into forms she could process and appreciate. Their shared explorations had become more than just excursions; they were expeditions into the heart of their mutual curiosity, a joint venture into the vastness of their shared existence.

He would sometimes bring her gifts, not of manufactured trinkets, but of the forest's bounty. A perfectly formed bird's nest, found abandoned, its intricate weaving a marvel of natural architecture. A cluster of wild strawberries, their sweetness a concentrated burst of sunshine. A smooth, water-worn stone, its surface cool and calming to the touch. Truly would receive these offerings with a gratitude that radiated from her, her smiles genuine and bright, her soft exclamations of delight a melody that Abel found himself cherishing. He learned that her happiness was contagious, a vibrant energy that made the very air around them feel lighter, more alive.

He had even begun to mimic some of her more human mannerisms, not consciously, but as a natural extension of their developing bond. When she expressed concern, a slight tremor in her voice, he would sometimes tilt his head in a way that mirrored her questioning gaze. When she laughed, a sound that always filled him with a strange, resonant warmth, he would sometimes emit a low, rumbling chuckle, a sound that vibrated deep within his chest, a shared expression of mirth. These were not acts of mimicry for the sake of imitation, but rather the organic responses of a being who was slowly, cautiously, opening his heart to another.

The forest, under the quiet spell of their unlikely alliance, seemed to respond in kind. The animals grew less skittish in their presence, as if sensing the gentle nature of their interactions. The sunlight, filtering through the leaves, seemed to paint the glade with a warmer hue whenever they were together. The ancient trees stood as silent witnesses to their burgeoning friendship, their gnarled branches reaching towards the sky as if in benediction. Abel and Truly, two souls from vastly different worlds, had found solace and understanding in the quiet heart of the wilderness, their bond a testament to the enduring power of connection, a whispered promise of hope in a world that often felt defined by division. Their alliance, though unspoken and unconventional, was the strongest of covenants, a silent vow to protect and cherish the fragile sanctuary they had discovered together.

3

YEARS OF WHISPERS AND WILDNESS

The passage of time, measured not by ticking clocks or shifting suns, but by the slow, deliberate cycles of nature, began to weave Truly and Abel's lives into a shroud of shared experience. The vibrant, embrace of summer had been their initial sanctuary, a time of exploration and the blossoming of their unlikely trust. Now, as the days began to shorten and the air took on a brisk, invigorating edge, they found their sanctuary transforming, mirroring the grand spectacle of autumn's arrival. The familiar greens of the forest canopy began to ignite, first with subtle blushes of crimson and gold, then with an blaze that painted the hillsides in hues of amber, russet, and fiery orange.

Truly, her usual solitary walks now punctuated by Abel's silent companionship, found a new layer of wonder in this seasonal metamorphosis. He would often pause, his great form a shadowed sentinel against the vibrant backdrop, and his amber eyes would follow the lazy drift of a single falling leaf. There was an understanding in his stillness, a quiet acknowledgment of the earth's surrender to the coming cold, a process he seemed to observe with an ancient, ingrained patience. He would sometimes gently nudge a fallen maple leaf towards her with his massive finger, its veins intricate as a roadmap, and Truly would accept it, its dryness a stark contrast to the dewy freshness of summer. She learned to recognize the subtle shift in the forest's scent, the earthy musk of decaying leaves, the sharp tang of pine needles, the faint, sweet perfume of late-blooming wildflowers clinging defiantly to life. Abel, in his silent way, pointed out the changing patterns of the wildlife: the frantic gathering of nuts by squirrels, the migratory flights of birds etching V-shaped patterns against the vast sky, the increased vigilance of deer as their coats thickened. He showed her how certain plants, having shed their blossoms, now bore clusters of berries, their jewel-toned hues a promise of sustenance through the leaner months. He would gently pluck a deep red hawthorn berry and offer it to her, its tart sweetness a sharp, awakening flavor on her tongue.

Their meetings, once dictated by the exploration of a new connection, had solidified into a steadfast ritual. As autumn's colors began to soften, yielding to the muted palette of late fall, a chill permeated the air. The forest floor became a thick carpet of fallen leaves, rustling with every step, a symphony of dry whispers that accompanied their quiet conversations. Abel, his shaggy hide offering a natural camou-flage against the darkening woods, became an even more imposing, yet comforting, presence. He would often sit with Truly by their usual meeting spot, his massive form a warm, living bulwark against the encroaching cold. He would clear a patch of ground with a sweep of his hand, creating a small, sheltered space where they could sit, the fallen leaves forming a surprisingly soft cushion.

Truly found herself increasingly drawn to confide in him, her voice often a hushed murmur against the sighing wind. The turbulent un-dercurrents of her young life, the lingering shadows of her isolated childhood, the uncertainties of her future, these were things she could speak of to Abel with a freedom she had never experienced. He listened without judgment, his amber eyes reflecting the fading sunlight, his quiet presence a profound reassurance. She spoke of the loneliness that still sometimes visited her, the ache for a connection she had never truly known. She confessed her hopes, whispered dreams of finding her place in the world, of being accepted, of finding a love that was as steadfast and true as Abel himself. He offered no advice, no platitudes. Instead, he would sometimes emit a low, resonant rumble from deep within his chest, a sound that Truly had come to understand as a form of empathy, a vibration that seemed to resonate with the very core of her being. He would occasionally reach out a colossal hand, not to touch, but to hover near her, a silent testament to his unwavering presence. His stillness was more eloquent than any human utterance, conveying a wisdom that transcended words. He taught her, through his silent example, the enduring strength of resilience, the quiet dignity of existence, and the profound beauty of simply *being*.

As the last evidence of autumn's color faded, the world outside their secluded haven transformed once more. Winter descended, cloaking the Ozarks in a blanket of pristine white. The familiar paths became obscured, the babbling brook froze into an ice covered plain, and the forest seemed to hold its breath, hushed and still. Yet, even in this stark, monochrome landscape, Truly and Abel continued their ritual. Their meetings became more precious, their shared warmth a stark contrast to the biting cold. Abel, his thick hide providing ample protection, would guide Truly through the snow-laden woods, his knowledge of the terrain unwavering even when the landscape was utterly trans-formed. He showed her the delicate tracery of animal tracks left in the fresh snow; each print a story whispered in the quiet of winter.

He pointed out the hardy evergreens, their boughs heavy with snow, and the dormant life that lay hidden beneath the frozen surface, a testament to nature's enduring power.

During these frigid encounters, Truly found herself sharing even deeper vulnerabilities. The quiet desperation that sometimes clawed at her, the fear that she was inherently flawed, unlovable, these were the ghosts she wrestled with in the solitude of her cottage. Abel's unwavering gaze, his steady presence, became a balm to her wounded spirit. He was a silent observer of her emotional landscape, his understanding profound. He would sometimes gently nudge her with his massive head, a soft, comforting pressure, as if to say, "You are not alone." He taught her that strength could be found not only in outward displays of power, but in the quiet fortitude of endurance, the unyielding spirit that perseveres through hardship. He was a living embodiment of the earth's ancient resilience, and in his presence, Truly began to find a reflection of that same strength within herself.

Their secret remained their own, a precious pact held within the embrace of the ancient woods. It was a treasure they guarded fiercely, a sanctuary from a world that would likely misunderstand, perhaps even condemn, their bond. Truly knew, with a certainty that settled deep in her bones, that Abel was more than just a creature of myth; he was her confidant, her protector, her truest friend. He had seen her at her most vulnerable, her most afraid, and had offered her nothing but acceptance and quiet solace. In return, she had offered him the simple, yet profound, gift of her trust, her company, and the burgeoning affection of her young heart. The shared silence between them, once filled with apprehension, was now a comfortable blanket, woven with unspoken understanding and a deep, abiding respect.

And then, as if the earth itself exhaled a sigh of relief, winter began to recede. The snow melted, revealing the first tentative shoots of green pushing through the thawing soil. The frozen streams began to chuckle and flow, their icy grip loosened. Spring had arrived, ushering in a season of vibrant rebirth, a renewal that mirrored the blossoming hope within Truly's own heart. Abel and she would return to their glade, now carpeted with wildflowers, their delicate petals unfurling in a joyous explosion of color. The air was alive with the chirping of birds, the buzzing of insects, the rustle of new leaves.

In this season of awakening, Truly felt a new surge of confidence. Abel's steadfast presence had nurtured a quiet strength within her. She spoke of her dreams not as fragile wishes, but as possibilities. She spoke of the future, no longer with trepidation, but with a sense of purpose. Abel, in his gentle way, encouraged this burgeoning self-assurance. He would bring her the first ripe berries of spring, their sweetness a vibrant herald of the coming abundance. He would lead her to ancient trees, their bark rough and gnarled, and with a sweep of his hand, indicate the new buds appearing on their branches, a silent promise of life renewed. He was teaching her to see the cyclic nature of existence, that endings were merely preludes to new beginnings, that even in the harshest of winters, life persisted, waiting for its moment to bloom. Their shared sanctuary, weathered through the changing seasons, had become more than just a meeting place; it was a crucible where their bond had been forged and tempered, a testament to the enduring power of connection that transcended the boundaries of species, of worlds, of understanding. The whispers of secrecy had woven themselves into the very fabric of their shared existence, a silent vow held within the wild heart of the Ozarks, a promise of enduring friendship that would weather every season to come.

Abel's protectiveness was a force of nature, as instinctual and unwavering as the turning of the seasons. As Truly navigated the years of her youth, a subtle shift occurred in the silent guardian's vigil. No longer was his watch simply a passive presence at the periphery of their shared glade. Now, whenever Truly ventured close to the tangled borders of the forest, to the edge where the wild embrace of his domain met the more unpredictable world of humankind, his senses were hyper-alert. He would melt into the dappled shadows, a sentinel of moss and shadow, his amber eyes, usually filled with a gentle curiosity, now sharpened with a primal vigilance. He had, over their years of companionship, developed an unnerving ability to discern the subtle, almost imperceptible signs of human aggression. It wasn't just the boisterous laughter that might spill from the distant village, or the metallic clang of a blacksmith's hammer; it was something deeper, a resonant disharmony that humans often carried with them.

He could sense the predatory glint in a stranger's eye, a cold, calculating flicker that was absent in the innocent curiosity of a child. He could feel the harshness that tightened the muscles in a person's jaw, the almost aggressive stance they adopted when they felt threatened or, worse, when they intended to inflict harm. These were not learned behaviors, but ancient instincts, honed by generations of his kind who had learned to navigate the perilous landscape of interaction with the two-legged creatures who often brought disruption and destruction. Now, those instincts, so potent and deeply ingrained, were singularly focused on Truly. She was the fragile human connection, the unexpected bond that had woven itself into the very fabric of his being, and his primary directive had become her safety. He was a silent guardian, an unseen shield, ensuring that the sanctuary they had carved out for themselves remained inviolate, a haven where she could explore and grow without the shadow of fear.

There were times Truly felt it, a prickling sensation on the back of her neck, a feeling of being watched, not with malice, but with an intense, unwavering focus. She would pause, scanning the dense foliage, catching a fleeting glimpse of movement, a shade deeper than the surrounding shadows, or the brief, unmistakable gleam of those luminous amber eyes. She understood, without needing words, that Abel was near, his immense presence a comforting reassurance that often dispelled any lingering unease. He never intruded, never startled her, but his watchful gaze was a constant, silent promise:

You are not alone. You are safe.

One crisp autumn afternoon, a group of young men from the village, their faces flushed with the bravado of drink and the recklessness of youth, ventured deeper into the woods than usual, their raucous laughter and stumbling footsteps disturbing the natural quiet. Truly, drawn by the scent of late-blooming honeysuckle, had wandered a little further from their usual meeting place, her attention caught by a particularly vibrant patch of crimson toadstools. She was engrossed in sketching their intricate patterns in her worn notebook when the sound of their drunken shouting pierced the air, growing closer. Her heart gave a nervous lurch. She knew those voices, the careless swagger they carried, the way they sometimes leered at women they passed on the road.

From his concealed vantage point behind a thicket of ancient oaks, Abel stiffened. The low growl that rumbled in his chest was almost imperceptible, a vibration that seemed to shake the very earth beneath him. He recognized the discordant energy radiating from the approaching humans, the volatile mixture of arrogance and menace. Their intentions were not innocent exploration; their trespass was fueled by a careless disregard for the wild, and potentially, for any solitary soul they might encounter. His gaze, usually soft when turned towards Truly, narrowed with a protective fire. He watched as the young men stumbled into the clearing, their eyes scanning the area with a coarse curiosity. One of them, a burly fellow with a sneer etched onto his face, pointed vaguely in Truly's direction, his voice carrying a rough, taunting edge. "Lookee here, lads! A lost little doe, all by herself. Might be some fun to be had."

A chill, colder than the autumn air, traced its way down Truly's spine. She instinctively clutched her sketchpad closer, her mind racing. She knew she should retreat, melt back into the trees, but a part of her, fueled by Abel's silent, steadfast presence, felt a flicker of something akin to defiance. She would not be easily intimidated. However, before she could decide on a course of action, a subtle shift occurred in the air. The birdsong, which had been gradually silenced by the intruders, ceased altogether. The rustling of leaves underfoot, which had accompanied the young men's clumsy progress, suddenly stopped. An unnatural stillness descended upon the glade, a silence so profound it felt heavy, charged with an unseen power.

The young men faltered, their bravado evaporating in the face of this sudden, unnerving quiet. They looked around, their swagger replaced by a nervous unease. The lead man, his face pale beneath his stubble, muttered, "What was that? Did you hear that?" Another, his eyes wide, stammered, "It's... it's like everything just... stopped." They could not see Abel, his mastery of camouflage absolute, but they could feel him. The air around them seemed to thicken, to press in, carrying with it an invisible weight of ancient power and immense displeasure. A low, guttural sound, like the grinding of stones deep within the earth, emanated from the shadows. It was not a roar of aggression, but a warning, a deep, resonant rumble that vibrated in their very bones, speaking of territorial boundaries and consequences for their trespass.

Panic bloomed on their faces. The bravado was gone, replaced by a primal fear. They scrambled backward, tripping over each other in their haste to escape the oppressive atmosphere. Their raucous laughter was replaced by choked gasps and panicked shouts of "Let's get outta here!" They didn't need to see the source of the unsettling power; they simply knew they were unwelcome, and that an ancient force had made its displeasure known. Truly watched them flee, their retreat far more hasty than their approach. As the last echoes of their panicked footsteps faded, the birds cautiously resumed their chirping, and the natural symphony of the forest slowly returned.

Truly let out a shaky breath, her heart still thrumming against her ribs. She looked towards the dense foliage where she knew Abel was hidden, a profound sense of gratitude washing over her. She couldn't see him, but she knew he was there, his silent, unwavering protection a shield against any perceived threat. She whispered into the quiet air, "Thank you," a simple offering of thanks to her unseen guardian. A moment later, a single, perfect crimson toadstool, dislodged from its spot by the fleeing men, tumbled gently from the branches above and landed at her feet. It was Abel's way of acknowledging her, a silent message:

You are seen. You are cared for.

This incident solidified something within Truly. It wasn't just a feeling anymore; it was a certainty. Abel was her protector. His instincts, so powerful and so finely tuned, had recognized the potential danger long before she had fully registered it herself. He hadn't needed to reveal himself, to unleash his full might. His mere presence, the subtle emanation of his protective aura, had been enough to drive away the threat. He had used his power not for violence, but for deterrence, a testament to the depth of his understanding and the restraint of his immense strength. He understood the fragility of her human form, the vulnerability that came with her species, and he dedicated himself to mitigating those risks.

He continued to refine his watchfulness. He began to recognize the specific scents that signaled human presence, the acrid tang of sweat, the lingering smell of woodsmoke clinging to clothes, the metallic scent of tools. He learned to distinguish the hurried, purposeful tread of a hunter from the aimless wanderings of a lost traveler. He could differentiate the sharp, aggressive bark of a village dog from the playful yaps of a pet. These were not mere observations; they were data points, processed by an ancient, intuitive intelligence, all filtered through the lens of safeguarding Truly. If he detected anything that veered from the neutral or benign, his senses would zero in, his focus unwavering until the potential threat had passed or was sufficiently deterred.

There were days Truly would explore the fringes of the woods, gathering herbs or sketching wildflowers, and she would sense his nearby presence. A sudden stillness in the undergrowth, a pair of eyes watching from the deep shade, a shadow that moved with an unnatural grace. He would never approach directly unless he deemed it absolutely necessary, but his vigilance was a constant, comforting blanket. He was a ghost in the periphery of her vision, a guardian woven into the very essence of the forest. He had learned to anticipate her movements, to understand the rhythm of her explorations. He knew when she was likely to be near the edges of his domain, and it was then that his protectiveness would swell, a silent tide of awareness washing over the woods.

He understood that humans, even those who meant no harm, could be unpredictable. A child could wander too far, a lost traveler could become disoriented, or, as she had already experienced, a group of boisterous, ill-intentioned individuals could trespass. His role was to be the buffer, the unseen force that redirected potential dangers away from her. He had no desire to interact with other humans; their presence often carried energy that he found unsettling. But for Truly, he was willing to step beyond his usual solitude, to extend his vigilance to the very borders of her world.

His protectiveness was not a cage, but a carefully constructed perimeter of safety. He understood that Truly needed to explore, to learn, to experience the world beyond their glade. He facilitated this freedom by ensuring that her journeys into the less protected areas were as safe as possible. He would guide her away from treacherous terrain, his presence a silent warning that would make her pause and reconsider her path. He would sometimes leave a trail of large, distinctive paw prints, leading her away from areas where he had detected the unsettling scent of human activity or the presence of dangerous predators that might pose a risk to her. He was teaching her, in his own way, about the dangers of the wild, not to instill fear, but to foster respect and caution.

He learned to read the cues of her moods as well. If she seemed anxious or preoccupied, he would remain closer, his presence a more tangible reassurance. If she was relaxed and joyful, he would allow himself a little more distance, his watchful gaze still present, but less intensely focused. He was an astute observer, a master of non-verbal communication, and he translated these observations into action, adjusting his protective stance accordingly. His love for Truly, though unspoken, was expressed in every silent vigil, every watchful glance, every subtle redirection of potential harm. It was a fierce, primal protectiveness, a testament to the profound bond that had formed between a creature of myth and a young woman finding her place in the world. He was her wild heart's guardian, and she, unknowingly, had become the most precious treasure he had ever been tasked to protect.

The afternoon sun, a golden orb through the thinning canopy, painted dappled patterns on the forest floor. Truly, with Abel, a silent, immense shadow at her side, found herself drawn further into the woods than she had ever dared venture before. The familiar comfort of their glade, a sanctuary carved from mutual understanding, was now a receding memory. Today, a new chapter was unfolding, one whispered on the breeze and etched in the ancient, crossing roots that snaked across their path. Abel's usual hyper-vigilance had softened, replaced by a quiet curiosity that mirrored her own. The primal alertness that had flared when the drunken villagers intruded was now a subtle, underlying current, a constant awareness that spoke of a deeper, more complex world than she had ever imagined.

He had begun to lead her, not with spoken words, but with subtle gestures, a shift in his weight, a tilt of his massive head towards a barely discernible trail. It was a world revealed through instinct and observation woven from the silences between rustling leaves and the ancient language of the forest itself. He showed her the 'paths of the elders,' as she would later come to think of them, faint impressions in the earth, worn smooth by generations of passing feet, too narrow for human stride, too deliberate for mere animal passage. He would pause at the edge of these almost invisible highways, his amber eyes, now alight with a gentle pride, meeting hers. He didn't invite her onto them, not directly. Instead, he'd trace their route with a massive finger, outlining a journey through the dense woods, a silent explanation of routes taken, of journeys completed, of lives lived within these ancient boundaries.

Their exploration was a careful dance. Abel's primary directive remained Truly's safety, a foundational truth that underpinned every step. But this was no longer solely about warding off external threats. It was about sharing, about offering a glimpse into his own existence, a tentative unveiling of the world that shaped him. He led her not into the heart of his hidden clan's domain, for that remained a sacred, inviolable space, but to the very edges of its influence. He showed her the boundaries, marked not by fences or stone walls, but by the subtle shifts in the forest's character. Here, the trees seemed to lean in, their branches intertwined in a more intimate embrace. The undergrowth, while still wild, held a curated neatness, as if tended by unseen hands. The air itself felt different, charged with a quiet energy, a resonance that spoke of presence, of life, of a community that moved in harmony with the natural world.

He would stop by a cluster of particularly ancient, moss-laden oaks, their trunks wider than three men could encircle. He'd run a calloused hand over the rough bark, a gesture of deep respect, and then, with a soft grunt, he would rap his knuckles against a specific section of the wood. A hollow, resonant sound echoed through the stillness, a deep thrum that seemed to vibrate not just in the air, but in Truly's very bones. He repeated the action, tapping out a simple, rhythmic pattern. Then, he'd pause, listening intently. A moment later, from a seemingly impossible distance, a similar rhythmic drumming answered. It was a call and response, a conversation carried on the wind, a testament to a communication system far more intricate and subtle than Truly had ever conceived. He watched her face, his gaze searching for understanding, for comprehension of this silent, primal dialogue.

He showed her the communal foraging grounds, patches of land where berries grew in improbable abundance, where the choicest roots were clustered, and where the sweet, dew-kissed leaves of certain plants were always plentiful. He didn't pluck the fruits himself, not while she was near. Instead, he'd gesture towards them, a silent invitation to observe. He'd then pick up a fallen branch, its wood softened and hollowed by time and moisture, and begin to beat a steady, percussive rhythm against its side. The sound, he conveyed through a series of gestures, was a signal. It was a message to his kin, a notification that resources were available, a call for gathering, for sharing. It was a tangible demonstration of their communal spirit, of a society built on cooperation and mutual support, a stark contrast to the often-competitive nature of human villages.

As he tapped, Truly watched the forest with new eyes. She began to notice things she had previously overlooked. A faint disturbance in the dew-laden grass, too deliberate for wind. A cluster of perfectly ripe berries, arranged almost artfully on a broad leaf. The sudden silence of a flock of birds, as if they had collectively received a warning.

These were the subtle signs, the whispered clues of Abel's kin, the Bigfoot, moving through their world. He was revealing to her not just his territory, but the very fabric of his existence, a testament to the profound trust that had blossomed between them.

He pointed out specific trees; their bark marked with intricate patterns. These weren't carvings made by human hands. They were natural markings, enhanced by the subtle touch of Bigfoot fingers, like a signature, a territorial marker, a message left for those who understood its language. He'd run his fingers along the lines, his touch reverent, and then he'd mime scratching an itch, a surprisingly human gesture that made Truly smile. It was his way of showing her that these markings were not just symbols, but functional, practical elements of their lives, like trail markers or signposts in their vast, untamed world.

The concept of 'clan' was something Abel conveyed through actions rather than words. He would point to a distant ridge, then make a sweeping gesture encompassing a wide expanse of forest. He'd then bring his hands together, interlocking his fingers in a gesture of unity, of togetherness. He showed her a series of large, communal nesting sites, hollowed-out areas beneath ancient trees, lined with soft moss and dried leaves. These were not individual homes, but shared spaces, places where the clan gathered, where young were raised, where stories were told, and where the collective wisdom of generations was passed down. He mimed the act of sharing food, of huddling together for warmth, of protecting the vulnerable. It was a powerful, unspoken lesson in community, a stark contrast to the often-isolated lives humans led.

He guided her through areas where the forest floor was littered with the discarded husks of nuts and the gnawed remnants of edible roots. These were not random piles of debris. They were evidence of communal feasts, of shared harvests. He pointed to a particularly large, smooth stone, worn flat on its surface. Through gestures, he explained that this was a gathering stone, a place where important decisions were made, where disputes were settled, where the elders of the clan convened. He showed her how the moss around the stone was worn away, evidence of countless gatherings over countless years.

Abel's world, as he was revealing it to Truly, was one of ancient traditions, of deep connection to the land, and of a complex social structure that valued cooperation above all else. He showed her how his kin communicated not just through sound, but through scent marking, through subtle shifts in posture, through the very way they moved through the forest. He mimed the act of leaving a scent marker on a tree, a signal of passage, of presence, of intention. He explained, through a series of expressive gestures, that these scent trails were like an invisible map, guiding others, warning them of dangers, and announcing arrivals.

He also demonstrated their mastery of camouflage. He would point to a patch of dense foliage, then with a silent grace, he would seem to melt into it, his massive form becoming one with the shadows and leaves. He would remain still for long moments, an almost imperceptible part of the forest, until he chose to reappear, a ghost emerging from the green. This was not just for concealment; it was a fundamental aspect of their survival, their way of blending seamlessly with their environment, of becoming one with the wild. He showed her how they could mimic the rustling of leaves, the creak of branches, the chirping of birds, a symphony of natural sounds that allowed them to move undetected.

There were times when Abel would pause, his massive head tilted, listening to something Truly couldn't perceive. He would then make a series of short, sharp gestures, a rapid staccato of movements that conveyed a sense of urgency. He'd then gently, but firmly, steer her in a different direction, away from a particular area. She learned to trust these silent directives implicitly. Later, she would sometimes catch the faintest scent of smoke, or hear the distant, muffled sounds of human activity, confirming that he had indeed guided her away from potential danger, from the intrusion of the human world.

He never revealed the exact location of his clan's primary settlement. That was a boundary he would not cross, a secret he guarded with the ferocity of a parent protecting a child. But he showed her enough to paint a vivid picture of a hidden, thriving society. He showed her the ancient hunting grounds, where game was managed with respect, where no creature was hunted unnecessarily. He showed her the medicinal herb gardens, tended with care, their bounty shared amongst the clan. He showed her the sacred groves, places of contemplation and reverence, where the elders communed with the spirits of the forest.

Each revelation was a carefully measured step, a testament to Abel's growing trust in Truly. He was not just her protector; he was becoming her guide, her interpreter of the wild. He was revealing to her not just his world, but a deeper understanding of her own connection to nature, a connection she had always felt but had never fully articulated. He was showing her that the forest was not merely a collection of trees and animals, but a living, breathing entity, populated by beings of immense wisdom and profound connection, beings like himself, who lived in harmony with its rhythms, and who guarded its secrets with their very lives.

He would sometimes sit with her at the edge of a clearing, his massive form exuding a sense of quiet contentment. He would watch the play of sunlight on the leaves, the flight of a butterfly, the scurry of a squirrel. In these moments, he wasn't the formidable guardian or the keeper of secrets. He was simply a creature at peace in his natural world, and he was sharing that peace with her. He would reach out, not to touch her, but to gently brush a fallen leaf from her hair, a gesture of tenderness that spoke volumes. These shared moments of quiet observation, of silent communion, were as significant as any grand revelation. They were the threads that wove their bond tighter, the unspoken promises of a shared future, a future where the boundaries between their worlds, though still respected, were becoming increasingly permeable, softened by the warmth of trust and the enduring power of understanding. He was offering her a glimpse, a privileged window into a world she could never fully enter, but a world she could now, with him as her guide, begin to truly comprehend.

The sunlight, once a source of comfort, now felt like a spotlight, highlighting Truly's growing unease. The glade, her childhood sanctuary, had begun to feel like a cage, its familiar boundaries constricting with each passing day. The whispers had started subtly, at first. Casual observations from other girls her age, tinged with an unspoken judgment. "Truly's always off in the woods," they'd murmur, their voices laced with curiosity that quickly morphed into suspicion. "What is she even doing out there all alone?" Alone, that was the word that stung the most. They couldn't fathom the silent companionship she found amongst the ancient trees, the profound connection she shared with Abel, a being so far removed from their world, yet so much more understanding than any human she knew.

Her mother, bless her well-meaning heart, would often try to steer her back towards what she considered normal. "Truly, dear, Mrs. Gable is having her quilting bee on Saturday. You should go. It's important to... connect with people your own age." Connect. The word felt hollow. How could she connect with girls who spoke of embroidered cushions and local gossip when her mind was filled with the scent of pine needles and the silent language of the forest? How could she explain the quiet strength she felt when Abel's massive hand rested, not on her shoulder, but beside her, a silent promise of protection? They wouldn't understand. They couldn't. Their world was one of predictable routines, of social niceties, of carefully constructed illusions. Hers, increasingly, was becoming one of raw truth, of instinct, of a bond that transcended words.

The village itself seemed to shrink around her, its once-charming paths now feeling claustrophobic. The baker's wife, a woman whose smile used to be a warm invitation, now offered a strained, tight-lipped greeting, her eyes lingering on Truly's slightly disheveled appearance, the faint smudges of earth on her worn boots. The blacksmith, usually jovial, would fall silent when she approached, his hammer falling still, his gaze following her with an unnerving intensity. It was as if her solitary wanderings had cast a strange shadow, marking her as an outsider, a deviation from the accepted norm.

She tried, she really did, to bridge the chasm. She'd sit in on the afternoon gatherings, forcing a smile, nodding along to conversations about the price of grain or the upcoming harvest festival. But her thoughts would drift, replaying Abel's silent gestures, the way he'd point out a rare mushroom or trace a particular pattern on a tree trunk. She'd recall the sheer, unadulterated joy of running through a sun-filled clearing, Abel's quiet amusement at her clumsy attempts to mimic his silent grace. These memories were a balm, a secret reservoir of peace in a sea of unspoken expectations.

The girls at the village well, their laughter echoing with a carefree abandon Truly once shared, now spoke of suitors, of dowries, of the future they all were expected to build within the village walls. They'd eye her with a mixture of pity and disdain. "Still no interest, Truly?" Lilli, her childhood friend, would ask, her tone a careful balance of concern and something harder to define. "You're not getting any younger. You need to think about settling down." Settling down. The phrase conjured images of dusty rooms, of stifled dreams, of a life lived within carefully prescribed boundaries. It was a life that felt utterly alien to her, a life that was already slipping away with every moment she spent with Abel, with every secret shared under the ancient canopy.

The weight of these expectations was a heavy cloak. It pressed down on her shoulders, making her movements stiff, her smiles forced. She longed to explain, to tell them about the world that was opening up to her, a world of ancient wisdom, of a deep, intrinsic connection to the earth, of a being who saw her not for her potential as a wife or a daughter, but as herself. But the words caught in her throat, tangled with the fear of ridicule, of disbelief, of the inevitable condemnation. How could she explain a Bigfoot? How could she convey the profound gentleness of a creature so often depicted as a monstrous legend? They would think she was mad. Perhaps, in their eyes, she was.

Her solitude, once a choice born of a yearning for peace, was now becoming an enforced isolation. The very people who were supposed to be her community were slowly, subtly, pushing her away. They didn't understand her newfound quietness, her occasional faraway gaze, the way her heart would quicken at the distant call of a hawk, a sound that Abel had taught her to interpret. They saw her withdrawal as aloofness, her love of the woods as a peculiar eccentricity. They couldn't see the vibrant, expanding world that held her captive, a world that made their concerns seem so... small.

This growing chasm between her inner life and the outer reality created a gnawing loneliness. It was a different kind of loneliness than she had ever known. It wasn't the absence of company, but the absence of understanding. It was the silent ache of being fundamentally disconnected, of holding within her a truth that could not be shared. The woods, her sanctuary, became her only true refuge. The rough bark of a tree under her hand, the soft rustle of leaves, the steady, silent presence of Abel, these were the things that grounded her, that reaffirmed her reality.

She would find herself staring out of her small bedroom window at the dark line of the forest against the night sky, an ache in her chest. She'd imagine Abel moving through those trees, a silent guardian, his senses alive to the night. And she would feel a pang of longing, a deep yearning to be there, with him, away from the stifling expectations of the human world. The fear of discovery, of the consequences that might arise if her connection to Abel were ever revealed, added another layer to her growing anxiety. It was a secret she guarded fiercely, a precious, dangerous thing that made her both incredibly rich and profoundly vulnerable.

The contrast was stark, almost painful. In the woods, with Abel, she was seen, truly seen. He communicated with her not through words, but through shared experiences, through silent acknowledgments of her presence, through gestures that conveyed a depth of feeling she had never encountered. He taught her to read the subtle signs of the forest, to understand its rhythms, its language. He showed her a world where beings lived in harmony with nature, where strength was tempered with gentleness, and where community was built on mutual respect, not social obligation.

Back in the village, she was an enigma, a puzzle they couldn't solve. Her quietness was interpreted as defiance, her independence as a rejection of their values. The simple act of going for a walk was met with suspicious glances. The boys who once teased her playfully now averted their eyes, a newfound awkwardness in their interactions. It was as if her connection to the wild, her secret friendship, had rendered her invisible to them, or worse, a subject of whispered speculation.

She found herself retreating further into herself, the stolen moments with Abel becoming even more precious. They were an anchor in the storm of her adolescent life, a reminder that there was a world beyond the confines of the village, a world where she belonged, even if she couldn't fully articulate why or how. She learned to compartmentalize, to switch between the facade of the compliant village girl and the quiet observer of the wild. But the strain of maintaining this duality was beginning to show. Her smiles felt thinner, her laughter more brittle.

The villagers, in their own way, were creating the very thing they seemed to fear: an outcast. By judging her unspoken choices, by withdrawing their warmth, they were pushing her towards the very wilderness they cautioned her against. Truly understood, with a growing clarity, that her path was diverging from theirs, irrevocably. The wild was calling to her, not just through Abel, but through a part of her own soul that was finally awakening, a part that resonated with the ancient rhythms of the earth, a part that found solace and belonging not in the chatter of human society, but in the profound silence of the forest.

She remembered a particular afternoon, the air thick with the scent of rain and damp earth. She had been helping her mother mend fishing nets by the river, the task monotonous and soul-crushing. Lilli and a few other girls were there, their conversation a relentless stream of village gossip. Truly's hands moved mechanically, her mind a thousand miles away. Suddenly, a flash of movement in the trees across the river caught her eye. It was Abel, a fleeting glimpse of dark fur against the green, his eyes, even from that distance, seemed to meet hers. A wave of warmth washed over her, a silent acknowledgment, a shared secret. Lilli nudged her. "Daydreaming again, Truly? You'd better pay attention, or you'll snag your fingers." Truly offered a weak smile, but her heart was already elsewhere, soaring with the freedom she felt in those fleeting moments of connection. The riverbank, with its incessant drone of human voices, suddenly felt like a cage.

The isolation wasn't just about being misunderstood; it was about the slow erosion of her sense of self. The constant unspoken judgments chipped away at her confidence, making her question her own instincts, her own desires. Was she wrong to find solace in the woods? Was it truly so strange to feel a deeper connection to a creature of legend than to the girls who had grown up beside her? These questions, left unanswered, festered, creating a quiet despair that even Abel's presence couldn't entirely dispel.

He could offer her protection, companionship, and a window into a world of profound beauty and wisdom, but he couldn't shield her from the realities of human society. He couldn't quell the whispers, couldn't mend the growing rift between her and her community. And in that inability lay a new kind of vulnerability for Truly. She was caught between two worlds, belonging fully to neither. The wild offered her freedom, but it also meant a future of continued isolation from her own kind. The village offered a semblance of belonging, but it meant sacrificing the truest part of herself. This was the shadow of human society, a complex, suffocating force that made the quiet sanctuary of the woods all the more alluring, and all the more tragically necessary. Her time with Abel was not just a precious escape; it was becoming a vital lifeline, the only place where she felt truly seen, truly alive, in a world that increasingly threatened to make her disappear.

The air in the shadowed grove, usually a balm to Truly's spirit, now hummed with a disquiet she couldn't quite shake. It wasn't the rustling leaves or the distant murmur of the stream; it was a subtler, more primal dissonance, emanating from the very beings she had come to know and, in Abel's case, to cherish. Abel himself was a constant, a steadfast anchor in her increasingly complex world. His silent presence, the way he'd instinctively shift his weight when she grew tired, the gentle rumble in his chest that served as a form of silent reassurance, these were constants she relied on. But even he, her confidant, her protector, was bound by ties that stretched far beyond their shared glades, ties that were beginning to chafe against the edges of their burgeoning affection.

4

THE CLAN

His kin. The word itself felt alien on Truly's tongue, yet the reality was now undeniably present. She had caught brief glimpses of them, fleetingly at first, shadows moving with unnatural grace at the periphery of her vision, the silent watchers of her clandestine meetings with Abel. They were larger, more imposing than he, their eyes holding a depth of ancient caution that sent a shiver down her spine. And their suspicion of her, Truly realized with a sinking heart, was not a mere curiosity. It was a deep-seated mistrust, a prejudice as old as the towering oaks that shaded their hidden domain. She felt it in the way their gazes, when they dared to meet hers, lingered not with anger, but with a chilling assessment, as if she were a blight, an unwelcome intrusion into a carefully guarded sanctuary.

Abel tried to bridge the gap. He would speak to her, in his own way, through a series of gestures and low, rumbling vocalizations that she was slowly, painstakingly learning to interpret. He'd point towards his family, a subtle incline of his massive head, and then trace a line in the air, a sweeping motion that conveyed a sense of deep-rooted history, of unshakeable tradition. He'd then turn to her, his dark eyes holding a flicker of something akin to regret, a silent acknowledgment of the divide. He was loyal to her, of that she had no doubt. His every action spoke of a burgeoning affection, a genuine fondness that warmed her to her core. Yet, that same loyalty was a double-edged sword, for it meant he was caught, as if in a trap of his own making, between the human girl who had somehow captured his attention and the ancient pacts that bound him to his clan.

"They do not understand," he had conveyed to her one crisp autumn afternoon, his voice a deep tremor in the quiet air, the words a mixture of translated thoughts and instinctual understanding. He had gestured towards a group of his kind, observing her from a distance with an unnerving stillness. "They see... danger. They see the outside. They fear what they do not know." His massive hand, usually so gentle in its touch, clenched slightly, a subtle expression of his internal conflict. "They have protected our ways for generations. They believe... you disrupt the balance."

Truly absorbed his words, the weight of them settling heavily upon her. She understood his family's apprehension, on a purely rational level. She was a human, a creature of a world that had a long and often brutal history with the wild, with those who lived outside the established order. Her own people, for all their perceived civility, harbored their own fears and superstitions, their own ways of marking and ostracizing what they didn't comprehend. The villagers' wary glances, their hushed whispers when she passed, she had seen it all. And now, she saw it mirrored in Abel's own kind, although with a different, perhaps more primal, set of fears.

"It's not your fault, Abel," she murmured, reaching out to touch his arm, her small hand dwarfed by the thick, coarse fur. He flinched slightly, not from her touch, but from the awareness that they were observed. "I don't want to cause trouble for you or your family."

He let out a soft huff, a sound that might have been a sigh. "Trouble is... already here. You are here. And I... I wish for you to be." The admission, simple and profound, hung in the air between them. He was acknowledging the impossible, the undeniable pull he felt towards her, a pull that defied the ingrained warnings of his ancestors.

This growing affection, she realized, was not a simple matter of two individuals finding solace in each other. It was a seed, planted in fertile ground, but carrying with it the inherent danger of a storm. Abel's family saw it as a threat, a crack in the fortress walls that protected their existence. Their disapproval was a palpable thing, a cold current that flowed beneath the surface of their interactions, even when they were outwardly neutral. They were the keepers of tradition, the guardians of their people's secrecy, and Truly represented an unknown variable, a potential catalyst for change that they deeply feared.

There was one elder, a matriarch whose fur was the color of ancient moss and whose eyes held the glint of a thousand winters, who was particularly vocal in her disapproval. Truly had only seen her from afar, a stooped, formidable figure observing from the shadows. Abel had conveyed her sentiments with a somber finality. "She speaks of the old ways, of the blood oaths. Of the purity of our lineage. She says... you are a lure. A trap. A weakness we cannot afford."

The words stung, not because they were unexpected, but because they confirmed Truly's deepest anxieties. She wasn't just an anomaly; she was a potential existential threat. And Abel, caught in the crossfire, was beginning to show the strain. His playful antics, his moments of quiet contemplation with her, were becoming tinged with a subtle anxiety. He would scan the tree line more frequently, his ears twitching at sounds only he could discern. He was constantly aware of the watchful eyes, the unspoken judgments, and the weight of his dual loyalties was etched onto his usually placid features.

"He believes I can protect you," Abel communicated, his gaze fixed on the distant, shadowed slopes where his clan dwelled. "He is... one of the few. He understands that I would not risk myself, or my kin, for something I did not believe in. But the others... they see only a human. A fleeting creature with a short lifespan and a dangerous curiosity." He paused, a deep rumble vibrating in his chest. "They do not understand... what you are to me."

What was she to him? The question echoed in Truly's own heart. She was no longer just a lost girl finding refuge in the woods. She was a focal point of contention, a symbol of a potential shift in the established order. Her presence in Abel's life was not just a personal joy; it was a quiet rebellion, a subtle defiance against the ingrained rules of his world. And that rebellion, she knew, would not go unnoticed, nor would it be easily forgiven.

The implications were vast, stretching out before them like an uncharted forest path. If Abel's family grew more hostile, if their suspicion solidified into outright action, what then? Could Abel truly shield her from the collective will of his clan? Or would he be forced to choose, to sever the bond that had become so vital to both of them? The thought was a chilling one, a stark reminder of the precariousness of their situation. Their stolen moments of peace were overshadowed by the looming possibility of conflict, a conflict born not of malice, but of fear and a deep-seated need to preserve their way of life.

She saw the internal struggle play out in his eyes, in the tension in his broad shoulders. He was torn between the burgeoning, undeniable feelings for her and the ingrained sense of duty, the primal urge to protect his own. He had explained, in his unique way, the history of his kind, their need for secrecy, their vulnerability to the outside world. Humans, he had conveyed, had a way of destroying what they didn't understand, of exploiting what they feared. And his family, in their wisdom, had learned this lesson through painful experience.

"They worry," he had communicated, a low, almost sorrowful sound. "They worry that your presence will lead others to us. That it will expose our existence. That it will lead to... the end." He looked at her then, his gaze searching, vulnerable. "I do not believe this. But they... they have lived longer. They have seen more."

This was the true seed of future conflict. It wasn't just about Abel's family disliking her. It was about their deeply ingrained fear for the survival of their entire species, a fear that Truly, through her connection with Abel, inadvertently represented. Their prejudice was not irrational; it was a survival mechanism, honed over centuries of cautious existence. And Abel though he clearly cared for Truly, was still a part of that world, still bound by its imperatives. His affection for her was a powerful force, but could it truly override generations of ingrained caution and fear for the collective good?

Truly found herself watching him more closely, searching for signs of his internal debate. When they were alone, he was the same gentle, devoted companion. But in the presence of his kin, or even when they were merely in proximity, a subtle shift occurred. His posture would become more guarded, his movements more deliberate. He would instinctively position himself between her and the watchful eyes, a silent sentinel warding off unseen threats. It was a testament to his loyalty, but it also highlighted the pressure he was under, the constant negotiation between his heart and his heritage.

The whispers of his family were not spoken words, but a silent language of disapproval that permeated the air around them. It was in the way they would suddenly cease their movements when she approached, their massive forms freezing like statues. It was in the way their gazes would bore into her, not with overt hostility, but with an unnerving, dispassionate scrutiny. It was a cold assessment, a silent judgment that spoke volumes about their perception of her as an outsider, a potential danger to their hidden world. Abel, caught between these two worlds, was becoming a bridge that was being tested by the very forces it sought to connect. The loyalty he felt for Truly was undeniable, a bright spark in the gathering shadows, but it was a loyalty that would inevitably lead to trials, to difficult choices, and to a future that was far from certain. The wild, which had once offered her solace, was now presenting her with a danger that was both ancient and deeply personal.

5

THE UNWELCOME PROPOSAL

The crisp autumn air, usually a welcome embrace, now felt like a tightening noose around Truly's throat. The familiar scent of damp earth and decaying leaves, once a comforting balm, was now tinged with a subtle, acrid undertone of apprehension. It was the smell of change, the scent of a future she was not ready to face, a future being sculpted by hands that believed they knew what was best for her. Her eighteenth birthday had come and gone, a milestone that had felt more like a pronouncement than a celebration. With it, the whispers had begun, soft at first, like the rustle of dry leaves, but quickly gathering momentum, growing louder and more insistent with each passing day.

Her mother, usually a woman of quiet strength and gentle reassurances, had taken on a new, determined glint in her eyes. Truly noticed it first during supper one evening, a sharp, assessing gaze that lingered on her face longer than usual. Then came the hushed conversations between her parents, punctuated by knowing glances and the occasional conspiratorial smile that Truly was meant to be oblivious to. The words "settled," "secure," and "suitable match" began to drift through the cottage like phantom guests, unwelcome apparitions in her carefully constructed world.

"It's time, Truly," her mother had said, her voice laced with an urgency that made Truly's stomach tighten. They were sitting by the fireplace, the flames casting dancing shadows on her mother's face, accentuating the fine lines etched around her eyes. "You are a young woman now. A woman of... potential. We cannot have you wandering the woods indefinitely, chasing after... whims." The last word was spoken with a delicate, almost imperceptible curl of her lip, a subtle dismissal of Truly's deep connection to the wild, to Abel.

Truly swallowed, the lump in her throat making it difficult to speak. "But Mama, I am happy. I love it out there. It's... where I feel most myself." Her mother's sigh was a soft exhalation of exasperation. "Happiness is a fleeting thing, child. Security is what endures. And a good match, a *respectable* match, is the foundation of a secure future. Think of it, Truly. Think of what it means for our family. For your own standing in the community."

The community. The word itself felt heavy, laden with expectations Truly had never asked for. She imagined the familiar faces in the village square, the gossiping tongues, the veiled judgments. She saw herself, Truly, the weaver's daughter, who spent too much time in the woods, who was too quiet, too withdrawn. The idea of being tethered to one of the eligible young men her parents seemed to be considering sent a tremor of dread through her. Young Thorne, the blacksmith's son, with his boisterous laugh and perpetually soot-stained hands. Or perhaps Silas, the miller's apprentice, whose eyes always seemed to be darting around, as if constantly on the verge of some minor mischief. Their world felt so small, so suffocatingly predictable. It was a life of predictable sunrises and sunsets, of well-trodden paths and unchanging routines. A life devoid of the wild, untamed magic that pulsed through her veins whenever she was near Abel, whenever she was lost in the embrace of the ancient forest.

"They are... fine young men, Truly," her father chimed in, his voice a low rumble from his armchair. He was a man of few words, but his pronouncements carried weight. "Hardworking. Honest. They will provide for a wife, give her a good home." "But do I want a good home with someone I... don't feel anything for?" Truly's voice was barely a whisper, a fragile thing against the rising tide of their intentions. She looked at her parents, their faces earnest, their intentions, she knew, pure. They loved her, of that she had no doubt. They wanted the best for her, a life free from the hardships they had known, a life of comfort and stability. But their vision of "best" was a gilded cage, a comfortable prison from which she felt an overwhelming urge to escape.

Her mother's expression softened, a fleeting tenderness momentarily overriding her pragmatic concerns. She reached out, her hand cool on Truly's flushed cheek. "Oh, my sweet girl. Feelings... they can grow. Marriage is not always about the whirlwind romance you read about in those silly books. It's about partnership, about building a life together. And these young men... they are of our world, Truly. They understand our ways, our traditions. They would keep you safe, close to home."

Close to home. The words echoed the very thing she was beginning to fear most. The thought of being confined, of her horizons shrinking to the familiar cobblestones of the village, of her days dictated by the ringing of the blacksmith's hammer or the grinding of the miller's stones, was a bleak prospect indeed. She thought of Abel, of the vast, untamed expanse of the forest, of the freedom she found there, the exhilarating sense of belonging to something larger, something wilder, something that resonated with the deepest parts of her soul.

"But... what if I don't want to be kept close to home?" she ventured, her voice gaining a sliver of strength. "What if my heart... belongs elsewhere?" The unspoken addition hung heavy in the air: *with Abel.* She knew it was a dangerous path to tread, a seed of rebellion she was planting in the fertile ground of her parents' expectations.

Her mother's hand stilled on her cheek. The warmth vanished, replaced by a sudden coolness that made Truly shiver. Her mother's eyes narrowed, the softness replaced by a flicker of concern, or perhaps something akin to alarm. "Truly, you speak foolishness. There is no 'elsewhere' for a respectable young woman. Your place is here, with your family, building your own family. And these... these woods... they are no place for a woman of your age. It's not proper. And it's not safe."

The word "proper" landed like a stone, each syllable a judgment. Truly felt a familiar sting behind her eyes, a mixture of frustration and hurt. They didn't understand. They couldn't. How could she explain the profound connection she felt, the silent understanding she shared with Abel? How could she articulate the thrill of the chase, the scent of pine needles underfoot, the symphony of birdsong that was more eloquent than any human conversation? How could she describe the raw, untamed beauty that had captured her heart and refused to let go?

"I am safe, Mama," she said, her voice steadier now, fueled by a nascent defiance. "And... I am not just chasing whims. I am... learning. Exploring."

Her father cleared his throat, a subtle signal that the discussion was nearing its end. "Learning and exploring are well and good for a time, Truly. But life demands more. It demands responsibility. And the responsibility of a young woman of your age is to prepare for her future. A future that, whether you admit it or not, will involve a husband and a home." He looked at her directly, his gaze unwavering. "Your mother and I have spoken with Mr. Thorne. His son, Thomas, has expressed... an interest. He is a good boy, Truly. Strong. He will make you a fine husband."

The name echoed in the room, a death blow to Truly's burgeoning hopes. Thomas Thorne. He was a hulking young man, his face ruddy, his mannerisms clumsy and overbearing. He had once cornered her by the well, his gaze appraising her with an unsettling possessiveness that had sent a wave of revulsion through her. She had fled, her heart pounding, her breath catching in her throat. The memory resurfaced now, sharp and vivid, confirming her deepest fears. This was the future they envisioned for her? A future of unwanted advances and stifled dreams?

"I... I don't want to marry Thomas Thorne," she stated, her voice firm, betraying none of the turmoil raging within her.

Her mother's jaw tightened. "It is not about what you *want*, Truly. Not entirely. It is about what is sensible, what is proper, what is secure." She rose from her seat, her movements sharp and decisive. "We have given this a great deal of thought. Master Thorne is a respected man in the village. His son will inherit a thriving business. It is a good match for you. For all of us."

Truly remained seated, the warmth of the hearth no longer reaching her. She felt a chill creep into her bones, a premonition of the battles to come. The comfortable, predictable world her parents offered felt like a suffocating blanket, threatening to smother the wild spark that Abel had fanned into a flame. She knew, with a certainty that was both terrifying and exhilarating, that she could not accept this path. Her heart, her soul, belonged to the wild, to the shadows of the forest, and to the silent, rumbling affection of the creature who dwelled within its depths. The whispers of a match, meant to secure her future, were instead igniting a silent rebellion within her, a desperate yearning for a future that was entirely her own. The pressure to conform, to accept the life laid out before her, was immense, a tangible force pushing down on her, yet the thought of renouncing her freedom, of turning her back on the wild, felt like a betrayal of herself. She could feel Abel's presence even now, a comforting phantom in the back of her mind, a reminder of the world that truly called to her. And for that world, she knew, she would have to fight.

Her parents, mistaking her silence for reluctant contemplation, continued to elaborate on the perceived benefits of such a union. Her mother, ever the pragmatist, began to detail the practical advantages, the potential for a comfortable home, the social standing that would be elevated by marrying into the Thorne family. "Thomas is a good, honest lad," she repeated, as if the sheer repetition would somehow make it true in Truly's eyes. "He'll provide well. His father, the black-smith, has a good reputation, and his business is thriving. It's a stable future, Truly, something to be thankful for."

Truly's gaze drifted towards the window, her eyes scanning the darkening sky. The first stars were beginning to prick through the indigo canvas, distant and indifferent. She imagined Abel out there, under that same vast sky, his senses keenly attuned to the whisper of the wind, the rustle of leaves, the faintest tremor of the earth. He would be free, unburdened by the suffocating weight of societal expectations, his existence a testament to the raw, unadulterated beauty of the wild. A stark contrast to the carefully constructed lives of the villagers, lives that her parents were so eager for her to embrace.

"And what if I do not want a stable future?" Truly asked, her voice soft but firm, cutting through the drone of her mother's justifications. She turned from the window, her eyes meeting her mother's directly. "What if my heart longs for something... less stable, perhaps, but more... real?" Her mother blinked, a flicker of surprise, then annoyance, crossing her features. "Real? Truly, what are you talking about? A home, a husband, children, that is real. That is the fabric of life."

"But it's not the only fabric, Mama," Truly countered, feeling a surge of boldness. "There are other ways of living. Other kinds of... belonging." She thought of the ancient trees, the hidden glades, the silent communion she shared with Abel. These were not mere pastimes; they were integral to her very being. To abandon them would be to abandon a part of herself. Her father sighed, a sound of weary resignation. "Truly, your mother is right. We want what is best for you. And what is best is security. We have worked hard to provide you with a good upbringing, to ensure you have opportunities. This is an opportunity. Thomas Thorne is a decent young man, and his family is well-regarded."

"Decent is not the same as desirable, Father," Truly murmured, her gaze dropping to her hands, which were twisting in her lap. The thought of Thomas Thorne's clumsy advances, the pressure to conform to his expectations, filled her with a sense of unease that was almost unbearable. It was a future she could foresee with chilling clarity: endless days of domestic drudgery, punctuated by forced smiles and polite conversation, her spirit slowly wilting like a flower denied sunlight.

"He will keep you safe," her mother insisted, her voice taking on a pleading tone. "He will protect you. He will provide for you. You won't have to worry about... where your next meal is coming from, or if you'll have a roof over your head. We've seen too much hardship, Truly. We want a better life for you."

Truly understood their fear, the deep-seated desire to shield her from the struggles they had endured. But their vision of protection was a gilded cage, and she craved the freedom of the open sky. "I am not afraid of hardship, Mama," she said, her voice gaining strength. "And I am not without protection. I have... I have friends who look out for me." She didn't dare mention Abel by name, but the unspoken truth hung in the air between them, a silent testament to the wild guardian who watched over her. Her mother's eyes narrowed, suspicion replacing the pleading. "Friends? What friends, Truly? Besides the few village girls your age, who else do you even speak to?"

Truly hesitated, her mind racing. How could she explain Abel? How could she convey the depth of his quiet devotion, the unspoken promises held within his steady gaze? To mention him would be to invite a storm, to expose him to the very dangers his family feared. The thought of his kin, their ancient mistrust of humans, filled her with a fresh wave of dread. She couldn't risk bringing that kind of scrutiny upon him, upon their hidden world.

"Just... people," she said vaguely, hoping to deflect the questioning. "People who... understand the woods." Her father's expression hardened. "Truly, this talk of 'understanding the woods' is precisely what concerns us. It is not a proper pursuit for a young woman. You should be focused on your needlework, on learning to manage a household, on preparing for marriage. Not... wandering through the trees."

The accusation, though subtly phrased, stung. They saw her connection to the wild as a deviation, a flaw in her character, rather than an integral part of her identity. "The woods are a part of me," she said, her voice barely above a whisper, but imbued with a quiet conviction. "They are where I feel most alive. And I cannot simply... abandon that." Her mother wrung her hands. "But Truly, think of your future! Think of the stability, the security! Thomas Thorne is a good, strong man. He will give you a good life. A safe life." "Safe is not the same as happy, Mama," Truly repeated, the words feeling truer now than ever before. She thought of Abel, of the quiet strength in his gaze, the unspoken understanding that passed between them. Their connection was something far more profound, far more real, than any superficial courtship with a village lad. It was a connection that spoke to her soul, a wild, untamed love that blossomed in the heart of the ancient forest.

Her father sighed again, the sound heavy with a weariness that suggested this was a battle he was not prepared to win tonight. "We will speak of this again, Truly. But understand this: we have your best interests at heart. And we believe that a good marriage is in your best interests." He stood, signaling the end of the conversation. "Now, go. It is late. And tomorrow, Master Thorne will be expecting an answer regarding Thomas's... intentions."

6

A UNKNOWN SUITER

Truly rose, her legs feeling stiff, her heart heavy with a nascent sense of rebellion. She offered a polite, albeit strained, nod to her parents and turned to leave the room. As she walked towards the stairs, she could feel their eyes on her, a tangible pressure, a silent plea for her to conform. But as she ascended into the quiet darkness of her room, her mind was already racing, not with thoughts of Thomas Thorne and domesticity, but with the image of a towering, fur-clad figure, his dark eyes filled with a love that transcended words, a love that echoed the wild, untamed spirit of the forest itself. The proposals might be unwelcome, the expectations suffocating, but Truly knew, with a certainty that settled deep within her bones, that she would not be easily swayed. Her heart was already pledged, not to a man of the village, but to a wilder, more ancient world. The path ahead was uncertain, fraught with potential conflict, but for the first time, Truly felt a flicker of fierce determination. She would not be a pawn in her parents' ambitions, nor a victim of societal expectations. Her future, she decided, would be her own to forge, and it would be one steeped in the wild magic that had captured her heart. The whispers of a match were turning into a roar of defiance, and Truly, for the first time, was ready to roar back.

The suffocating weight of her parents' expectations pressed down on Truly, a tangible force that made each breath a conscious effort. The very air in the cottage seemed to thicken with unspoken demands, with the specter of a future she desperately wanted to avoid. She had managed to deflect the immediate pressure regarding Thomas Thorne, leaving her parents to stew in their disappointed silence, but she knew this was only a temporary reprieve. The village remained a hive of matchmaking gossip, and her parents, driven by their own fears and desires for her security, would undoubtedly present other candidates. The thought was enough to send a shiver down her spine, a phantom chill that had nothing to do with the autumn air.

She found solace, as always, in the woods. Each step on the familiar forest floor, each breath of pine-scented air, was a balm to her frayed nerves. She sought out Abel, her silent guardian, her confidant. He was there, a comforting presence just beyond the veil of human perception, his deep, rumbling affection a steady anchor in the turbulent sea of her life. He would emerge from the shadows, his massive form a reassuring silhouette against the ancient trees, his dark eyes, eyes that held an intelligence and depth that surpassed any human she knew – fixed on her with an unwavering intensity. He didn't speak in words, but in the rustle of leaves, the twitch of an ear, the soft pressure of his immense head nudging her hand. And in these silent exchanges, Truly felt understood, truly seen, in a way no one else in her village ever had.

One crisp afternoon, as Truly sat by the edge of a sun-dappled clearing, idly weaving a crown of wildflowers, she felt a prickle of unease, a disturbance in the usual harmony of the woods. It was a subtle shift, like a discordant note in a familiar melody. Abel, who had been dozing peacefully at her feet, his great body blending almost seamlessly with the undergrowth, stirred. His ears swiveled, catching sounds imperceptible to Truly, and a low growl, barely audible but laced with warning, rumbled in his chest. His fur bristled, and his gaze, usually filled with quiet devotion, was now sharp, scanning the perimeter of their sanctuary.

Truly's heart quickened. Abel's instincts were rarely wrong. He was attuned to the forest's pulse, to the presence of any living thing that dared to tread its sacred paths with ill intent. "What is it, Abel?" she whispered, her voice barely disturbing the stillness. He didn't answer, but nudged her gently, urging her to her feet. "Come," the gesture seemed to say. "We should move."

As Truly rose, her eyes followed Abel's intense stare towards the denser thicket of trees. A figure was emerging, stepping out from behind the gnarled trunk of an ancient oak. Truly's breath hitched. It wasn't one of the village hunters, nor a woodcutter. This man was... different. He was tall, with a broad frame that spoke of physical labor, but there was a swagger in his gait, a certain self-assuredness that bordered on arrogance. His clothes were well-made, of good quality wool, a shade of deep forest green that made him blend too easily with his surroundings. He had dark, unruly hair that fell across his brow, and his eyes, when they landed on Truly, were a startlingly bright blue, sharp and assessing, like a hawk's.

He stopped a few paces away, a slow, predatory smile spreading across his lips. "Well, well," he said, his voice a low baritone, smooth but with an undercurrent of something rough, something that grated on Truly's nerves. "Look what the forest has brought me. A little bird, strayed from her nest."

Abel, hidden now, let out a guttural growl, a sound that vibrated through Truly's very bones. He moved in preparation to stand directly in front of her, a solid wall of fur and muscle, his stance protective, defiant if needed. His eyes, usually so gentle when directed at Truly, were now blazing with an intensity that would have sent any normal man fleeing.

The newcomer, however, did not flinch at the sounds around him, the feeling of another close by. He merely chuckled, a sound that was devoid of genuine amusement. "Easy there" he said, his gaze flicking over the tree line in the direction of Abel with a mixture of curiosity and disdain. "I mean no harm. Not to the lady, at least."

Truly felt a tremor of apprehension run through her. There was something about this man, Silas, as she would soon learn his name, that set her teeth on edge. It wasn't just his sudden appearance, or Abel's strong reaction. It was the way he looked at her, a possessive gleam in his bright blue eyes, as if he already owned her, as if she were a prize to be claimed. It was a look that spoke of entitlement, of a man accustomed to taking what he wanted. "Who are you?" Truly asked, her voice surprisingly steady, bolstered by Abel's presence nearby. She kept her gaze fixed on Silas, refusing to let his unnerving stare unnerve her.

He bowed his head, a theatrical gesture that did little to endear him. "Silas," he replied. "Silas Croft. And I am, or rather, will soon be, a suitor for your hand, fair maiden." The words hit Truly like a physical blow. *Suitor.* The word tasted like ash in her mouth. Her parents had spoken of matches, of respectable unions, but they hadn't mentioned anyone new. And this man, Silas Croft, with his rough charm and unsettling possessiveness, felt like the antithesis of anything she might consider. "You... you are mistaken," Truly stammered, her mind racing. "I am not betrothed, and I have no intention of entertaining... proposals."

Silas's smile widened, revealing a flash of white teeth. It was not a kind smile. "Oh, but I assure you, my dear Truly," he said, taking a step closer, oblivious to Abel's low, menacing growl. "Your parents and I have had... discussions. They are quite amenable to the idea. As am I. You see, I have heard much about the weaver's daughter. A beauty, they say. A quiet girl, with a certain... wildness about her. A wildness that, I believe, I can tame."

The word 'tame' struck Truly like a lash. Tame? She was not a wild creature to be broken and controlled. She was a spirit of the forest, fierce and free. Abel let out a more insistent growl, his hackles rising. He took a step forward, his massive form The rustling of the forage sent, a clear warning to the intruder. Silas's eyes narrowed, his gaze finally acknowledging the sheer power of the creature which lay just out of sight. There was a flicker of something in his eyes, surprise, perhaps, or a grudging respect, quickly masked by a renewed wave of arrogance. "A loyal companion," he mused, his eyes glinting as he assessed the forest looking for the source of the comotion. "But a beast is a beast, and a man is a man. And a man's claim will always supersede that of a wild animal."

Truly felt a cold dread seep into her bones. This was precisely the kind of arrogance, the kind of dismissive attitude towards the natural world, that she found so abhorrent in some of the villagers. Silas

Croft seemed to embody it all. He saw the woods as something to be conquered, the creatures within them as beasts to be subdued, and women, like herself, as prizes to be claimed and tamed. "You do not understand," Truly said, her voice trembling slightly, but with a newfound resolve. "Abel is not just a beast. And I am not yours to claim."

Silas took another step, ignoring Abel's furious rumble. He reached out, his hand moving towards Truly as if to touch her cheek. It was a bold, presumptuous move that sent a jolt of pure revulsion through her. Abel reacted instantly, a thunderous roar erupting from his chest as he surged forward. The sheer force of the movement sent Silas stumbling backward, his eyes wide with shock and anger. "By the gods!" Silas spat, regaining his footing. He glared at Abel, now a shadow, his face contorted with fury.

Abel stood his ground, a low, menacing growl emanating from him. He was ready to defend Truly with his life, his protective instincts fully engaged. The raw, untamed power radiating from him was palpable, a force of nature unleashed. Truly stepped forward, placing her hand up, a silent plea for restraint. She knew he could easily tear Silas apart, but she didn't want that. She didn't want violence. But she also knew she couldn't allow Silas to continue his forward advance. "Leave," she said, her voice clear and firm, cutting through the tense air. "Leave this forest, and do not return. I have no interest in you or your... proposal."

Silas's bright blue eyes narrowed, a dangerous glint appearing in them. He straightened his tunic, his expression a mask of cold fury. "You think you can dismiss me so easily, girl?" he sneered. "You think you can hide away in these woods forever, with your... pet monster or whatever it is?" He gestured dismissively towards Abel's location. "The world outside this forest has its rules, and you will learn them. Your parents have agreed. This is a formality. I will be back." With a final, contemptuous glare towards Abel, Silas turned on his heel and disappeared back into the thicket, the rustling of leaves his only parting comment.

The moment he was gone, Abel moved from his hidden refuge and nudged Truly gently, a soft whine of concern escaping him. He licked her hand, his rough tongue a comforting sensation against her skin. Truly sank back onto the mossy ground, her legs suddenly weak. The encounter had shaken her deeply. Silas Croft's possessiveness, his entitlement, his utter disregard for her feelings and for Abel's presence, had all combined to create a chilling premonition. "He'll be back, Abel," she whispered, her voice heavy with dread. "He said he will be back." Abel responded with a low rumble, a sound of reassurance. He settled down beside her, his warm body a solid presence against her side, his vigilance unwavering. He would not let Silas Croft harm her. Truly knew this with a certainty that resonated deep within her soul.

As Truly sat there, leaning against Abel's formidable strength, she felt a profound sense of gratitude for her wild guardian. He was more than just a protector; he was a symbol of the life she cherished, the freedom she craved. Silas Croft represented the antithesis of that life, a dark shadow cast by the world she was trying to escape. His rough charm was a façade, his possessiveness a dangerous undercurrent that threatened to engulf her. She understood now, with a terrifying clarity, why Abel had reacted so strongly. Silas Croft carried an aura of darkness, a tangible malevolence that even Truly, with her limited understanding of such things, could sense. It was a palpable energy that pricked at

Abel's protective instincts, warning him of a genuine threat. This was no mere village suitor; this was something far more insidious.

The encounter left Truly with a knot of anxiety that tightened with each passing moment. Silas Croft's claim, however flimsy, was a new complication in her already precarious situation. Her parents' willingness to entertain his suit, despite her obvious discomfort, was a painful confirmation of their priorities. They saw stability, social standing, and financial security as paramount, even if it meant sacrificing her happiness, her freedom, and her connection to the wild world she loved.

She knew she would have to be strong. She would have to find a way to resist Silas Croft and the pressures that his courtship represented. And she knew, with unwavering certainty, that Abel would be by her side, a silent, unwavering sentinel, his presence a constant reminder of the wild strength and profound love that existed beyond the confines of human expectation. The woods had offered her refuge, but now they had also become a battleground, and Truly braced herself for the fight ahead. The scent of pine and damp earth, once a comfort, now carried the faint, acrid tang of a looming conflict. Silas Croft had entered the picture, and Truly's world had irrevocably shifted.

The air in the cottage, once merely heavy with unspoken expectations, now vibrated with a sickeningly cheerful acceptance. Truly's parents, their faces alight with a peculiar blend of relief and triumph, spoke of Silas Croft not as a potential husband, but as a certainty. The word "betrothal" had been spoken, sealed not with vows, but with a handshake between her father and Silas, a gesture that felt like a betrayal to Truly. Her protests, once a torrent of desperate pleas, had dwindled to a choked whisper, lost in the whirlwind of their newfound plans. They saw the offer from Silas not as an imposition, but as a golden opportunity, a secure future unfurling before them, a future where their daughter would be... taken care of. The sheer speed with which they had embraced the idea was a testament to their ingrained desire for her to settle, to conform, to be placed within the rigid framework of a respectable marriage.

Truly watched them, her heart a leaden weight in her chest. Her mother, usually so pragmatic, was now effusive, discussing dowry fabrics and the guest list with a flutter of excitement that Truly found grotesque. Her father, his brow furrowed with the usual worries of a farmer, seemed to shed years, his smile wider and more genuine than she had seen it in a long time. He spoke of Silas's supposed 'good standing' in the neighboring villages, of his 'connections,' and the 'advantage' this union would bring. Advantage. The word echoed in Truly's mind, a cold, hard sound. Was her life, her happiness, simply a commodity to be bartered for advantage? The thought was a bitter draught, and she swallowed it down, lest it choke her.

"He is a good man, Truly," her mother said, her voice softening as she noticed the stark pallor of her daughter's face. "He will provide for you. You will want for nothing." "But I do not want him, Mother," Truly whispered, the words barely audible. "I do not want this." Her mother sighed, a sound of weary resignation. "There are things, Truly, that are more important than fleeting desires. Security. Stability. A name that will command respect. Silas Croft offers you all of that. And he is... quite taken with you, despite your... spirited nature." She gave Truly a pointed look, a reminder of her earlier defiance. "He sees potential. He believes he can... mold you."

The word 'mold' sent a fresh wave of revulsion through Truly. Mold. Like clay. Like something inanimate, to be shaped according to another's will. She was not clay. She was a living, breathing entity, with her own thoughts, her own desires, her own spirit. And Silas Croft, with his arrogant certainty, intended to break it.

7

—— ⋅ ——

UNSEEN TEARS

The days that followed were a blur of suffocating activity. The cottage buzzed with preparations. Bolts of fine linen were brought out, fabrics Truly had only dreamed of touching, now destined for Silas's new wife. Her mother, caught up in the fervor, hummed as she stitched intricate patterns, her fingers flying across the cloth. Invitations were being drafted, sealed with wax bearing her father's family crest. Truly was consulted on trivial matters, the color of the ribbons for her hair, the style of her wedding gown, but never on the fundamental choice of her life. Her opinions were deemed irrelevant, her feelings secondary to the grand pronouncements of her parents and the swift finality of Silas Croft's proposal.

Each conversation, each planning session, felt like another nail in the coffin of her freedom. She tried to voice her concerns, to highlight the unsettling intensity in Silas's eyes, the possessive way he had looked at her, the sheer audacity of his claim. But her words fell on deaf ears. Her parents, blinded by their own ambitions, dismissed her anxieties as girlish jitters, the natural apprehension of a young woman about to embark on married life. "You'll grow to love him, Truly," her father said, his tone patronizing. "A good marriage is built on respect and shared goals, not on fanciful notions of passion."

Passion. Truly yearned for it, for a connection that ignited her soul, not one that extinguished it. Silas offered something else entirely, possession. A gilded cage. She saw it in the way he had spoken to her, the condescending smile that suggested he already knew her better than she knew herself. He had seen her in the woods, a place of wildness and freedom, and had declared his intention to 'tame' her. That was not love; that was conquest.

Her only respite, her only sanctuary, remained the ancient woods. As the wedding date loomed, a mere few weeks away, Truly found herself retreating into their embrace with increasing desperation. The familiar scent of damp earth and pine needles, the dappled sunlight filtering through the canopy, the symphony of birdsong, these were the only things that felt real, the only things that offered her solace. Here, under the watchful eyes of the ancient trees, she could shed the suffocating pretense of happiness, the forced smiles, the polite acquiescence.

Abel, sensing her distress, was her constant companion. He would emerge from the shadows, his great form a comforting presence, his dark eyes filled with an understanding that transcended words. He would lay his head in her lap, his rumbling purr a low, resonant vibration that soothed her jangled nerves. He didn't judge her, didn't offer platitudes. He simply *was present*. He was her anchor in a world that was rapidly spinning out of control, a silent testament to the wildness that Silas Croft so desperately wished to extinguish.

"They've accepted, Abel," she whispered one afternoon, her voice thick with unshed tears, as she stroked his velvety ear. "My parents.

They've agreed. I'm to marry Silas Croft." Abel whined softly, nudging her hand with his nose, a silent offering of comfort. He understood. His instincts, sharp and clear, had warned him of Silas's dark intentions from the very first encounter. He had sensed the possessiveness, the arrogance, the underlying threat. And now, his quiet guardian was to be taken from him, bound to a man who represented everything antithetical to Truly's true nature.

She confessed her fears to him, the anxieties that clawed at her in the quiet hours of the night. "I don't want to be his wife, Abel. I don't want to be 'tamed.' I want to be free. I want to be... me." She buried her face in his warm fur, inhaling his earthy scent, a scent of the wild, untamed world she belonged to. "He looked at me like I was a prize he had won. Like I was something to be owned. And my parents... they just smiled and nodded." Abel shifted, nudging her away from his fur and looking her directly in the eye. His gaze was steady, reassuring, and a fierce protectiveness radiated from him. It was as if he were saying, *I will not let him break you.*

Truly found a strange strength in his gaze. He was a creature of the wild, a being of immense power and loyalty. If he believed in her, if he stood by her, perhaps she could find the courage to stand by herself. She began to spend more time in the woods, not just seeking solace, but actively observing, learning, absorbing the wisdom of the natural world. She watched how the deer navigated the treacherous terrain, how the birds built their nests with meticulous care, how the trees stood tall and unyielding against the fiercest storms. She saw resilience, adaptation, and a quiet strength that did not rely on brute force or outward displays of power.

She practiced her weaving, her fingers flying with a renewed purpose. She wasn't just creating cloth; she was weaving her own destiny, thread by thread. She poured her frustration, her fear, and her burgeoning defiance into the intricate patterns. Each knot, each loop, was a silent rebellion against the fate that was being thrust upon her. She imagined her own strength, her own spirit, woven into the fabric, an invisible shield against the encroaching darkness of Silas Croft's influence.

Her parents, mistaking her quietness for acceptance, grew more relaxed. They saw her weaving, her walks in the woods, as the natural activities of a bride-to-be preparing for her new life. They didn't see the fierce resolve hardening in her eyes, the quiet determination that was taking root in her heart. They didn't see that her retreat into the woods was not an act of surrender, but a strategic withdrawal, a gathering of strength before a battle she was determined to fight, even if she had to fight it alone.

The looming wedding was a constant, oppressive presence, a storm cloud on the horizon of her life. Truly felt a growing sense of claustrophobia, the walls of the cottage pressing in on her, the expectations of the village a suffocating blanket. Her conversations with her parents became strained, punctuated by silences that spoke volumes. They wanted her to be happy, they said, but their definition of happiness was a narrow, restrictive one, a life devoid of passion and freedom. Silas Croft, with his charm and his wealth, represented the pinnacle of that definition, and Truly found herself increasingly unable to reconcile their vision with her own.

She would sit by the window, watching the birds jump from branch to branch, their effortless flight a painful reminder of her own impending confinement. The laughter of the village children playing in the distance, once a joyous sound, now seemed to mock her. They were free to roam, to explore, to simply *be*. Truly, on the other hand, was bound by duty, by expectation, by a proposal she had never asked for.

One evening, as the sun dipped below the horizon, painting the sky in hues of fiery orange and soft lavender, Truly sat with her parents. The air was thick with unspoken tension. Her mother cleared her throat, her voice gentle but firm. "Silas has arranged for a carriage to take you into the market town tomorrow, Truly. He wishes to purchase your wedding jewelry. He spoke of a beautiful sapphire necklace he saw there, and... he said it would perfectly complement the color of your eyes."

Truly's stomach churned. The idea of Silas choosing jewelry for her, of him dictating what would adorn her body, felt like another violation. "I... I don't need new jewelry, Mother," she said, her voice tight. "What I have is sufficient." Her father sighed, a sound of exasperation. "Truly, this is not a matter of necessity, but of custom. Silas wishes to honor you. He is a generous man." "Generous with what he considers mine," Truly muttered, the words escaping before she could stop them. Her mother's face tightened. "Do not be ungrateful, Truly. Silas Croft is offering you a life most girls in this village can only dream of. He is of good breeding, he is wealthy, and he clearly cares for you." "Cares for me?" Truly's voice rose, betraying her carefully constructed composure. "He wants to own me! He wants to put me on display, to adorn me like a... like a prize. He sees me as a possession, not a person!" Her hands clenched into fists on her lap. "And you, both of you, you are just letting him! You are handing me over like a package!" Her father's face darkened. "That is enough, Truly! You will show respect to Silas, and you will show respect to your parents. We have made our decision. This marriage is for your own good. You will go with Silas tomorrow, and you will accept his gifts with gratitude."

Truly looked at them, her heart aching with a profound sense of disappointment. They saw only the benefits, the societal advantages, the fulfillment of their own aspirations. They couldn't, or wouldn't, see the suffering they were inflicting on their own daughter. The weight of their expectations, once a heavy burden, now felt like an iron vise, crushing her spirit. She knew, with a chilling certainty, that Silas Croft was not merely a suitor; he was a symbol of everything she fought against, everything she feared. And her parents, in their misguided desire for her security, were actively making her downfall possible. The woods, her only refuge, suddenly seemed miles away, and the path back to her own free spirit, a treacherous and uncertain one. The wedding was no longer just an event; it was a looming threat, a manifestation of her loss of control, and Truly felt a cold dread settle deep within her, a premonition of a future she desperately wanted to escape.

Abel observed the bustling activity surrounding the cottage with a growing disquiet that settled deep in his ancient bones. From his vantage point, partially concealed by the thick, gnarled branches of an ancient oak at the edge of the clearing, the scene was display of joyous preparation that felt profoundly wrong to his instincts. He saw Truly's mother, her face flushed with an almost frantic excitement, directing village women as they carried bundles of herbs and flowers into the cottage. He saw her father, his usual stoic demeanor replaced with a broad, almost giddy smile, accepting congratulations from passing neighbors. They moved with a purpose, a shared delusion of happiness that Abel couldn't comprehend.

His gaze, however, was invariably drawn to Truly. She moved among them with a forced grace, her smiles brittle, her eyes holding a distant, haunted look. He watched as Silas Croft, that insufferable peacock, draped himself around her like a possessive shadow. The man's every gesture, from the way his hand lingered too long on her arm to the smug self-satisfaction etched on his face, screamed ownership. Abel's hackles rose, a low growl vibrating in his chest, a sound he had to stifle, lest it betray his presence.

He had witnessed their interactions before, of course. Each time Silas visited, Abel's unease had deepened. He had seen Silas's eyes, sharp and calculating, sweep over Truly as if she were a piece of property to be appraised. He had heard the veiled threats couched in honeyed words, the subtle manipulations designed to chip away at her spirit. He had seen Silas's jaw tighten, his voice drop to a menacing whisper when he thought no one else could hear, words of ownership and expectation that Truly met with a stoic silence that broke Abel's heart.

One afternoon, Silas had cornered Truly by the well, his body angled towards her, effectively blocking her path. Abel, hidden deeper in the woods, had watched with mounting fury. Silas had leaned in, his voice a low rumble that Abel could just discern. "You will learn to be a proper wife, Truly," he had said, his tone laced with an impatience that belied his supposedly loving intentions. "You have a wild streak, a stubbornness that needs to be tamed. But I have the patience, and the means, to ensure you become the lady of my household, just as I envision."

Truly had stood rigid, her face pale but her chin held high. "I am not a wild creature to be tamed, Silas," she had replied, her voice surprisingly steady. "I am myself." Silas had let out a short, dismissive laugh. "Such spirit. It's what makes you so... appealing. But it will be put to good use. You will learn to channel it, to direct it for my benefit, and for ours. You will not disappoint me, Truly. I will not *allow* you to." He had then reached out, his fingers closing around her wrist with a grip that was far too tight. Truly had flinched, a subtle tremor that only Abel, with his heightened senses, could detect. Silas had merely tightened his hold, his eyes locking with hers, a silent assertion of power. "We will make a fine pair," he had murmured, a possessive possessiveness in his tone. "You, my beautiful, spirited wife. And I, your devoted husband."

Abel had felt a primal urge to surge forward, to rip Silas limb from limb, to tear him away from the human he had sworn to protect. But he knew he couldn't. His nature, his very essence, was to be a silent guardian, a protector from the shadows. Direct intervention, especially in the affairs of humans, was fraught with peril, not just for him, but for Truly. His appearance would likely scare her, alienate her further from her family, and confirm Silas's already inflated sense of importance. He was a force of nature, not a meddler in human squabbles.

So he watched, a silent sentinel, his massive form coiled with a tension that mirrored Truly's own. Each day, as the wedding preparations intensified, his frustration grew. He saw Truly's parents, caught in their own dreams of social advancement, oblivious to the subtle tyranny unfolding before them. They saw Silas's wealth, his status, his apparent admiration for their daughter, and mistook it for love and security.

They didn't see the possessiveness, the underlying control, the way Silas was already attempting to bend Truly to his will.

He saw Silas bring gifts, a glittering assortment of trinkets and finery. He watched as Silas presented Truly with a delicate silver locket, its surface intricately engraved with intertwined initials. Truly had accepted it with a polite, distant smile, but Abel had seen the way her fingers had trembled as she touched the cold metal. He saw Silas lean in, whispering something in her ear that made her flinch subtly, her eyes darting nervously towards her parents. Silas had then placed a proprietary arm around her shoulders, pulling her close for a brief, suffocating embrace that Truly endured with a stiff spine.

Abel's heart ached with a helplessness he had never known. He was a creature of immense power, capable of defending Truly from physical harm, but this was a different kind of threat, a subtler, more insidious one that preyed on her spirit and her will. He was torn. His loyalty to Truly, a bond forged in shared moments of quiet companionship and mutual understanding, warred with the ingrained caution of his kind. He was meant to be her protector, but how could he protect her from her own family's decisions, from the societal pressures that were so alien to his world, from the calculated machinations of a man like Silas Croft?

He spent hours observing Truly's routines, searching for any sign of a plan, any flicker of rebellion that he could subtly encourage. He saw her retreating to the woods, her solace, her sanctuary. He watched her weaving, her fingers moving with a desperate intensity, as if she were trying to weave herself a way out of this suffocating reality. He saw the fierce concentration in her eyes, the way she poured all her frustration and fear into the intricate patterns. He sensed a growing resolve within her, a quiet strength that was beginning to bloom, but he also saw the crushing weight of expectation that threatened to suffocate it before it could fully blossom.

He observed Silas's interactions with the villagers. The man was charming and generous with his coin, which seemed to have bought him a great deal of goodwill. Silas spoke of his future with Truly as a foregone conclusion, of the grand house he would build, the influence they would wield. He basked in the admiration, unburdened by any apparent awareness of Truly's inner turmoil. He saw her as a beautiful, docile prize, an addition to his esteemed household, not as a partner with her own thoughts and desires.

One evening, Abel watched as Silas presented Truly with a stunning sapphire necklace. The gemstones shimmered under the lamplight, a vibrant blue that was indeed reminiscent of Truly's eyes, but the gift felt like a brand, a declaration of ownership. Silas fastened it around her neck himself, his fingers brushing against her skin with an intimacy that made Abel's fur bristle. "It is perfect, my dear," Silas said, his voice dripping with satisfaction. "It will make you look even more radiant on our wedding day. A true jewel for my new bride."

Truly's smile was a fragile thing, barely touching her eyes. "It is... beautiful, Silas," she managed, her voice a little breathless. She kept her gaze fixed on the shimmering stones, avoiding his eyes. Silas, however, seemed to misinterpret her reaction. He beamed, mistaking her polite acquiescence for genuine delight. He then turned to Truly's parents, his chest puffed out with pride. "You see? She approves. She will make a wonderful wife. I am most fortunate." Truly's father clapped Silas on the back, his gruff voice full of pleasure. "And we are fortunate, Silas, that you have chosen our Truly. She is a good girl, though she can be… a little headstrong at times. But you will soon tame that." He winked, a gesture that made Truly visibly shrink.

Abel felt a wave of despair wash over him. They were so eager to believe the charade, so blind to the reality. They saw a successful match, a secure future, and were unwilling to acknowledge the potential unhappiness it would bring their daughter. Silas's possessive touch, his condescending words, Truly's increasingly withdrawn demeanor, none of it registered. They were too caught up in the grand vision of their daughter's ascent. He saw Truly retreat to her room that night, the sapphire necklace still around her neck, but her shoulders slumped. She paced the floor, her movements agitated. He could almost feel her despair radiating through the thin walls of the cottage. She paused at the window, looking out into the darkness, and Abel knew she was looking for him, seeking solace in the thought of his silent vigil.

He remained there, an unwavering presence, a guardian from the wild, his heart heavy with the burden of his inability to directly intervene. He was a creature of instinct, of fierce loyalty, and the sight of Truly's quiet suffering, of Silas's encroaching control, was a torment. He could only watch, a silent witness to the unfolding drama, his very essence screaming in protest against the fate that was being woven for the human he had come to cherish. His vigil was a distant one, filled with a gnawing frustration, a profound sense of powerlessness that went against his very nature, a silent vow to protect his human, even from the shadows, even when his heart ached with the inability to do more. He was a ghost in their lives, a spectral presence unseen and unheard, yet his watchful gaze never wavered, his loyalty unwavering, his hope for Truly's escape a silent, burning ember in the encroaching darkness. He would remain, a sentinel of the wild, until the moment he could finally act, or until his heart could bear witness no longer.

The air in Oak holler was thick with the scent of celebratory baking and the hum of excited whispers. Banners, woven with wildflowers and promising good fortune, fluttered from every cottage window, their cheerful colors a stark contrast to the grey knot of dread tightening in Truly's chest. Each knot tied in the colourful ribbons, each flower pressed into a bouquet, felt like another strand binding her to a future she desperately wished to escape. Her mother, her face alight with an almost frantic joy, flitted from room to room, her movements as energetic as a hummingbird's. "Truly, darling, did you polish the silver as I asked? Silas's mother will expect a gleaming table, and we must make a good impression. Your father is out with Mr. Croft, discussing the arrangements for the reception feast. They are ordering the finest wines, you know. And the roast... oh, it will be a spectacle!"

Truly nodded, her voice a breath of sound barely audible above the cheerful din. "Yes, Mother. The silver is done." She traced a finger over the cool, smooth surface of a silver goblet, the reflection distorted and wavering. It looked like her own face, pale and drawn, a stranger staring back from the polished surface. She saw the expectation in her mother's eyes, a desperate hope for a prosperous future, for a daughter settled and secure. It was a weight she had carried for years, a heavy cloak woven from good intentions and the fear of disappointing those she loved. Her parents saw Silas Croft as salvation, a solution to their modest standing, a man who could offer their daughter a life of comfort and respectability. They saw his wealth, his lineage, his assured presence, and mistook it for affection. They saw the polished veneer, the charming smiles he offered them, and failed to see the predator beneath.

Her father, a man of few words but deep affections, had been equally enthusiastic, albeit in his own quieter way. He had clapped Silas on the shoulder with a gruff warmth, his pride evident in the slight puff of his chest. "She's a good girl, Silas. A bit quiet, perhaps, but with a good heart. And strong hands, useful for managing a household." He had meant it as a compliment, a testament to her capability, but Truly had felt a chill. "Strong hands for managing a household." It sounded less like a description of a beloved daughter and more like an appraisal of a skilled laborer, a valuable asset to be directed and utilized. She understood her father's desire for her security, his worry about her future, but his inability to see *her*, the real Truly, not the wife-in-waiting, was a pain sharper than any she had imagined.

This distance between what her family saw and what was true felt like a growing void. They celebrated the engagement as if it were a triumph, a meticulously planned victory. They spoke of Silas's generosity, his grand plans for their future, the prominent position Truly would hold as Mrs. Silas Croft. They saw the tangible benefits, the social climbing, the financial security, and lauded Silas as a prize catch. They saw the gleaming future reflected in the sapphire necklace he had so possessively fastened around her throat, a vibrant blue that matched her eyes, yet felt like a brand of ownership. They mistook her polite silence, her hesitant smiles, for contentment, for the demure acceptance of a bride-to-be. They could not, or would not, see the tremor in her hands as she reached for his arm, the way her breath hitched when his gaze lingered too long, the subtle flinch when his voice dropped to a possessive murmur.

The worst, perhaps, was the dismissal of her feelings, the gentle but firm redirection whenever she dared to hint at her unease. "Nonsense, Truly," her mother would say, her voice laced with a hint of exasperation. "Silas is a good man. He adores you. You'll see. You're just nervous, and that's perfectly natural. It's a big step, but he will take such good care of you. He's so much older and wiser, he'll guide you." Guidance. The word itself felt like a gilded cage. Silas's 'guidance' felt more like a carefully orchestrated campaign to mold her into someone she was not, someone pliable and obedient, a reflection of his own desires.

She remembered a conversation with her father just last week, a moment when a sliver of her true self had broken through the facade. They had been walking by the river, the late afternoon sun dappling through the leaves. "Father," she had begun, her voice trembling slightly, "I... I am not sure I am ready for this." He had stopped, his gaze kind but uncomprehending. "Ready for what, child? Ready to be married? Of course, you are. Silas is a fine prospect. He will provide for you better than any man in Oak Holler. You'll have a grand house, servants... you won't have to worry about a thing." He had patted her hand, a gesture meant to soothe, but it only deepened her despair. "But I don't... I don't love him, Father," she had whispered, the words tasting like ash. He had frowned, his brow furrowing. "Love? Love comes after marriage, Truly. Duty and companionship, that's what builds a strong marriage. Silas is a good man. He'll be a good husband. Don't be foolish. This is a good match, the best we could have hoped for."

Foolish. The word echoed in the cavern of her heart. Was it foolish to yearn for something more than a comfortable arrangement? Was it foolish to wish for a connection built on genuine affection, not societal obligation? Her parents, blinded by the promise of status and security, saw only the surface. They saw a young woman on the cusp of a prosperous life, and their concern was only that she might, through some childish whim or romantic folly, jeopardize it. They couldn't grasp that her unease was not mere nervousness, but a deep-seated premonition, a primal instinct screaming danger.

This disconnect only amplified her isolation. While the villagers offered congratulatory smiles and offered well-intentioned advice on wedding cakes and fine linens, Truly felt adrift in a sea of happy delusion. Their jovial greetings, their toasts to her future happiness, felt like a mockery of her inner turmoil. They saw a bride, a symbol of burgeoning prosperity for Oak Holler, and projected their own hopes and dreams onto her. They saw Silas as a benefactor, a man of means and ambition who would elevate not just his own standing, but the standing of those connected to him. And Truly, their daughter, was the key to this elevated future.

She found herself retreating more and more to the quiet sanctuary of the woods, the place where her true self felt safe to breathe. There, beneath the watchful gaze of ancient trees, she could shed the pretense. She could let the tears fall, let the frustration gnaw at her, and she could remember the silent understanding that existed between her and Abel. He, at least, saw. He saw the tremor in her hand when Silas touched her, he saw the forced brightness of her smile, he saw the silent plea in her eyes. He didn't offer platitudes or dismiss her fears; he simply *saw*.

She would often sit by the roots of his oak, her back pressed against the rough bark, and let the quiet strength of his presence seep into her. She imagined his immense form, hidden from view, his golden eyes watching her with an understanding that transcended words. He was a creature of a different world, a world of instinct and ancient wisdom, and he seemed to grasp the subtle nuances of human emotion that eluded those closest to her. His silent guardianship was a solace, a confirmation that she was not entirely alone in her struggle. He was a witness to her truth, a silent ally in a world that seemed determined to twist it.

She recalled an afternoon spent by the stream, weaving a crown of wildflowers, her fingers clumsy with unshed tears. Abel had emerged from the trees, his massive presence radiating a quiet reassurance. He had nudged a fallen branch with his snout, nudging it closer to her, as if offering a silent apology for the harshness of the world. He hadn't spoken, of course, but his presence had been a balm. He had sat with her, a silent, colossal shadow, his steady breathing a counterpoint to the frantic thumping of her heart. In that moment, she had felt a connection more profound than any she shared with the people of Oak Holler. Abel understood the language of the heart, the unspoken fears, the quiet despairs. He didn't need words to acknowledge the weight crushing her.

Her parents, however, saw her occasional disappearances into the woods as a sign of her youth, her girlish daydreaming. "She's just letting off steam," her mother would say, waving a dismissive hand. "A few weeks as Silas's wife, and she'll be too busy managing his grand estate to be wandering in the trees." The thought sent a shiver down Truly's spine. Managing his grand estate. She imagined herself overseeing servants, hosting lavish dinners, always playing the part of the dutiful wife, while her own spirit withered and died. It was a vision of a gilded emptiness, a life of outward prosperity and inner desolation.

The constant pressure to be cheerful, to project an image of joyful anticipation, was exhausting. She learned to smile on command, to nod at the right moments, to murmur affirmations that felt like lies on her tongue. Each congratulatory word, each well-meaning touch from a villager, felt like another brick in the wall being built around her heart. They were so eager for Silas's prosperity to reflect on them, so keen to be associated with his rising fortunes. Truly, the instrument of their communal advancement, was a secondary consideration.

Even the gifts, meant to symbolize affection and commitment, felt like shackles. The sapphire necklace, the delicate silver locket etched with intertwined initials, they were beautiful, undeniably so, but they represented a future she dreaded. When Silas had presented the locket, his fingers had brushed her skin, a touch that sent a jolt of revulsion through her. He had leaned in, his breath warm against her ear, murmuring something about how soon those initials would be hers to bear, not just on a piece of jewelry, but on her very being. Truly had forced a smile, her heart pounding against her ribs, and the locket had felt like a brand, searing itself into her skin.

Her mother had cooed over the gifts, admiring the craftsmanship, exclaiming over the generosity. "Such a thoughtful man, Silas is," she had said, her eyes shining. "He knows how to spoil a woman. You're a lucky girl, Truly. Truly lucky." Truly had simply nodded, her gaze fixed on the glittering trinkets, each one a tangible reminder of the trap she was in. The more they celebrated, the deeper her despair grew. The more they lauded Silas, the more she yearned for the silent, unconditional acceptance she found in Abel's watchful presence. He was the only one who saw her truth, the only one who understood the suffocating weight of expectation, and the chilling horror of a future she did not want. He was her silent sentinel, her only comfort in a world that refused to see her tears.

8

A MARRIAGE OF SHADOWS

The dawn of her wedding day broke not with the gentle caress of sunlight, but with an oppressive, suffocating weight. Truly felt it settle upon her like a shroud as her eyes fluttered open, the familiar quilt of her childhood bedroom doing little to ward off the encroaching chill. The air, usually alive with the morning songs of Oak Holler's birds, seemed to hold its breath, a hushed reverence for a ceremony that felt more like a funeral for her own spirit than a celebration of a new beginning. Her mother, ever bustling, entered with a tray laden with delicate pastries and a cup of herbal tea, her face a mask of forced gaiety. "Awake, my darling! The most important day of your life! You must eat, you must be strong."

Truly tried to swallow, but the tea tasted like bitter herbs and unspoken fears. Her mother's touch, as she adjusted the intricate lace of Truly's wedding gown, was firm, almost possessive, as if trying to physically stitch her daughter into the role of Mrs. Silas Croft. The gown itself, a cascade of ivory silk and delicate embroidery, felt like a cage, its beauty a cruel mockery of her inner turmoil. Each pearl sewn into the bodice, each thread painstakingly woven, represented a promise of a future she did not desire, a life she felt utterly unprepared to embrace. She caught her reflection in the polished surface of her dressing table mirror, and a stranger looked back, a pale, hollow-eyed girl adorned for sacrifice.

Downstairs, the wedding preparations were in full swing, a whirlwind of activity that Truly felt disconnected from. The scent of rose petals, intended to sweeten the air, only added to the cloying atmosphere. Her father, his face etched with a mixture of pride and a subtle, almost imperceptible anxiety, stood beside Silas Croft, his hand resting on the groom's shoulder. Silas, impeccably dressed, exuded an aura of confident ownership. His smile, directed at Truly's father, was sharp and knowing, a private jest shared between men who understood the transactional nature of the union. When his gaze finally landed on Truly, it held a proprietary glint, a silent assertion of his claim. He didn't see her fear; he saw his prize, secured.

The procession to the village chapel was a blur of expectant faces, eager to witness the union of Oak Holler's most prominent family with the wealthy outsider. Children scattered petals, their laughter a discordant chime against the somber melody of Truly's heart. Friends and neighbors offered congratulations, their words like stones dropped into a deep well, each one amplifying the echo of her despair. "You look radiant, Truly!" "A perfect match!" "Silas is such a fortunate man!" She offered weak smiles, her voice a whisper when she managed to murmur a reply, her focus elsewhere.

She couldn't help but scan the edges of the crowd, her eyes drawn to the familiar, dense line of the forest. A flicker of movement, a shadow detaching itself from the ancient trees. There, standing sentinel at the very fringe of the woods, where the manicured village gardens gave way to untamed wilderness, was Abel. He was cloaked in his natural camouflage, his massive form a testament to the primal world he inhabited, yet his presence was unmistakable. His amber eyes, usually so full of intelligent curiosity or gentle warmth, were clouded with a profound sadness, a heavy understanding that pierced through Truly's carefully constructed composure. He was a silent observer, a witness to this human ritual that felt so alien, so wrong.

The chapel was small, its stone walls usually imbued with a sense of peace and sanctity, but today they felt constricting, charged with tension. The air was thick with the scent of incense and wilting lilies. Silas's hand, as it took hers, was cool and firm, his grip tightening possessively, possessively, as if to ensure she wouldn't flee. His thumb brushed over the knuckles of her hand, a gesture that was meant to be reassuring but felt like a brand, a mark of ownership being pressed into her skin. Truly shivered, a tremor that had nothing to do with the chapel's cool air. She could feel the weight of Silas's attention, the expectation in his gaze, and it was suffocating.

The vows were spoken, Truly's voice barely audible, a fragile thread of sound lost in the solemn pronouncements. She repeated the words of devotion, of loyalty, of lifelong commitment, each syllable a betrayal of her own heart. She looked at Silas, his face serene, his eyes fixed on her with an intensity that made her skin crawl. He was a stranger, a man who saw her as a possession, a jewel to be added to his collection, and the reality of this union, sealed with the pronouncements of the village priest, crashed down upon her with crushing force. Her parents beamed, their relief visible, their dream of elevated status finally realized. They saw the outward show, the perfect scene from a fantasy, and were oblivious to the silent screams trapped within their daughter's throat.

As the ceremony concluded, and the pronouncement of husband and wife echoed through the chapel, Truly felt a profound sense of disorientation. She was no longer Truly of Oak Holler, the girl who found solace in the rustling leaves and the companionship of wild things. She was now Mrs. Silas Croft, bound by law and expectation to a man she did not love, a man whose touch sent shivers of revulsion down her spine. Silas led her from the chapel, his arm firmly around her waist, pulling her close, an almost imperceptible tightening of his grip that spoke volumes. He guided her into the bright sunlight, the cheers of the villagers a deafening roar, a celebration of her capture.

Her gaze, however, instinctively drifted back to the treeline. Abel was still there, a steadfast, solitary figure against the vibrant green. He hadn't moved. His posture was one of deep contemplation, his powerful frame conveying a sense of immense stillness, as if he were absorbing the very essence of the somber occasion. He was a creature of instinct, of the wild, and this formalized human bonding, this exchange of vows and societal blessings, must have seemed like a strange and alien ritual to him. Yet, his unwavering presence was a silent acknowledgment of their connection, a testament to the bond they shared that transcended words and ceremonies. He was her anchor in this sea of forced happiness, a silent promise that even in this darkest of moments, she was not entirely alone.

Truly raised her hand, a subtle, almost imperceptible gesture, a flicker of her fingers in his direction. It was a silent plea, a desperate farewell, an unspoken acknowledgement of the divide that had opened between their worlds, now seemingly insurmountable. His amber eyes met hers across the distance, and in their depths, she saw a reflection of her own despair, a mirrored anguish that confirmed the depth of his concern. He understood. He saw the forced smile on her lips, the tremor in her chin, the hollowness behind her eyes. He saw the possessiveness in Silas's grip, the way he steered her away from the familiar comfort of her home and into the unknown territory of his life.

The reception was held in the village square, tables groaning under the weight of food and drink. Laughter, music, and the clinking of glasses filled the air, a vibrant display of celebration that felt utterly alien to Truly. Silas, ever the gracious host, moved through the crowd, accepting congratulations, his charm a practiced, superficial veneer. He would occasionally pull Truly close, a possessive gesture that drew admiring glances, and she would force a smile, her heart a leaden weight in her chest. She felt like an exhibit, a trophy, her discomfort masked by the celebratory sounds.

Later, as the sun began to dip below the horizon, casting long shadows across the square, Silas led Truly away from the revelry. "Come, my wife," he murmured, his voice smooth and polished, his arm still a vice around her waist. "Our carriage awaits. We have a journey to undertake." Truly's stomach clenched. The journey. The unknown. The further separation from everything she knew and loved. As they approached the waiting carriage, a magnificent black conveyance drawn by two powerful steeds, she stole one last glance towards the forests edge. Abel was gone. He had retreated into the shadows, his silent vigil ended, leaving her to face this new, terrifying chapter alone. Yet, even in his absence, she felt the echo of his concern, a phantom warmth against the encroaching cold. He had witnessed the sealing of her fate, and his heavy heart surely mirrored the desolation in her own. He knew, as she did, that this marriage was not a union of hearts, but a subjugation, a binding of shadows that promised to engulf her light. The carriage door opened, a gaping maw inviting her into a future she could only dread.

The ornate carriage, a symbol of Silas's wealth and Truly's supposed good fortune, lurched into motion, the rhythm of the horses' hooves a somber drumbeat against the darkening landscape. Truly sat beside Silas, a suffocating silence clinging to them like the velvet upholstery. The forced gaiety of the wedding reception had evaporated with the setting sun, leaving behind a chilling reality. Silas's hand, which had rested lightly on her knee during the journey from Oak Holler, began to drift, his fingers tracing the delicate embroidery of her gown. It was not a gesture of tenderness, but one of assessment, as if he were cataloging the finery he now owned.

"You are a beautiful bride, Truly," Silas said, his voice a low purr that did nothing to warm the air between them. "A truly exquisite prize." He paused, his gaze sweeping over her with an unnerving intensity. "And now, you are mine. All mine."

Truly flinched inwardly. The possessiveness in his tone, so thinly veiled, was more alarming than any outright aggression. She remembered the glint in his eyes at the chapel, the possessive assertion that had chilled her to the bone. This was not the charming suitor who had courted her with promises of a shared life in their new home. This was a man who saw her as an acquisition, a conquest to be subdued and displayed.

As the carriage rattled on, leaving behind the familiar, comforting silhouette of Oak Holler and the beckoning darkness of the forest, Silas's demeanor shifted subtly. The practiced charm began to crack, revealing a core of something hard and unforgiving. He spoke of their new life, of the Ozark cabin, painting a picture of idyllic isolation, but his words were laced with an undertone of control. He outlined her duties, her expected behavior, her role as Mrs. Silas Croft, wife to a man of influence and means. Each pronouncement was delivered as a matter of fact, as if her desires or opinions were irrelevant, mere trifles to be swept aside.

"You will learn to appreciate the quiet," he stated, not as an invitation but as a decree. "The solitude of the mountains is good for a woman. It keeps her focused, away from the frivolous distractions of the village. No more gossiping with your friends, no more wandering through those woods." He let out a short, humorless laugh. "Those days are over, Truly. You belong to me now. Your world is here, with me." Truly's breath hitched. The forest, her sanctuary, the place where she found peace and connection with nature, was to be forbidden? Her friends, the few she held dear, were to be distanced? A cold dread seeped into her bones; more profound than any fear she had felt before. The carriage was not just transporting her to a new home; it was carrying her into a gilded cage.

When the carriage finally pulled to a stop, Truly looked out at the cabin Silas had described. It was nestled deep within a dense forest, the towering trees obscuring much of the sky. The structure itself was sturdy, built of dark logs, with a wide porch and a single chimney spewing a thin plume of smoke. It was undeniably picturesque, a scene ripped from the pages of a romantic novel, yet Truly saw only the looming shadows, the isolation, the absence of any sign of life beyond the immediate, suffocating enclosure.

Silas stepped down from the carriage first, his movements confident and purposeful. He extended a hand to Truly, his grip firm as she stepped down onto the rough-hewn porch. The air here was thin and sharp, carrying the scent of pine needles and damp earth. It was a far cry from the familiar, gentle air of Oak Holler, and it felt alien, unwelcoming.

Inside, the cabin was sparsely but expensively furnished. A large stone fireplace dominated one wall, and heavy, dark wood furniture filled the main living area. It was tidy, almost sterile, devoid of any personal touches that might suggest a lived-in space. It felt more like a hunting lodge, a temporary dwelling, than a home. "This will be our haven, Truly," Silas announced, his voice echoing slightly in the quiet space. He circled her, his gaze lingering on her wedding gown. "You will have everything you need. I will provide for you. You need only to be a good wife."

He turned to her, his smile now a tight, controlled expression that didn't reach his eyes. "And tonight," he continued, his voice dropping to a lower register, "we begin your education." The meaning of his words settled upon Truly with the weight of a physical blow. The tenderness, the chivalry, the whispered promises of affection, all of it had been a carefully constructed facade. The man standing before her was not the man she had been led to believe he was. The wedding night, meant to be the consummation of a loving union, was to be a lesson in submission.

Silas's touch, when he finally reached for her, was not gentle. His hands, rougher than she had imagined, pulled her close, his grip possessive, bruising. He dismissed her with a wave of his hand and a curt instruction to remove her wedding gown, his gaze burning into her with an intensity that stripped away her last vestiges of comfort. He saw not his bride, but a prize to be claimed, an object to be dominated.

The ensuing hours were a blur of fear and humiliation. Silas's temper, once he felt secure in his dominion, proved to be as volatile as a summer storm. His words, sharp and cutting, chipped away at Truly's spirit. He belittled her, ridiculed her upbringing, her naivete, her supposed lack of sophistication. He mocked her quiet nature, her love for nature, her connection to the wild. "Such a naive little thing," he sneered, his breath hot against her ear as he forced her to kneel before him. "Did you truly believe that all that romantic nonsense about true love applied to someone like you? You are a commodity, Truly, and I have paid a handsome price for you. You will behave accordingly."

He spoke of his own perceived superiority, of his power and his wealth, emphasizing how she had been elevated by marrying him. He twisted her genuine emotions into weaknesses, her sensitivity into foolishness. Every attempt Truly made to assert herself, to voice a simple preference or a quiet protest, was met with derision and a tightening of his control. He isolated her, not just from her past life, but from any possibility of connection within their new surroundings. He made it clear that her world was now confined to the cabin walls, to his presence, to his dictates.

Sleep offered little respite. The cabin, once intended to be a symbol of their shared future, now felt like a prison. The silence, which Silas had so lauded, was now punctuated by the echoes of his harsh words and Truly's stifled sobs. The heavy furniture seemed to press in on her, the thick walls a barrier against any hope of escape. The rough-hewn beams of the ceiling, illuminated by the flickering lamplight, seemed to twist and writhe like the tendrils of the despair that had begun to engulf her. "You are mine now, Truly," Silas would repeat, his voice a low growl that vibrated through the floorboards, a constant reminder of her captivity. "And I will mold you into what I desire. You have no choice but to obey."

Truly clung to the fading memories of Oak Holler, to the scent of her mother's garden, to the rustling symphony of the forest, to the comforting presence of Abel, a silent sentinel at the edge of her former world. These memories were fragile embers in the encroaching darkness, all she had to hold onto as the reality of her marriage to Silas Croft, a marriage of shadows, began to truly take hold. The charade of courtship was over. The honeymoon, if it could even be called that, was a cruel mockery. This was Silas's true nature, revealed in the brutal intimacy of their wedding night, and Truly knew, with a chilling certainty, that her life had irrevocably changed. She was no longer the free-spirited girl of Oakhaven, but a captive, bound by promises made under duress and by the iron will of a man who saw her not as a partner, but as property. The Ozark cabin, once a dream, had become her cage, and the key was held firmly in Silas's possessive hand.

The days that followed bled into a monotonous cycle of unspoken rules and stifled emotions. Silas enforced his control with an iron fist, his pronouncements becoming the law of their isolated existence. Truly's meals were often taken in silence, Silas observing her with a detached, critical eye. If she dared to speak of her home, of her family, his expression would darken, and he would launch into a tirade about her ingratitude, her foolish sentimentality. "Your family is weak, Truly," he'd sneer, swirling a glass of amber liquid. "They sent you away for a better future, did they not? This is your better future. Marriage to me. Stop clinging to the past. It will only hold you back."

He curtailed her movements with meticulous precision. The porch was permitted, but the woods were strictly forbidden. He would grant her brief walks, always under his watchful eye, during which he would lecture her on the dangers of the wilderness, on the untamed impulses that lurked in its depths, mirroring, he implied, the base instincts of those who lived outside of civilization. It was a subtle but persistent attempt to condition her, to make her fear the very things she had once loved.

He controlled her appearance, dictating the gowns she wore, the way she styled her hair. He insisted on a constant air of refinement, a polished exterior that masked the turmoil within. Yet, beneath this veneer of domesticity, he was constantly testing her, probing for any sign of defiance. A misplaced word, a hesitant glance, a moment of lost focus could trigger a storm of his displeasure.

One afternoon, as Truly was attempting to mend a tear in one of Silas's shirts, a task he had assigned her with pointed emphasis on its necessity, she pricked her finger. A small bead of blood welled up, crimson against her pale skin. She gasped, her mind flashing back to a similar incident years ago, when Abel had nudged her hand with his damp muzzle, offering a silent comfort as she had bandaged a scraped knee. The memory was so vivid, so potent, that for a moment, Truly's gaze drifted out the window, her eyes seeking the familiar green of the tree line, a phantom longing for his presence.

Silas, who had been observing her from his armchair, his eyes glinting with a predator's patience, noticed the shift in her demeanor. He rose; his steps deliberate as he approached her. "What is it, my dear?" he asked, his voice deceptively mild. "Lost in thought? Thinking of those woodland creatures again, perhaps?" Truly's heart hammered against her ribs. She quickly turned back to her sewing, her hands trembling slightly. "No, Silas. I simply pricked my finger."

He reached out, his fingers brushing against hers, and Truly instinctively pulled away. His eyes narrowed, a flicker of dark anger crossing his face. "Do not presume to recoil from my touch, Truly. You are my wife. My touch is your privilege." He snatched the shirt from her grasp, examining the tiny stain. "And you are clumsy. Useless, even. Perhaps I overestimated your capacity for even the simplest of domestic tasks."

The criticism, sharp and unwarranted, stung more than the prick of the needle. Truly felt tears prickling her eyes, but she fought them back. Silas's cruel words, his constant belittling, were designed to break her spirit, to erode her self-worth. She wouldn't give him the satisfaction of seeing her weep. He tossed the shirt back onto the table, the movement abrupt. "You will rest now," he commanded. "And reflect on your duties. I will not tolerate incompetence." He strode out of the room, leaving Truly alone with the suffocating silence and the stinging remnants of his contempt.

Later, as dusk began to settle, casting long, eerie shadows across the cabin's interior, Silas returned. He was in a different mood, his eyes alight with a possessive gleam that Truly had come to associate with his desire to assert his ownership. He spoke of their isolation not as a punishment, but as an advantage. "This is perfect, Truly," he murmured, pouring himself another drink. "No one to see us. No one to interfere. Just you and me, and the vast wilderness that you will learn to fear, and I will learn to master." He raised his glass in a mock toast. "To our future. A future built on strength, on control, on absolute obedience." He began to speak of his business dealings, of his plans to expand his influence, but his words were less about ambition and more about dominance. He saw the world as a series of battles to be won, of people to be subjugated. And he included Truly in this worldview, not as an equal, but as a prize that he had conquered and would now keep under his firmest control.

Truly listened, her gaze fixed on the dancing flames in the fireplace, searching for a flicker of warmth that was so absent in her new life. She thought of the days she had spent exploring the woods, her heart light, her spirit free. She remembered the way Abel's golden eyes would reflect the sunlight, full of a gentle understanding, a quiet companionship that was more profound than any words Silas could ever utter. He was a creature of the wild, and in his silent presence, Truly had felt a connection to something pure and untamed. Now, she was trapped in a manufactured wilderness, a controlled environment designed to stifle her very essence. She stole a glance at Silas. He was oblivious to her inner turmoil, lost in his own self-aggrandizing narrative. His face, illuminated by the firelight, seemed harder, more ruthless than ever before. The charm, the veneer of respectability he had shown in Oak Holler, had completely dissolved, leaving behind a man driven by a deep-seated need for power and possession.

As the night deepened, Silas's demands became more overt. His touch was rough, his kisses demanding, devoid of any affection. He treated her as a plaything, an object to be used and discarded. Truly endured, her body a frozen vessel, her mind retreating to the furthest corners of her consciousness, seeking refuge in the echoes of a happier time. She whispered Abel's name in the darkness, a silent plea for strength, for remembrance of the wild, free spirit that was slowly being crushed within her.

The cabin, with its dark wood and oppressive silence, had become more than just a dwelling; it was a physical manifestation of Silas's dominion. Its walls, once intended to offer shelter and comfort, now seemed to press in on her, amplifying the whispers of his control, the echoes of his disdain. Truly, trapped within its confines, felt her own spirit begin to wither, the vibrant colors of her inner world fading to muted shades of grey. The marriage of shadows had begun, and Truly was slowly, irrevocably, being consumed by the darkness.

The boughs of the ancient oaks, cloaked in the twilight gloom, offered Abel a vantage point he had occupied for countless nights since Truly's departure. From this shadowed perch, the familiar scent of pine and damp earth did little to soothe the gnawing unease that had become his constant companion. His amber eyes, usually alight with the quiet wisdom of the forest, now burned with a restless, protective urgency. He had watched the ornate carriage recede, a harbinger of change, and since then, the whispers carried on the wind had been laced with a darkness that chilled him to the bone.

Tonight, the whispers had shifted into something tangible, something that vibrated through the very roots of the trees. Silas's voice, a rasp that grated against Abel's keen hearing, rose in a torrent of fury. It was a sound that never failed to send a ripple of apprehension through the surrounding fauna, but for Abel, it was a sound that tightened his chest with a primal fear. He strained to see through the deepening shadows that clung to the Ozark cabin, Silas's new domain, the place that had become Truly's prison.

He saw her then, a small, fragile figure silhouetted against the dim light of the cabin's interior. Even from this distance, he could discern the unnatural tension in her posture, the way her shoulders were hunched as if perpetually bracing for a blow. The light caught the sheen of unshed tears in her eyes, eyes that once sparkled with the joy of discovery, now clouded with a pervasive dread. Each subtle shift in her stance, each hesitant movement, spoke volumes of the suffocating control that had ensnared her.

Silas's tirade continued, a venomous stream of accusations and pronouncements that Abel couldn't fully decipher, but the intent was clear. It was an assault, designed to break, to demean, to assert absolute dominion. The deep, resonant growls that rumbled in Abel's chest were a testament to his barely suppressed rage. He had always been a creature of patience, his clan's ancient teachings emphasizing restraint, the observation of cycles, the wisdom of waiting. But the sight of Truly's palpable suffering, the raw fear etched onto her delicate features, was testing the very core of his being.

He remembered the few times Silas had ventured out of the cabin, always with Truly trailing a few paces behind, her gaze fixed on the ground. Abel had observed Silas's possessive hand on her arm, the way he would subtly steer her, guiding her movements as if she were a recalcitrant hound. The casual cruelty in Silas's demeanor, the cold assessment in his eyes as he surveyed his surroundings, had always made Abel's hackles rise. But now, witnessing the direct impact of that cruelty on Truly, the deep, personal anguish he could sense radiating from her, the prejudices his clan held against humans seemed a distant, irrelevant echo.

His clan elders spoke of the inherent deceit of humankind, their fleeting loyalties, their destructive tendencies. They warned of the dangers of forming bonds with such creatures, of the inevitable heartbreak that such alliances would bring. Yet, Abel had always found a quiet solace in Truly's presence, in her gentle spirit and her profound connection to the natural world. She was different, a beacon of warmth in a world often perceived by his kind as harsh and unforgiving. And now, this different human, this keeper of his own heart's unspoken affections, was being systematically broken.

The protective instincts that lay dormant within him, instincts honed by generations of guarding their territory and their kin, surged with an unprecedented force. He was a creature of the wild, a being of instinct and subtle communication. He could not directly intervene in the human dramas unfolding within the cabin's walls, not without risking exposure, not without potentially exacerbating Truly's precarious situation. The thought of his clan's wrath, of the consequences of such a blatant disregard for their laws, was a chilling prospect. But the thought of Truly, alone and afraid, trapped in a cycle of abuse, was a far greater torment.

He grasped a branch, his claws digging into the bark, a low whine escaping his throat. His usual calm was fractured, replaced by a desperate need to act. He was a guardian, a protector by nature, and to stand by and witness this slow torture was an unbearable agony. He thought of the ancient power that flowed through his veins, the inherent connection he shared with the earth, the subtle influence he could wield over the natural world. Could he use it? Could he somehow disrupt Silas's hold, offer Truly a sliver of respite, a glimmer of hope?

The prejudices of his clan, the ingrained fear of human entanglement, felt paper-thin against the immense weight of Truly's suffering. He had always been the anomaly, the one who felt a deeper connection to the world beyond his own kind. Now, that connection was proving to be a double-edged sword, offering him a profound empathy that was simultaneously his greatest strength and his most debilitating weakness. He was powerless to stop the torment directly, and this helplessness was a bitter pill to swallow.

He watched as Truly flinched again, her body recoiling from Silas's unseen proximity. The sound of Silas's voice softened, taking on a new, sinister tone that Abel recognized as a precursor to a different kind of violation. His fur bristled, a guttural growl building in his chest. The restraint that had served him for so long was fraying at the edges, worn thin by the constant barrage of Truly's misery. He needed a plan, a way to breach Silas's defenses, to offer Truly an escape, however temporary. The forest had always been his sanctuary, his domain, and within its embrace, he would find a way to fight for her. The desperation that fueled him was a potent force, pushing him to consider actions he had never before contemplated, all for the sake of the woman who had inadvertently captured his wild heart. He knew, with a certainty that resonated deep within his bones, that he could no longer simply watch. He had to find a way to intervene, to disrupt the suffocating darkness that was slowly consuming Truly, before she was lost to it entirely. The prejudices of his clan felt like distant thunder compared to the immediate, deafening roar of his own protective fury. He was a guardian, and he would not stand idly by as his charge was destroyed. The whispers of the forest, once a balm to his spirit, now seemed to carry the echoes of Truly's silent pleas, urging him to action, to find a way out of this agonizing stalemate.

The sunlight that once greeted Truly as a familiar friend now felt like a mocking spotlight, exposing her to a world that seemed to have forgotten her. Her visits to the forest, once the highlight of her meager existence, became agonizingly infrequent. The ancient oaks, once her haven, now seemed to loom with judgment, their branches heavy with the unspoken disapproval of her prolonged absence. Silas's suffocating presence had a way of leaching the color from everything she touched, including the vibrant memories of her time spent in Abel's company.

When she did manage to steal away, the stolen moments were shrouded in a veil of profound sadness. The easy laughter that had once flowed between her and Abel was replaced by hesitant whispers, by the ragged edges of her despair. Her words, once full of hopeful inquiries about the forest's secrets and the creatures that inhabited it, now spoke of a life slowly dimming, of ambitions turning to dust, and of dreams withering on the vine. "Abel," she would begin, her voice barely audible, her gaze fixed on the fallen leaves beneath her feet, "the sunlight... it doesn't feel the same anymore. It's as if a shadow has settled over everything."

She would recount fragmented tales of her days, not of grand adventures or intriguing discoveries, but of the monotonous weight of

Silas's control. She spoke of the way he watched her, his gaze like a physical restraint, of the subtle manipulations that chipped away at her will, of the constant undercurrent of threat that made even the simplest tasks feel like navigating a minefield. "He... he doesn't understand why I long for the quiet," she confessed one afternoon, her voice trembling. "He sees it as a weakness, a defiance. He says my fascination with the woods is childish, that I should be grateful for the comforts he provides, even if those comforts are... confined."

The cage Silas had built for her was indeed luxurious, filled with fine fabrics, expensive trinkets, and an abundance of food. But it was a cage nonetheless, its bars forged from possessiveness and a deep-seated insecurity that manifested as cruelty. Truly would explain, her eyes brimming with unshed tears, how Silas would twist her words, misinterpret her actions, and use her deepest desires against her. "He tells me I'm lucky to have him," she whispered, her voice thick with a sorrow that seemed too heavy for her slender frame. "That no one else would tolerate my... my peculiar nature. And sometimes, when he's in one of his moods, I almost believe him."

Abel, in his quiet, watchful way, would listen, his amber eyes never leaving her face. He could sense the erosion of her spirit, the subtle dimming of the light that had once shone so brightly within her. He would offer what comfort he could, a soft rumble in his chest that spoke of solidarity, a gentle nudge of his head against her hand that conveyed his unwavering presence. He couldn't speak human words, but his actions, his steadfast loyalty, spoke a language that Truly understood implicitly. "I used to dream of exploring every corner of this forest," she murmured, tracing the intricate patterns of moss on a fallen log. "Of learning the names of every plant, of understanding the language of the birds. Now... now my world has shrunk to the walls of that house. The forest feels so far away, even when I'm standing right here." She sighed, a sound that seemed to carry the weight of all her unfulfilled longings. "I miss the wildness, Abel. I miss feeling... free."

The contrast between her current reality and the life she once knew was stark, and the realization of this chasm was a constant source of pain. She spoke of how her visits to Abel had become clandestine affairs, snatched moments of reprieve where she had to constantly glance over her shoulder, her heart pounding with the fear of discovery. Each rustle of leaves, each snapping twig, would send a jolt of panic through her, for she knew that if Silas caught her, the consequences would be severe. He had made it clear that her excursions were a privilege, not a right, and that any perceived transgression would be met with swift and unpleasant retribution.

"He demands my attention constantly," Truly explained, her gaze drifting towards the dense canopy of trees, as if searching for an escape route that wasn't there. "He wants to know where I am, who I'm with, what I'm thinking. There's no space for my own thoughts, my own desires. It's as if I'm expected to exist solely for his amusement, for his validation." She hugged herself, a shiver coursing through her despite the mild autumn air. "The days blur into one another. They are filled with the same routines, the same suffocating silence broken only by his commands or his... pronouncements."

Even the simple act of gathering wildflowers, something she once relished, had become fraught with anxiety. Silas would scrutinize her bouquet, dissecting her choices, questioning her motives. "Why these particular flowers, Truly?" he'd ask, his voice laced with suspicion.

"Do they remind you of someone? Or something you shouldn't be remembering?" The joy was gone, replaced by a gnawing apprehension that her every innocent action was being judged, interpreted as a betrayal.

Her conversations with Abel, though brief and infrequent, became an anchor in the turbulent sea of her despair. She would pour out her heart, finding solace in his silent, attentive presence. Even though he was a creature of the wild, a being bound by his own laws and limitations, his unwavering loyalty was a potent antidote to Silas's manipulative words. She knew he couldn't intervene directly, that the gulf between their worlds was too vast for him to bridge without immense risk. Yet, the simple fact of his existence, of his steadfast friendship, offered a glimmer of hope in the encroaching darkness.

"Sometimes," she would admit, her voice barely a whisper, "when I feel like I can't bear it any longer, I close my eyes and imagine you here. I imagine the scent of the pines, the feel of the moss beneath my feet. It's a small thing, I know, but it's enough to remind me that there's still beauty in the world, that not everything is tainted by... by him." She would look at Abel, her eyes pleading for understanding, for reassurance. "You are the only one who sees me, Abel. Truly sees me. Everyone else... they only see what Silas wants them to see."

She confessed the growing weariness that had overtaken her very bones. The constant vigilance, the emotional manipulation, the suppression of her own identity, it was all taking its toll. "My spirit feels... brittle," she would say, her voice thin and reedy. "Like a dried leaf that could crumble at any moment. I try to hold onto the memories of who I was, of what I dreamed of, but they seem to fade with each passing day." The laughter that had once come so easily now felt like a distant echo, a sound from another life. The spark of curiosity that had drawn her to the forest, to Abel, was flickering precariously.

One particularly bleak afternoon, after a heated argument with Silas that had left her trembling and hollow, Truly found herself at the edge of the woods. She didn't venture deep, her fear of being caught overriding even her desperate need for solace. She sat on a sun-warmed rock, the familiar scent of pine needles a faint comfort. Abel, sensing her distress from his vantage point, approached cautiously.

Truly looked up, a weak smile gracing her lips. "Oh, Abel," she sighed, her voice laden with exhaustion. "He's made it so difficult to even breathe freely. He says my fascination with this place is a sign of my inadequacy, that I'm trying to escape my responsibilities. He doesn't understand that this is where I feel... whole." She picked up a smooth, grey stone, turning it over and over in her palm. "I feel like I'm losing myself, Abel. Bits and pieces of me are just... disappearing."

She spoke of the subtle ways Silas chipped away at her resilience. It wasn't always overt shouting or physical threats; often, it was a constant drip of belittling comments, of dismissive remarks about her intelligence, her capabilities, her very worth. He would praise her when it suited him, only to withdraw his affection abruptly, leaving her confused and desperate to regain his favor. This emotional pendulum swing was, in its own way, more damaging than outright abuse, as it fostered a crippling dependency and a constant fear of displeasing him.

"He tells me I'm too sensitive," she confessed, her gaze fixed on a distant hawk circling lazily in the sky. "That I overreact to everything. He makes me doubt my own feelings, my own perceptions. Am I really seeing things clearly, Abel? Or am I just... imagining it all?" Her voice cracked, and she pressed her knuckles to her eyes, willing the tears to stop. She felt a profound sense of shame for her vulnerability, for her inability to break free from Silas's influence.

The thought of Abel, of his silent strength and unwavering presence, was a lifeline. "You're the only one who believes me," she whispered, stroking his thick fur. "You don't judge me. You just... are. And that's more than I can say for anyone else in my life right now." She leaned her forehead against his, drawing strength from his solid, unwavering form. "I don't know how much longer I can keep pretending. The fight is... it's becoming too much."

Her words were not a plea for Abel to act, for she knew the impossibility of such a request. They were, however, a testament to the profound impact his friendship had on her, a beacon of hope in her increasingly bleak existence. Even as her spirit dwindled, the thought of Abel, of their shared quiet moments in the forest, of his steadfast loyalty, served as a fragile reminder that she was not entirely alone. It was a sliver of light, a whisper of resilience, in the face of overwhelming despair, a testament to the enduring power of connection, however distant, however constrained. The forest, and the bond she shared with its silent guardian, remained the last glimpse of her former self, a private sanctuary where the echoes of her true spirit could still be heard.

9

FRACTURED RESPONSABILITIES

The ancient forest, a tapestry of emerald and gold, had always been Abel's sanctuary. But lately, the rustling leaves seemed to carry a different tune, a murmur of discontent that prickled his fur. His visits to the edge of the human settlement, once brief and driven by a desperate concern for Truly, were becoming longer, more frequent. He found himself drawn to the faint trails of smoke that curled from chimneys, to the distant, discordant sounds of human life, a stark contrast to the forest's natural symphony. He observed the people, their hurried movements, their strange rituals, their vulnerability laid bare under the indifferent sky. And with each observation, a seed of unease, a quiet rebellion, began to sprout within him.

It was Lyra, her fur the color of moonlit snow, who first voiced the clan's growing apprehension. Her eyes, usually pools of gentle curiosity, now held a sharp, assessing glint as she cornered him near the Great Oak. "Abel," she began, her voice a low growl that vibrated with unspoken accusation, "your scent... it is tinged with the scent of *them*. You linger too long at the boundary. The elders have noticed."

Abel shifted, his massive frame suddenly feeling too large, too conspicuous. He could feel the weight of unseen eyes upon him, the collective disapproval of his kin coalescing like a gathering storm. He had always been a creature of instinct, of deep-seated loyalty to the clan and their traditions. But Truly's plight had woven a thread of empathy into his being, a strange and potent force that pulled him in a direction utterly alien to his nature. "I... I am merely observing, Lyra," he rumbled, the words feeling hollow even to his own ears. "There are... changes at the edge of our territory. We must be aware."

Lyra's ears flattened against her skull. "Aware? Or entangled? Your focus has shifted, Abel. Your attention is divided. The clan senses it. The younger ones mimic your gaze towards the human lands, their curiosity a dangerous flame. The elders speak of it in hushed tones, their disapproval a palpable chill in the den." She stepped closer, her gaze intense. "They say you are forgetting your place. That your heart beats to a rhythm not of the forest, but of the two-legged creatures and their noisy, fragile world."

He could offer no adequate defense. How could he explain the gnawing ache he felt when he pictured Truly's fading light, her spirit slowly being extinguished by the suffocating attentions of her human mate? How could he convey the urgent, primal need to intervene, to shield her from a pain he understood all too well, though its source was of a different kind? He knew the ancient laws, etched into the very soul of their kind: keep to the shadows, observe, but never interfere. The history between their kind and humans was a bloody tapestry, woven with threads of betrayal, fear, and loss. To cross that boundary, to offer succor to one of *them*, was to court disaster, to risk the fragile peace that had been painstakingly maintained for generations.

Later, he sought out Elder Maeve, her fur a grizzled testament to her years, her wisdom a guiding light for the clan. He found her by the ancestral stream; her gaze fixed on the water's surface as if reading secrets within its flow. He approached with due reverence, lowering his head in a gesture of respect. "Elder Maeve," he began, his voice deep and resonant, "Lyra speaks of the clan's concern. I... I do not wish to cause disharmony." Maeve turned, her ancient eyes, like polished amber, held a profound sadness. "Disharmony, Abel, is already upon us. It is in your restless pacing, in the way your gaze drifts towards the forbidden horizon. It is in the subtle shift of your allegiance. You have always been a fierce protector of our lands, a loyal son of the forest. But lately, your heart seems to be pulling you elsewhere."

She rose, her movements slow but deliberate, and walked to the edge of the water, her shadow falling across the smooth stones. "The humans. They are a volatile species, Abel. Their emotions are as unpredictable as a summer storm. They grasp and they consume. They forget. They betray. Our history with them is long and bitter, filled with pain and sorrow. Our ancestors paid dearly for their trust. They taught us to be wary, to remain distant, to never let their world bleed into ours." Her voice grew stern, the gentleness replaced by a steely resolve. "They are not like us. Their lives are fleeting, their loyalties shallow. They are driven by greed and by a need for control. To involve yourself with one of them... it is a dangerous path. It is a betrayal of your lineage, of the very essence of what it means to be a creature of this forest."

Abel felt a familiar ache in his chest, a deep-seated conflict that tore at his very being. "But Elder Maeve," he pleaded, his voice thick with emotion, "she suffers. She is trapped, her spirit fading. I have seen it. Her human mate... he suffocates her. He uses his power to bind her, to dim her light. She longs for freedom, for a breath of clean air, for a moment of peace. Is it not our way to protect the vulnerable?"

Maeve let out a soft, sorrowful sigh. "We protect our own, Abel. We protect the balance of the forest. The struggles of the humans are their own. To interfere is to invite their chaos into our world. You cannot save them all. You cannot mend every broken spirit. To try is to risk your own well-being, and in doing so, the well-being of the entire clan. Think of the consequences. If your involvement is discovered... it will bring ruin upon us all." She looked at him, her gaze piercing. "You walk a precipice, Abel. Between your kin and your... compassion. This human female, she has somehow ensnared your empathy. But empathy, unchecked, can be a dangerous weapon. It can lead you astray. It can blind you to the greater threats, to the needs of your own kind."

The weight of her words settled upon him, heavy and suffocating. He understood the elders' fears. He had witnessed firsthand the destructive nature of human ambition, the casual cruelty that could be born from ignorance and fear. He had seen how they encroached upon the forest, felling ancient trees, scarring the earth with their settlements. But the memory of Truly's desperate eyes, the fragile hope that flickered within them when she spoke of him, haunted his thoughts. He spent days wrestling with his conscience, the conflict a constant, gnawing presence. He patrolled the forest's borders with a new vigilance, his senses heightened, his instincts screaming at him to retreat, to sever the connection. Yet, his paws seemed to carry him closer to the human settlement, his heart a battlefield of conflicting loyalties.

One evening, as the sun bled hues of orange and purple across the sky, he saw her. Truly, cloaked in shadow, had managed to slip away from her home. She stood at the very edge of the treeline, her form silhouetted against the fading light. She looked frail, a ghost of the vibrant woman he remembered. Her shoulders were slumped, and she clutched a shawl tightly around herself, as if warding off a chill that had nothing to do with the evening air.

He approached cautiously, a knot of anxiety tightening in his gut. The clan's warnings echoed in his mind, a chorus of caution and disapproval. But the sight of her, so alone and desolate, overrode all his reservations. He stopped a few paces away, his golden eyes fixed on her, a silent question in their depths. Truly's head snapped up, her eyes, wide and startled, found him. A flicker of relief, so profound it was almost painful to witness, crossed her face. "Abel," she whispered, her voice ragged with emotion. She took a hesitant step towards him, then another, until she was close enough to reach out and touch his massive head. "I... I couldn't stay away," she confessed, her voice trembling. "He... he is always watching. His words... they are like chains. He speaks of my duty, of my position, but all I feel is the weight of his possessiveness. He claims to love me, but his love is a cage. He restrains me, Abel. He smothers me." Tears began to stream down her face, unchecked. "I feel like I am disappearing. Like I am being erased."

Abel nudged her gently with his head, a low rumble of comfort emanating from his chest. He could feel the tremor that ran through her, the fear and despair that emanated from her like a noxious vapor.

The clan's warnings about human volatility, about their capacity for causing harm, felt both true and yet... incomplete. Truly was not the source of this harm; she was its victim. "He says I am ungrateful," she sobbed, her body wracked with silent tremors. "That I have everything a woman could desire. And I... I try to believe him. But the silence in that house... it screams. His constant scrutiny... it grinds me down. I miss the forest, Abel. I miss the wildness. I miss... I miss *me*."

He could offer no words of human comfort, no platitudes to assuage her pain. His role was to be a silent sentinel, a steadfast presence. He pressed his flank against her leg, a grounding force against her instability. He could sense the inner turmoil that raged within her, the desperate struggle for survival against an invisible enemy. "The elders... they speak of the dangers," he finally managed, his voice a low growl, the human words feeling clumsy on his tongue. "They warn me. They say... to disassociate. To forget. That our worlds should never mix." Truly let out a small, broken laugh that held no humor. "I understand," she whispered, her voice barely audible. "They are right to be wary. My world... it is tainted. He has made it so. But Abel," she lifted her tear-streaked face to meet his gaze, her eyes pleading, "you are the only part of my old life that still feels real. You are the only one who sees me, not as Silas's wife, but as... Truly."

The weight of her reliance, the depth of her despair, pressed down on him. He was caught between the ancient wisdom of his clan and the raw, undeniable suffering of a single human. He was a creature of instinct, yet this situation demanded more than instinct. It demanded a choice, a path that would inevitably lead to conflict. He looked back towards the dark, impenetrable depths of the forest, the home he had always known. He could almost hear the whispers of his ancestors, the rustle of disapproval in the leaves. But then he looked at Truly, her vulnerability a stark contrast to the stoic strength of his kin, and he felt a pull that was as ancient as the earth itself: the urge to protect, to offer solace to those in need, regardless of their species. "I cannot abandon you," he rumbled, the words a solemn vow. "But I must be... discreet. The clan's eyes are upon me. Their disapproval... it is a heavy burden." Truly reached out, her hand resting on his broad forehead, her touch surprisingly steady. "I know," she whispered. "And I am grateful. More grateful than words can express. Just... knowing you are here. It is enough to keep a small ember of hope alive."

As she turned to go, melting back into the encroaching darkness of her own world, Abel remained, a solitary figure at the edge of two realms. The scent of pine and damp earth mingled with the faint, lingering scent of human sorrow. He knew he had crossed a line, a subtle but significant boundary. He had chosen empathy over tradition, compassion over caution. And he knew, with a certainty that chilled him to the bone, that this precarious balancing act, this marriage of shadows, would not go unnoticed for long. The clan's disapproval was not just a murmur; it was a gathering tide, and he was standing at its very edge, vulnerable and alone.

10

THE BREAKING POINT

The moon, a sliver of white in the ink-black sky, offered no solace to the small cabin nestled at the forest's edge. Inside, the air crackled with a tension so thick it felt as if the very walls were straining to escape. Truly, her breath catching in ragged gasps, pressed herself against the rough-hewn wood of the cabin, trying to make herself small, invisible. But Silas's rage was a storm that could not be outrun. His voice, usually laced with a possessive sweetness that had once fooled her, was now a venomous hiss, each word a shard of ice digging into her raw nerves.

"You think I don't see it, Truly?" he snarled, his eyes burning with a feverish jealousy that seemed to consume him from within. "That lingering scent of the forest... the way you look towards the trees as if they hold some secret solace, you can't find here, with me." He stepped closer, his shadow engulfing her. "You yearn for something else, don't you? Something wild and untamed. Something *better* than what I offer." Truly flinched, a small, involuntary tremor passing through her. She tried to speak, to deny his accusations, to explain that her longing was for a freedom she'd once known, a life before his suffocating grip had tightened around her. But the words caught in her throat, strangled by the fear that had become her constant companion. "Silence," Silas commanded, his voice dropping to a dangerous low. "Your silence speaks volumes, woman. It confirms my every suspicion. You pine for him, don't you? For that... beast who haunts your dreams." He laughed, a harsh, grating sound that grated on Truly's ears. "Do you think I am blind? I see the way your eyes linger on the tree line, the phantom caress of the wind on your skin as if you expect him to materialize from the shadows."

He advanced, his fists clenching and unclenching at his sides. The small cabin, once a refuge, now felt like a cage, the suffocating confines amplifying the terror that coiled in Truly's stomach. She could hear the distant hoot of an owl, a mournful cry that seemed to echo the despair in her own heart. She imagined Abel, her silent guardian, just beyond the trees, perhaps sensing her distress, perhaps torn by the ancient laws that forbade him from interfering. The thought was a faint spark of hope, quickly extinguished by the crushing reality of her situation. "You think your beast can give you freedom, don't you?" Silas spat, his breath hot and foul against her face. "He whispered tales of the wild, of a life unbound by the chains of civilization. But you are mine, Truly. Mine to command, mine to control. You belong to me, and no one, not even some creature of the woods, can change that."

His hand shot out, not with the casual cruelty of previous outbursts, but with a deliberate, calculated force. He grabbed her arm, his fingers digging into her flesh, leaving angry red marks. Truly cried out, a sharp, pained sound that was swallowed by the indifference of the night. The struggle was desperate, a silent ballet of pain and fear. She twisted, bucked, trying to wrench herself free, but Silas was stronger, fueled by a jealous rage that seemed to lend him unnatural strength.

She stumbled backward, her head striking the wooden frame of the hearth. The impact sent a jolt of pain through her skull, blurring her vision. Silas loomed over her, his face a mask of fury, his eyes wild and unseeing. He saw only betrayal, only the threat of losing the prize he believed he possessed. "You will never be free of me, Truly," he vowed, his voice a guttural growl. "I will break you. I will make you understand that your world begins and ends with me." The words were a physical blow, striking at the last vestiges of her spirit. The cabin seemed to spin around her, the rough-hewn planks blurring into a swirling vortex of despair.

The scent of damp earth and pine needles, usually a soothing balm to Abel's senses, was now laced with an acrid tang of fear. He pressed himself deeper into the thicket, the rough bark of an ancient oak scraping against his skin, a sensation he barely registered. The sounds of the cabin, muffled by distance and the rustling leaves, were a symphony of dread. He could hear Truly's cries, faint and choked, like a trapped bird beating its wings against a cage. And then there was Silas's voice, a guttural snarl, laced with a venom that even Abel, from his vantage point, could feel prickling his own hackles. It was the sound of a predator cornered; of a man consumed by a darkness Abel had only ever heard of in hushed, fearful whispers.

The warnings of his elders, the ingrained fear of the 'two-legs,' felt distant and insignificant now, like echoes from another lifetime. The raw, visceral terror emanating from the cabin, the unmistakable sound of a soul being systematically broken, drowned out all reason, all ingrained caution. He saw, in his mind's eye, Truly's delicate form being crushed, her spirit extinguished. The image was an unbearable agony, a violation of everything he stood for, of the protective instincts that pulsed through his very being.

He was Abel, of the Current River Basin. He was a protector. And he could no longer stand idly by while a human soul, his friend, was devoured. The choice, a monumental one that would shatter his world and potentially cost him everything, was no longer a choice at all. It was a necessity, a primal call to action that his very essence could no longer resist. His heart hammered against his ribs, a furious drumbeat of defiance. The ancient laws, the fear of reprisal, the ingrained prejudice, they were paper shields against the storm that was brewing within him. Truly's life, her very soul, was more important than any of it.

He took a deep, shuddering breath, the scent of Silas's rage a potent motivator. The air vibrated with the raw violence of the scene unfolding within the flimsy walls. He could almost taste the metallic tang of fear and the suffocating miasma of human desperation. His beast nature surged to the forefront, shedding the veneer of controlled restraint. The urge to protect, to defend, to guard, to *fight*, was an all-consuming fire. He was no longer just an observer. He was a participant, about to step from the shadows and into the heart of a conflict that had been brewing for far too long.

He lowered his head, his powerful shoulders bunching. The forest floor, thick with fallen leaves, would offer some cover for a moment, but not for long. Silas's rage was a beacon, drawing Abel closer. He could feel Truly's terror like a physical blow, a searing pain that propelled him forward. He was so close now, the sounds of their struggle growing more distinct, the desperate, muffled sobs of Truly a gut-wrenching counterpoint to Silas's enraged roars. Each sound was a lash, driving him onward, past the point of no return.

His mind raced, not with fear, but with a cold, calculated resolve. He knew the risks. He knew the consequences. But the thought of Truly suffering any further was a pain he could not endure. He had always felt a pull towards her, a strange, protective instinct that went beyond his duty as a guardian. He had watched her from afar, a silent, unseen presence, his heart aching with a sympathy he couldn't articulate. Now, that sympathy had ignited into a fierce, unyielding determination.

He would not let Silas break her. He would not allow the darkness to consume her light. The laws of his people, the fear of ostracism, the deep-seated animosity towards humans, they all paled in comparison to the immediate, desperate need to save Truly. He could feel the weight of centuries of ingrained prejudice and caution warring with the raw, undeniable urge to protect. But the latter was winning, a tidal wave of instinct and emotion crashing against the frail barriers of tradition.

He could feel the shift within him, the primal beast embracing the higher calling of a guardian. The ancient warnings of his clan, the fear of reprisal, the deep-seated prejudice against humans, all of it crumbled in the face of Truly's palpable terror. He knew, with a certainty that resonated to the core of his being, that he could not stand by and witness her destruction any longer. A decision was being forced upon him, not by logic or reason, but by the undeniable pull of empathy and the fierce, protective instinct that had always simmered beneath the surface of his calm demeanor. He could hear Truly's muffled cries, Truly's pleas for mercy, Truly's spirit being chipped away piece by piece, and with each sound, his resolve hardened. He knew he had to intervene. The consequences, merely an afterthought.

The wind howled around the small dwelling, a mournful, relentless gale that seemed to buffet the very timbers of the cabin. It was as if the forest itself was trying to tear it down, to expose the darkness festering within. Branches scraped against the roof, a percussive accompaniment to the sounds of distress that Abel could now distinctly hear. The soft, muffled sobs that had reached him from a distance were now clearer, laced with a desperate terror that twisted his gut. And beneath it all, the low, guttural rumble of Silas's voice, a sound that spoke of cold fury and absolute control.

Abel slowed his approach, melting into the deeper shadows cast by the gnarled oaks at the edge of the clearing. He moved with a predatory grace, his powerful form a dark silhouette against the moonlit undergrowth. Every nerve ending was alight; his senses stretched to their absolute limit. He could smell the damp earth, the pine needles, the faint, sweet scent of wild honeysuckle struggling to bloom in the encroaching chill. But overriding it all was the sharp fear, the cloying aroma of human desperation, and the musky, aggressive scent of Silas himself.

He observed the cabin, cataloging its weaknesses, its strengths. A single door, crudely fashioned from rough-hewn planks. Small, shuttered windows, offering little in the way of egress or ingress. The timbers were weathered, showing signs of age and disrepair, but the structure held firm against the gale. It was a meager defense, but one that Silas, in his current state of rage, would likely exploit to its fullest extent.

The forest watched. The ancient trees seemed to hold their breath, their leaves stilling their rustling dance. The wind, which had been a tempest, now died down to a mere whisper, a soft exhalation that carried the sounds from the cabin with unnerving clarity. It was as if the natural world, sensing the critical juncture, had fallen silent, reserving its energy for the inevitable release. The air vibrated with an almost unbearable tension, a coiled spring ready to snap.

The wind, as if recognizing his intent, suddenly swirled around him, carrying him forward, a silent escort. The branches of the trees, previously still, now thrashed wildly, their movements a dramatic flourish to his charge. The forest was no longer holding its breath; it was exhaling, a collective sigh of anticipation, of acknowledgment. It understood. It had always understood. And now, it was lending its ancient strength to his cause. He was the embodiment of its wild heart, its fierce protector, and he was about to bring the breaking point to Silas, not Truly.

The splintering wood of the cabin door was a punctuation mark in Truly's desperate pleas. Each crack, each groan of tortured timber, sent a fresh wave of ice through her veins. Silas's shadow loomed over her, a tangible weight pressing down, stealing the very air from her lungs. She could feel the tremor in his hands as he gripped her arm, the raw, unreasoning fury radiating from him like heat from a forge. Her world had shrunk to this single, terrifying room, to the suffocating presence of the man who had once promised her a different kind of life. "Silas," she whispered, her voice a dry, rasping sound, barely audible above the ragged rhythm of her own heart. She forced herself to meet his gaze, to search for any flicker of the man she had thought she knew, any trace of the gentleness that had once drawn her to him. But there was only a wild, unfocused rage, a storm cloud obscuring any familiar features. "Please. Silas, stop."

He didn't answer, his grip tightening until white knuckles stood out against his tanned skin. His chest heaved, the labored breaths a guttural counterpoint to her desperate entreaties. He was a cornered animal, his pride wounded, his possessiveness twisting into something ugly and dangerous. And she was the unwilling target of his violent tempest. "You're... you're hurting me," she managed, the words catching in her throat. The pressure on her arm was unbearable, bruising already blooming beneath his rough touch. Her eyes welled with tears, hot and stinging, but she fought to keep them from falling. Tears only seemed to fuel his anger. "Just... calm down. We can talk." Talk. The word felt like a mockery in the face of his escalating violence. There was no reasoning with this version of Silas, no logic he would accept. He was a creature of pure impulse now, his mind consumed by a consuming paranoia, a desperate need to assert his dominance. The cabin, once a refuge, had become a prison, the walls closing in, the rough-hewn timbers amplifying the sounds of his rage.

She longed, with an ache so profound it was a physical pain, for the forest. For the quiet rustle of leaves, the gentle sigh of the wind through the ancient pines, the comforting presence of Abel. His silent strength, his steady calm, it was the opposite of this chaos. She could almost feel his presence, a phantom warmth against her skin, a silent promise of protection that felt impossibly distant. The forest had always been her solace, a place where the world made sense, where nature's balance offered a balm to the hurts of human hearts. Now, it seemed to mock her with its remembered peace, its tranquil beauty a stark contrast to the ugliness unfolding within these four walls.

Silas finally spoke, his voice a low, dangerous growl that vibrated in her bones. "Talk? What is there to talk about, Truly? You think you can just defy me? You think you can deny me?" He dragged her, stumbling, across the room, his strength overwhelming her weakened resistance. The floorboards creaked beneath their weight, each step a jarring echo of her terror. He shoved her towards the rough-hewn table, its surface scarred and uneven. She braced herself, her hands flying out to catch her fall, but the impact was still jarring. The rough wood scraped against her palms, a sharp, stinging pain that mirrored the ache in her heart. "You belong to me," he hissed, his face inches from hers, his breath hot and foul against her skin. "You understand? Mine. And you will do as I say."

Truly squeezed her eyes shut for a fleeting moment, a silent prayer for an escape that felt increasingly unlikely. She imagined Abel, his powerful form a shield against this onslaught, his amber eyes burning with a protective fire. She pictured the serene depths of the forest, the dappled sunlight filtering through the leaves, the comforting scent of pine and damp earth. Those images were a fragile bulwark against the encroaching darkness, a desperate attempt to cling to sanity. "I... I understand, Silas," she choked out, forcing the words past the lump in her throat. It was a lie, a desperate attempt to placate him, to buy herself time, to find an opening. She knew, with a chilling certainty, that this was a breaking point, a precipice from which there might be no return. "You are right. I... I was foolish."

His grip loosened slightly, a flicker of something, triumph? in his wild eyes. But it was quickly replaced by a renewed wave of suspicion, his brow furrowed into a dark scowl. "Foolish? You think that's enough?

After what you did?" He gestured wildly, his arm knocking a crude earthenware jug from the table. It shattered on the floor, water and shards scattering across the rough planks. The sharp crash made Truly flinch, her body tensing in anticipation of further violence. "Silas, please," she pleaded, her voice cracking. "Don't. Let's just... let's just sit down. Let's try to be calm." She cast a desperate glance towards the window, a futile hope for a miraculous intervention. The glass was small, barred by thick wooden shutters, offering no escape, no glimpse of the outside world. The forest, her beloved forest, felt impossibly far away, its peace denied to her.

He laughed, a harsh, grating sound devoid of any humor. "Calm? You want calm, Truly? You think you deserve calm after... after what you did?" His eyes narrowed, and she could see the venom in his gaze, the poison of his wounded pride. He was spiraling, his emotions untethered, his grip on reality slipping with every passing moment. "I didn't... I didn't mean to," she stammered, her mind racing for any words that might soothe his rage. She thought of Abel's quiet strength, his understanding gaze. If only he were here. If only she could hear his calm, reassuring voice. "It was a mistake. I'm sorry." "Sorry?" he spat the word like a curse. "Sorry doesn't fix this, Truly. Sorry doesn't un-say what was said, un-do what was done." He paced the small room, his movements agitated, like a caged predator. The air crackled with his unrest. "You betrayed me. You think a whispered apology makes it all right?"

He stopped suddenly, his gaze fixing on her with an unnerving intensity. Truly's breath hitched. She knew that look. It was the prelude to something terrible. The quiet before the storm, but a storm that was already raging. The sounds of the forest outside, the gentle rustling of leaves, the distant murmur of the wind, seemed to recede, replaced by the deafening roar of Silas's fury. "You're going to learn, Truly," he said, his voice low and menacing. "You're going to learn what happens when you cross me. When you defy me."

He took a step towards her, and Truly instinctively recoiled, her back hitting the rough wall of the cabin. She could feel the splintered wood pressing into her skin, a minor discomfort compared to the dread coiling in her stomach. Her mind flashed back to Abel's warning, his concern for her safety. He had sensed this, hadn't he? He had felt the danger, the darkness that clung to Silas. "No, Silas, please," she whispered, her voice trembling. "Don't do this." She closed her eyes again, desperately trying to conjure the image of Abel's serene face, the strength in his gaze. She wished she could feel his presence, his protective aura. The quiet, intelligent understanding he always offered, a stark contrast to Silas's volatile emotions. The silence of the forest, she realized, was a precious thing, a testament to nature's order. This rage, this brutal assertion of power, was an affront to that order.

Suddenly, a sound from outside pierced the tense atmosphere. A sharp crack, louder than any twig snapping underfoot. It was followed by a low, resonant growl that seemed to vibrate through the very foundations of the cabin. Truly's head snapped up, her heart leaping with a sudden, impossible hope. Could it be? Silas's head whipped towards the door, his face a mask of confusion and then dawning alarm. His grip on Truly's chin faltered. "What was that?" he growled, his rage momentarily displaced by a prickle of unease.

The growl came again, closer this time, deeper, more powerful. It was a sound that spoke of ancient power, of primal force. Truly felt a thrill of anticipation, a desperate hope that her plea for silence, her unspoken longing for protection, had somehow been heard. She recognized the raw power in that sound, the controlled fury that was so unlike Silas's chaotic rage. "It's just an animal," Silas said, his voice lacking its earlier conviction. He pushed Truly away from him, the sudden release leaving her unsteady. She stumbled, catching herself on the table. "No," she whispered, her gaze fixed on the door, a newfound strength coursing through her. "It's not just an animal."

Another sound, this time a thunderous impact against the cabin door, shook the entire structure. Wood splintered, groaning under an immense force. Silas flinched, his eyes wide with a fear that Truly had never seen before. "Who's there?" he bellowed, his voice cracking with a sudden, uncharacteristic fear. "Show yourself!" The door shuddered again, and then, with a deafening roar of tearing wood, it burst inward. The force of the impact sent Silas stumbling backward, his eyes fixed on the dark, imposing figure silhouetted against the moonlit clearing.

Truly, her breath catching in her throat, stared in stunned silence. The ragged, desperate pleas that had filled the cabin moments before were silenced, replaced by the overwhelming presence of the protector she had silently invoked. The forest's plea for silence had been answered, not with quiet, but with a thunderous arrival. The breaking point had arrived, not for her, but for Silas.

The sound ripped from Abel's chest, a raw, untamed force that shattered the night's fragile stillness. It wasn't a roar of pain, though his heart was fractured by Truly's suffering. It was a roar of protective fury, a primal declaration that his silent vigil had reached its limit. The earth beneath the cabin seemed to tremble, the ancient trees of the forest momentarily holding their breath as the sound echoed through their branches. It was a sound that spoke of a bond deeper than words, a connection forged in the quiet understanding of the wild. Truly, who had heard Abel's hushed whispers and the gentle rumble of his contentment, had never imagined such a sound could emanate from him. It was the sound of a guardian unleashed, of a loyalty that would not tolerate injustice.

Silas, caught mid-stride in his menacing advance, froze. The rage that had contorted his features moments before flickered, replaced by a stark, uncomprehending terror. His eyes, wide and darting, scanned the splintered remains of the door, searching for the source of the terrifying vocalization. The sound had bypassed his ears and struck him directly in the gut, a visceral shockwave that momentarily paralyzed his every thought. The arrogance that had fueled his earlier aggression evaporated, replaced by a dawning, cold dread. He had heard the growls of predators in the deep woods, the territorial challenges of ancient beasts, but this... this was something else. This was a sound imbued with a power that seemed to transcend the natural world, a sound that promised retribution.

Truly, her own fear momentarily eclipsed by the overwhelming force of Abel's cry, felt a surge of hope so potent it was almost dizzying. The sound was a physical manifestation of her unspoken pleas, a tangible answer to her desperate longing for salvation. It resonated deep within her, a counterpoint to the suffocating darkness that Silas had woven around her. She could feel the vibration of it in the floorboards beneath her bare feet, in the very air she breathed. It was a promise of deliverance, a guarantee that she was not alone, that her suffering had not gone unnoticed. Her eyes, still stinging from unshed tears, fixed on the shattered doorway, her heart hammering a frantic rhythm of anticipation.

The raw power of Abel's roar seemed to physically push against the flimsy structure of the cabin. The timbers groaned, not from Silas's rough handling, but from the sheer sonic force that vibrated through them. Dust, previously invisible in the dim lamplight, danced in the disturbed air. The crude oil lamp on the table flickered wildly, casting erratic shadows that seemed to writhe with the intensity of the moment. The world outside, moments ago a silent, indifferent witness to Silas's cruelty, now seemed to hold its breath, acknowledging the profound shift that had just occurred. The breaking point wasn't just a figurative phrase anymore; it was a tangible event, heralded by a sound that would forever be etched into the memory of this cursed place.

Silas, his bravado crumbling, took a hesitant step back, his gaze still fixed on the gaping maw of the ruined doorway. He raised a trembling hand, as if to ward off an invisible blow. "What... what was that?" he stammered, his voice a thin, reedy echo of its former menace. He looked from the shattered door to Truly, a desperate plea for explanation in his eyes, but she could only offer a look of stunned awe. The question wasn't for her to answer. It was a challenge, a territorial dispute declared by a force he couldn't comprehend.

The silence that followed Abel's initial cry was heavy, pregnant with anticipation. It stretched, taut and vibrating, until Truly thought her own heart would burst from the strain. Then, a new sound emerged from the darkness outside, a sound of immense power and deliberate movement. It was the rhythmic crunch of heavy feet on the forest floor, each step deliberate, each stride measured, yet carrying an undeniable sense of urgency. The sounds drew closer, each footfall a drumbeat marking the approach of a force that had finally decided to intervene. The forest, which had always been Truly's sanctuary, was now sending its champion.

Silas scrambled backward, his movements clumsy and panicked. He tripped over a fallen stool, his hands flailing to regain his balance. The oil lamp swayed precariously, threatening to spill its flammable contents. He cursed under his breath, a string of venomous expletives that were lost in the growing symphony of approaching power. His eyes darted to the barred window, a futile hope for an alternative escape route, but the thick shutters remained resolutely closed, offering no solace. He was trapped, cornered by his own cruelty and the unstoppable force that was now at his doorstep. The paranoia that had fueled his actions now served him ill, turning his own worst fears into a terrifying reality.

The air grew colder, a palpable chill seeping into the cabin that had nothing to do with the night air. It was the breath of something ancient, something powerful, something that had watched and waited. Truly could feel it, a prickling sensation on her skin, a tightening in her chest that was not entirely of fear, but also of a profound, dawning relief. The energy in the room shifted, the oppressive atmosphere of Silas's rage dissipating, replaced by an aura of unwavering strength and protective intent. It was as if the very essence of the forest had coalesced into this single, powerful presence.

Then, a shadow detached itself from the deeper darkness of the forest. It was enormous, hulking, a silhouette against the faint moonlight that was more suggestion than clear form. It moved with a fluid grace that belied its immense size, a predator's stealth coupled with a guardian's unwavering purpose. Truly's breath hitched again. It was him. Abel. But not the Abel she knew from their quiet walks, the one who offered silent comfort and understanding. This was Abel as primal force, as protector, as a being of immense power finally roused to action.

11

THE CONFRONTATION

The shattered doorway yawned open, framing a silhouette that seemed to drink in the scant moonlight, growing larger, more imposing, with every passing second. Silas, his breath still catching in ragged gulps, felt his eyes drawn to the imposing figure that had emerged from the encroaching darkness. It was Abel, but not the quiet, watchful presence Truly had come to know. This was a being of primal power, a manifestation of the wild's deep, protective instincts, now unleashed. The air crackled with an almost tangible energy as he stepped fully into the meager light of the cabin, his immense form dwarfing the flimsy structure.

Abel's fur, the color of a storm-laden sky, seemed to absorb the gloom, making him appear as if carved from the very night itself. His muscles rippled beneath the dense coat, taut and coiled like a spring, ready to unleash devastation. But it was his eyes that truly held Silas captive. They were not the gentle, understanding pools of amber Truly had seen in quieter moments. These were molten gold, burning with an incandescent fury, a righteous anger that spoke of deep reservoirs of pain and a fierce, unyielding protectiveness. They fixed on Silas with an intensity that felt like a physical blow, an ancient condemnation that stripped away all pretense of bravado, leaving Silas exposed and trembling.

The raw power radiating from Abel was overwhelming. It wasn't just visual; it was a visceral sensation that vibrated through the very soles of Silas's worn boots, a chilling tremor that resonated deep within his bones. He felt his own carefully constructed arrogance crumble like dry earth under a flash flood. All his threats, his cruelty, his carefully orchestrated terror, seemed laughably insignificant in the face of this magnificent, terrifying guardian. The instinct to flee warred with a paralyzing awe, a primal fear that whispered of ancient transgressions and their inevitable reckoning. He had never encountered anything like this, not in the darkest corners of the wild he'd so often traversed. This was not just a beast; it was something more, something elemental, something that belonged to the very heart of the forest.

Abel's movement was deliberate, each heavy footstep a measured de-claration of presence. He didn't roar again, didn't need to. The silence that stretched between his arrival and his next movement was more potent than any sound. It was a silence pregnant with intent, with a promise of retribution that Silas could feel seeping into his very soul. He tried to summon a defiant retort, a curse to mask his terror, but his throat was constricted, his tongue thick and useless. His hands, which moments before had clutched a weapon with malicious intent, now hung uselessly at his sides, twitching with a fear he couldn't suppress.

Then, Abel lowered his great head, not in aggression, but in a slow, controlled descent that made Silas instinctively flinch. His amber eyes, still blazing, now held a specific focus, a piercing gaze that seemed to bore directly into Silas's core. A low growl, a sound that resonated more in the pit of Silas's stomach than in his ears, rumbled through the cabin. It was a sound that spoke of boundaries crossed, of sacred spaces violated, of a patience that had finally been exhausted. It was a warning, etched in the primal language of the wild, a promise that such trespass would not go unpunished.

Truly, witnessing this incredible display of raw power and protective fury, felt a surge of emotions so intense they threatened to overwhelm her. The fear that had been her constant companion for so long began to recede, replaced by a dawning sense of awe and a fragile, burgeoning hope. Abel's presence was a tangible shield, a living embodiment of her unspoken pleas for deliverance. She saw the flicker of his amber gaze briefly shift to her, a silent acknowledgment, a connection that spanned the chasm between fear and reassurance. It was a look that said, *I am here. You are safe.*

Silas, his eyes wide and darting between Abel and the now-barred window, seemed to search for an escape that didn't exist. He mumbled something incoherent, a desperate, choked sound that was swallowed by the heavy atmosphere. His gaze then found Truly, and for a fleeting moment, she saw a flicker of his old malice, a desperate attempt to reclaim some semblance of control. He opened his mouth as if to speak, perhaps to threaten, perhaps to plead, but Abel shifted his immense weight, a subtle movement that made Silas recoil as if struck. The protector's dominance was absolute, undeniable.

Truly, her voice finding a strength she hadn't known she possessed, stepped forward slightly, her gaze now steady on Silas. "He's right, Silas," she said, her voice clear and carrying a new, unwavering resolve. "You have gone too far. You have caused me pain. And now... now you will face the consequences." Her eyes, once filled with terror, now held a quiet defiance, a reflection of Abel's unwavering presence beside her. The fear was still a faint echo, but it was drowned out by a profound sense of liberation.

Abel's gaze remained fixed on Silas, his massive form a silent, unyielding sentinel. He hadn't physically touched Silas, hadn't threatened him with violence, yet his mere presence was more potent than any physical assault. Silas, utterly defeated, his bluster dissolved like mist in the morning sun, let out a choked sob. He looked less like a menacing tormentor and more like a cornered, pathetic creature, stripped of all his defenses by a power he couldn't comprehend. He made no move to attack, no desperate lunge, simply stood there, a quivering wreck beneath the unwavering gaze of the forest's guardian.

The oppressive atmosphere that Silas had woven around the cabin began to dissipate, replaced by the calm, potent aura of Abel's strength. The scent of damp earth and pine needles, usually a comfort, now carried an edge of wild power, of ancient forces stirring. The very walls of the cabin seemed to breathe easier, as if relieved of a suffocating burden. Truly felt a profound sense of peace settle over her, a peace that had been absent for so long, a peace that was earned through Abel's fierce loyalty and his willingness to finally reveal the true depths of his nature.

His eyes, still wide with a terror that had momentarily paralyzed him, narrowed, the molten gold gaze of Abel no longer an object of abject dread, but a raw, infuriating affront. Ownership. That was the word that echoed in the churning abyss of Silas's mind. He had carved out his dominion, had staked his claim, had bent Truly to his will through fear and coercion. And now, this... this *beast*... this creature of the wild, had the audacity to stand between him and what he considered his. It was not a protector; it was an intruder. A trespasser. An insolent obstacle that dared to defy *him*.

The primal aggression that had always simmered beneath Silas's carefully constructed veneer of control boiled over with the force of an erupting volcano. His mind, once a weapon of manipulation and cruelty, was now reduced to a single, burning instinct: to destroy the threat. His pride, a fragile thing built on the subjugation of others, recoiled at the idea of being defied, of being made to feel small and insignificant. This was not how his story was supposed to end. He was the predator, the master of his own narrative, and this wild guardian was attempting to rewrite it with its very presence.

With a choked snarl, Silas's gaze darted around the meager confines of the cabin, searching for anything, *anything*, that could serve his purpose. His hands, still trembling, clenched and unclenched at his sides, the phantom sensation of a weapon still clinging to them. But his eyes landed on the hearth, on the rough-hewn stone that framed the dying embers of the fire. There, leaning against the cold metal of the grate, was a heavy, wrought-iron poker. It was thick, solid, and bore the scorch marks of countless fires. It was a weapon.

A wild, almost manic gleam entered Silas's eyes. He lunged, his movements jerky and desperate, fueled by adrenaline and a terrifying sense of entitlement. His fingers closed around the cool, rough metal of the poker, the weight of it a comforting, familiar sensation. It was a tangible extension of his will, a tool of his dominance. Abel's silent, imposing presence was a challenge, an insult to everything Silas believed himself to be. He wouldn't cower. He wouldn't flee. Not again. Not ever.

The air crackled not with Abel's power, but with Silas's desperate, cornered rage. He felt a surge of exhilaration, a fleeting illusion of control returning as he hefted the poker. This was his chance. His final, desperate act of defiance against a force that threatened to dismantle his carefully constructed world, piece by agonizing piece. He didn't see the wisdom in Abel's gaze, the deep well of protectiveness. He saw only an enemy, an obstacle standing between him and Truly, the prize he believed he was entitled to.

He felt a tremor run through him, not of fear this time, but of anticipation. He was going to strike. He was going to reclaim his authority. He was going to remind this wild thing that some territories, some people, were not to be trifled with. The sheer audacity of Abel's intervention had ignited a dangerous, consuming fury within him. He was no longer the cold, calculating tormentor. He was a cornered animal, lashing out with the ferocity of a cornered wolf, ready to tear down anything that stood in its way, even if it meant tearing himself apart in the process.

The momentum of his lunge was powerful, a testament to the raw, unthinking energy that now consumed him. The poker was raised, a dark arc against the dim light, aimed not at Abel's head, but at the immense shoulder, a target that Silas believed would inflict the most immediate, debilitating pain. He envisioned the satisfying crunch of bone, the pained bellow that would surely follow, the moment when this wild protector would finally break, and Truly would be his again, cowering at his feet, her defiance extinguished.

But Abel didn't flinch. He didn't retreat. He didn't even seem to register the metallic glint of the poker as a threat. His molten gold eyes remained fixed on Silas, an ancient, unwavering stare that seemed to pierce through the rage, through the desperation, and into the very soul of the man. There was a profound sadness in that gaze, a weariness that spoke of ages of dealing with such darkness, such possessiveness. It was a look that Silas, in his blinding fury, could not comprehend. He expected fear, or pain, or a desperate defense. He received only an overwhelming sense of pity, and that, in its own way, was far more infuriating than any physical blow.

Silas let out another raw roar, a sound of frustration and pure, unbridled aggression. He was pouring every ounce of his being into this one desperate act. His muscles strained, his breath hitched, his entire focus narrowed to the single point of impact. He was the hunter, the aggressor, and this creature was simply in his way. The terror he had felt earlier had transformed into a blind, consuming need to prove himself, to reassert his dominance, to annihilate the threat that dared to challenge his will.

The air grew thick with anticipation, the very cabin seeming to hold its breath. Silas was a storm of destructive intent, a whirlwind of misplaced pride and brutal aggression. He was about to strike, to unleash the full force of his fury upon the creature that had dared to protect what he claimed. His mind was a canvas of destruction, his heart a black hole of possessiveness, and the heavy iron poker was the brush with which he intended to paint his final, violent masterpiece. The clash was imminent, a collision of primal rage and ancient guardianship, a moment where the illusion of control would be tested against the unyielding power of the wild.

Silas, fueled by a toxic cocktail of wounded pride and possessive rage, saw the poker in his hand not just as a weapon, but as an extension of his will. His vision, narrowed to a burning point of pure aggression, painted Abel as an obstacle, a brute standing between him and his perceived ownership of Truly. He lunged, his movements a desperate, uncoordinated flail, the wrought-iron poker a dark arc against the dim interior. He aimed for Abel's shoulder, a primal, instinctive strike born from a lifetime of inflicting pain and expecting it in return. He craved the satisfying crunch, the pained bellow, the visual confirmation of his dominance.

But Abel was not Silas. He was not a creature of desperation and brittle ego. He was an entity shaped by ages of observing the delicate balance of nature, by understanding the devastating consequences of unchecked aggression. His senses, honed by countless cycles of sun and moon, had registered Silas's every twitch, every shift in weight, every ragged breath. The blind fury that possessed Silas was a chaotic storm, easily anticipated by a mind that operated with the calm precision of a predator tracking its prey.

As the poker swung forward, Abel moved. It wasn't a flinch, not a step back to evade. It was a fluid, almost contemptuous shift of his massive form. His thick, fur-covered forearm, a shield of living muscle and bone, came up with a speed that belied its apparent bulk. The impact was not a clash of metal against flesh, but a controlled intercept. The wrought iron met the dense fur and sinew, and the sound that echoed through the cabin was not the sickening thud Silas had envisioned, but a dull clang, quickly absorbed by Abel's resilient form. The poker, instead of finding purchase, deflected sharply upwards, its momentum spent, leaving Silas momentarily off-balance, his roar of anticipation turning into a choked gasp of disbelief.

Abel's molten amber eyes, which had held a deep, unsettling sadness moments before, now flickered with a grim resolve. There was no malice in them, no desire for vengeance, only a profound, quiet determination. He had seen the glint of madness in Silas's eyes, had felt the raw, toxic energy radiating from the man, and understood, with the chilling clarity of instinct, the immediate and profound danger he posed to Truly. His purpose was singular: to neutralize the threat, to remove the source of the fear that had held Truly captive for so long. He was not here to fight, but to end.

With the poker deflected, Silas stumbled, his balance thrown by the unexpected resistance. It was a tiny opening, a sliver of opportunity that Abel seized with lightning speed. He didn't need to crush, didn't need to break. He needed to incapacitate. His immense strength, usually employed with the gentleness of a forest breeze, was now channeled with a focused intensity. His forearm, still braced against the deflected poker, swept downwards, not to strike Silas, but to sweep his legs out from under him.

The movement was so swift, so precisely timed, that Silas had no time to react. His feet, still planted from his forward lunge, were suddenly no longer beneath him. With a surprised yelp, he lost his footing, his body pitching forward. The poker, ripped from his grasp by the sudden shift in his center of gravity, clattered uselessly against the wooden floor. Silas's fall was awkward, ungainly, a stark contrast to the raw aggression he had projected moments before. He landed heavily on the worn rug, his breath knocked out of him, the air momentarily escaping his lungs in a wheezing gasp.

Before Silas could even begin to process the indignity of his fall, Abel was there. He loomed over the sprawled man, a silhouette of imposing power against the flickering firelight. His massive hands, each one capable of rending flesh from bone, were held not in aggression, but in a gesture of containment. He didn't strike again. He didn't need to. The sheer physical presence of Abel was enough to communicate the finality of the situation.

Silas, his face pressed against the rough fibers of the rug, tried to push himself up, his hands scrabbling for purchase. His muscles screamed, his ribs ached from the impact, but the real pain was the searing humiliation. Defeated. Not by a weapon, not by a show of equal strength, but by a single, precise action that had rendered him utterly powerless. He was a snared animal, his desperate struggle futile. He could feel Abel's gaze on him, a steady, unwavering pressure that seemed to penetrate his very being. It was not a look of triumph, nor of anger. It was something far more unsettling: a look of profound disappointment, of weary resignation.

Abel let out another low rumble, this one softer, more contemplative. It was a sound that spoke of a deep, ancient sadness, the kind that comes from witnessing the same destructive patterns repeat themselves across the ages. He had seen the fear in Truly's eyes, had felt the echoes of her suffering from his watchful distance. He had intervened only when the threat escalated from a subtle, insidious torment to an immediate, physical danger. Silas's lunge with the poker, fueled by a violent desperation, had been the final straw.

The struggle, if it could even be called that, was over. It had been a fleeting, brutal ballet of instinct and intent. Silas's clumsy, rage-fueled attack had been met with Abel's swift, decisive action, a testament to the vast difference in their capabilities. Silas, for all his bluster and cruelty, was a creature of limited, fragile power, driven by base emotions. Abel, on the other hand, was a force of nature, his power inherent, his movements guided by an ancient wisdom and an unwavering purpose.

Silas, still sprawled on the floor, managed to push himself onto his elbows. His chest heaved, his eyes, still wide with disbelief, darted between Abel's impassive face and the spot where the poker lay. He was trapped, not by chains or bars, but by the sheer, overwhelming presence of the creature before him. The primal urge to fight, to lash out, warred with a dawning, chilling realization: he was utterly outmatched.

Abel lowered himself slightly, his massive form settling onto his haunches. He was not a captor, nor a punisher. His role was that of a protector, a guardian. He observed Silas, his molten gold eyes reflecting the flickering flames, a silent assessment of the broken man. There was a weight to his stillness, a sense of inevitability that settled over the cabin like a shroud. Silas's reign of terror, built on fear and coercion, had finally met its end, not with a bang, but with the quiet, implacable force of the wild.

The air, once charged with Silas's frenzied rage, now held a different kind of tension, a stillness that spoke of resolution. Abel's actions had been swift, almost surgical. He had deflected, disarmed, and disabled, all without inflicting lasting harm. His objective was not to inflict pain, but to remove the immediate threat, to ensure Truly's safety. The raw power he possessed was immense, but it was wielded with a restraint that spoke of a deep understanding of consequence, of balance.

Silas let out a ragged sigh, a sound of defeat that seemed to drain the last vestiges of fight from him. He no longer saw a rival, a beast to be conquered. He saw an insurmountable force, a living embodiment of something far older and more powerful than his own twisted will. The pride that had fueled his aggression had been shattered, replaced by a gnawing sense of helplessness. Abel remained poised, his gaze steady. He was a silent sentinel, his very presence a declaration that the cycle of abuse had been broken. He had witnessed the subtle manipulations, the whispered threats, the suffocating control that Silas had exerted over Truly. He had seen the spark of defiance in her eyes slowly dim, replaced by a hollow weariness. And when Silas had finally revealed the true depth of his depravity, when his possessiveness had manifested in a clear intent to inflict physical harm, Abel had been forced into direct action.

Silas, still on the floor, finally found his voice, though it was a hoarse, broken whisper. "You... you can't... she's mine..." The words were a pathetic echo of his former arrogance, devoid of any conviction. Abel's reply was not in words, but in a subtle shift of his weight, a low, resonant sound that rumbled in his chest. It was a sound that conveyed an ancient truth, a truth that Silas, in his self-imposed blindness, had never understood. Some things, some lives, were not possessions. They were not to be owned or controlled. They were to be cherished, to be protected, to be set free.

The molten amber eyes of Abel fixed on Silas once more, and this time, there was a hint of something akin to pity in their depths. Silas had sought to dominate, to break, to possess. But in doing so, he had revealed the hollowness of his own spirit, the true poverty of his being. Abel, the embodiment of wild strength and ancient wisdom, had simply acted as nature intended: to restore balance, to shield the weak from the destructive impulses of the strong. The confrontation was over, and the wild had claimed its victory, not through bloodshed, but through the undeniable power of its inherent grace and unyielding protection. Silas, broken and defeated, was left to face the quiet, devastating truth of his own failure, under the watchful, unblinking gaze of a protector he could never hope to understand.

The silence that descended after Abel's decisive maneuver was not a peaceful one. It was a heavy, suffocating blanket woven from lingering adrenaline, the metallic tang of fear, and the sudden, stark absence of Silas's belligerent roar. Truly, who had instinctively recoiled, shrinking further into the shadows by the hearth, could still feel the phantom vibration of Abel's deep growl resonating in her bones. Her heart hammered against her ribs, a frantic drumbeat against the unnerving quiet. She watched Abel, his massive form still poised, his golden eyes fixed on Silas, who lay sprawled on the floor, his earlier fury seemingly leached out of him.

Silas, still grappling with the shock of his abrupt fall and the indignity of being disarmed with such effortless grace, attempted to regain his footing. A choked gasp escaped him as he scrabbled at the rough-hewn floorboards, his hands finding no purchase. He was a cornered animal, stripped of its weapons, its roar of defiance reduced to a ragged rasp. The poker, a symbol of his desperate aggression, lay abandoned several feet away, a dark, inanimate testament to his failed charge. Abel, his movements economical and precise, shifted his weight, his immense presence filling the small cabin, an unyielding wall of primal power. He was not a captor, not a judge, but a force of nature, an immovable object in Silas's path of destruction.

The air, filled with an unspoken tension, a silent exchange passing between the two men, or rather, between man and... something else. Silas's eyes, still wide with disbelief, flickered between the impassive, ancient gaze of Abel and the discarded poker. He saw not a beast to be vanquished, but an embodiment of an order far beyond his comprehension, an order that had just dismantled his carefully constructed world of dominance and fear with a single, fluid motion. Abel's golden eyes, pools of ancient wisdom and quiet power, held no malice, no vengeful glint, only a weary resolve, the kind that comes from witnessing the same destructive patterns repeat across the vast expanse of time. He had seen the fear in Truly's eyes, had felt the subtle, insidious erosion of her spirit under Silas's oppressive shadow. Silas's lunge, a sudden escalation from psychological torment to physical threat, had been the catalyst, the unforgivable transgression that had forced Abel's intervention.

Abel remained still, his golden gaze unwavering, a silent assessment of the disarmed aggressor. He was a guardian, a protector, and Silas's violent desperation had been a clear and present danger to the very person he was sworn to shield. Silas, still on his elbows, his breath coming in shallow, painful gasps, felt the sheer weight of Abel's presence pressing down on him, a physical manifestation of his defeat. The rage that had fueled his earlier aggression began to curdle into a bitter, gnawing helplessness. He was no longer the hunter, but the prey, caught in a snare of his own making.

It was at this precise moment, as Silas was attempting to push himself up, his limbs heavy with defeat and shock, that the critical error occurred. Abel, his instincts honed by countless cycles of predator and prey, his senses attuned to the slightest shift in equilibrium, saw Silas's unsteady movements. He saw the potential for Silas to regain his footing, to perhaps make another desperate, unpredictable lunge, however futile. Abel's primary directive was Truly's safety. While Silas was on the floor, he posed less of an immediate threat, but the possibility of him rearming or lunging again was not negligible. Abel's intention was to maintain the status quo, to keep Silas incapacitated and under his watchful, overwhelming presence.

As Silas's hands scrabbled against the floor, Abel instinctively moved. It was a subtle shift, a controlled adjustment of his massive weight. His goal was not to strike Silas, but to gently but firmly prevent him from regaining his footing, to keep him grounded and thus neutralized. He extended a broad, fur-covered hand, not to strike, but to apply a steadying, albeit firm, pressure against Silas's upper back. It was an action born of caution, a preemptive measure to ensure Silas remained harmless. He intended to guide Silas back to a supine position, to maintain his disarmed and destabilized state.

However, Abel, in his immense power, often had to calibrate his strength with extreme care. His inherent might was like the force of a tempest, capable of leveling forests. While he possessed an innate understanding of restraint, a whisper of his true power could still overwhelm a creature as fragile as Silas. Silas, already off-balance from his initial fall, was attempting to heave himself upwards with a surge of residual adrenaline. Abel's gentle, guiding pressure, meant to keep him down, instead found Silas at a precarious tipping point.

The hand, intended as a subtle nudge of containment, landed with a force amplified by the very nature of Abel's being. It wasn't a violent shove, but a significant push against Silas's already compromised balance. The sheer scale of Abel's strength, even when applied with the intention of minimal force, was far greater than Silas could anticipate or withstand in his current state. The weight of the hand, combined with the awkward angle of Silas's attempted rise, sent him lurching backward.

The movement was not a controlled retreat, but an uncontrolled stumble. Silas's legs, still trying to find a stable base, tangled beneath him. His arms flailed uselessly, attempting to regain some semblance of balance, but it was a lost cause. His eyes widened in a fresh wave of panic, a stark contrast to the furious aggression he had displayed moments before. He was no longer fighting Abel; he was fighting gravity, fighting his own compromised body, fighting the cruel twist of fate.

His stumble took him towards the back of the small, cramped cabin, a space cluttered with the necessities of their meager existence. His frantic attempts to regain his footing only propelled him further into the disarray. He tripped then, his heel catching on the edge of a thick, woven rug that lay spread across the floor. The rug, worn smooth with age and use, offered no resistance, no grip to counter his uncontrolled momentum.

The unexpected snag sent Silas's already unsteady body pitching forward, his arms windmilling uselessly in the air. There was no time for a yelp of surprise this time, no gasp of disbelief. Only the raw, guttural sound of a man falling, a sound that was cut short by an even more horrific noise. Silas's head struck the sharp, unforgiving corner of the heavy oak table that served as their rudimentary dining surface. The impact was sickeningly solid, a deep, resonant thud that echoed through the sudden, absolute silence of the cabin. It was not the sharp crack of bone, but a dull, heavy, final sound. The sound of something vital abruptly and irrevocably ceasing.

The struggle, the tension, the fear, all of it vanished in an instant. The air, so recently thick with the charged energy of confrontation, now hung heavy with a different kind of stillness. Truly, who had watched the scene unfold with bated breath, her hands clasped tightly at her throat, froze. Her eyes, wide and disbelieving, were fixed on Silas's still form. The sounds had ceased. The violent dance had ended, not with a victor and a vanquished, but with a sudden, stark, and terrifying finality.

Abel, his arm still extended, his amber eyes reflecting the flickering firelight, remained frozen for a moment, his own immense power momentarily overshadowed by the abrupt cessation of Silas's life force. His intention had been containment, not destruction. He had sought to neutralize a threat, to protect Truly. He had never intended for Silas's life to be extinguished, not like this. A low, mournful sound, almost a sigh, escaped his massive chest. It was a sound that spoke of regret, of a profound sorrow for the unintended consequence, for the fatal miscalculation that had resulted in the abrupt, brutal end of a human life. Truly's breath hitched. She could see Silas lying there, utterly still, his limbs splayed at an unnatural angle. The rough-hewn wood of the table corner, stained dark with age and use, seemed to pulse with the finality of the impact. The vibrant red of blood, stark against the muted tones of the cabin, began to bloom slowly from the wound on Silas's temple, a grim testament to the force of the collision.

The silence that followed Silas's abrupt, brutal end was not merely an absence of sound; it was a palpable entity, a suffocating shroud that wrapped around Truly and Abel, pressing in on them from all sides. The crackling of the hearth, moments before a comforting counterpoint to the tension, now sounded like the crackle of dry bones, a macabre soundtrack to the stillness. Truly's breath hitched again, a ragged, involuntary sound that seemed to tear through the quiet like a jagged shard of ice. Her vision, so recently focused on the desperate struggle, now swam with the horrific tableau before her. Silas. Still. Utterly, terrifyingly still.

Abel, his massive form still poised as if caught mid-motion, his great paw still hovering inches from Silas's inert form, seemed to shrink in on himself. The golden light in his eyes, which had burned with a fierce, protective fire just moments before, now flickered, dimming with a profound sorrow that seemed to weigh him down. He looked from the still figure of Silas to Truly, his gaze a complex tapestry of emotions. There was relief, undeniable and immense, that the threat to her had been neutralized. But it was intertwined with a crushing regret, a deep, guttural ache for the irreversible finality of what had occurred. He had intervened, as he was bound to do, as his very nature demanded. He had protected her. Yet, the act of protection had led to an end far more absolute than any mere defeat.

The air in the small cabin felt thick, stagnant, as if the very oxygen had been leached away by the shock. Truly could feel the tremor running through Abel's colossal frame, a low, resonating vibration that seemed to echo the frantic thumping of her own heart. It was not the tremor of anger, nor of exertion, but the deep, shuddering resonance of an immense being grappling with the devastating weight of consequence. He had intended only to subdue, to incapacitate, to ensure her safety. The physics of it all, the cruel, unforgiving nature of momentum and impact, had conspired against his intent, twisting his protective gesture into a fatal blow.

"Silas..." The name escaped Truly's lips as a whisper, barely audible, yet it seemed to shatter the fragile silence. It was not a cry of grief, not yet. It was a sound of disbelief, of dawning comprehension, the first tentative acknowledgment of a reality so stark and terrible it felt unreal. Her eyes, wide and unfocused, traced the unnatural angles of his limbs, the stillness of his chest. He was not breathing. The fire that had burned so fiercely in his eyes, that had fueled his venomous words and his violent actions, was gone. Replaced by a vacant, glassy stare that reflected only the dim light of the cabin.

Abel slowly, deliberately, retracted his paw. The movement was heavy, each inch a struggle against an invisible force. It was as if his very being was now burdened by the weight of Silas's extinguished life. He lowered himself to his haunches, his massive body folding with a grace that belied its size, but the movement was tinged with a deep weariness. His golden eyes, now soft and filled with an ancient sadness, finally met Truly's. "He is... gone," Abel rumbled, his voice a low, mournful sound that seemed to vibrate in the very timbers of the cabin. It was not an accusation, not a justification, but a simple, heartbreaking statement of fact. He had done what he had to do. He had fulfilled his purpose. But the cost... the cost was immeasurable. The relief of her safety was now irrevocably tainted by the spilled blood and the stolen breath.

Truly couldn't move. Her feet felt rooted to the floor, her body paralyzed by the horror of it all. She could feel the residual heat of the hearth on her face, a stark contrast to the icy dread that gripped her heart. The small cabin, which had always felt like a sanctuary, a place of refuge from the harshness of the outside world, now felt like a tomb. The walls seemed to press in, the low ceiling a suffocating weight. Every object, from the rough-hewn table to the simple wooden stool, now seemed to bear witness to the tragedy.

The adrenaline that had surged through her during Silas's attack began to ebb, leaving behind a profound exhaustion, a bone-deep weariness that settled over her like a damp cloak. Her hands, which had been clenched so tightly they had gone numb, slowly unfurled. She looked down at them, surprised to see them trembling uncontrollably. The image of Silas falling, of his head striking the table, was seared into her mind, a looping, horrific replay. The sickening thud, the abrupt silence, the blooming of blood, it was all too much to comprehend.

Truly finally took a step, a small, tentative movement away from the hearth, away from the lingering warmth that now seemed to mock her chilling reality. Her gaze fell upon the discarded poker, lying a few feet from Silas's body. It was a symbol of his aggression, his desperation, and now, it was simply an inert piece of metal, a relic of a conflict that had ended with such brutal efficiency. She remembered its weight in his hand, the glint of malice in his eyes as he'd lunged. And then,

Abel. The swift, almost effortless intervention. The amber eyes, steady and unwavering. The sheer, overwhelming power held in perfect, controlled restraint. Until it wasn't.

A shudder ran through her. She looked back at Abel. His massive head was bowed slightly, his golden eyes fixed on the floor. There was a profound sadness in his posture, a weariness that spoke of eons of witnessing the folly and the cruelty of sentient beings. He was not a beast of prey in that moment, but a guardian who had been forced to unleash his power, only to have it result in an unintended, irreversible tragedy. "Why?" The word was a choked gasp, a question that hung in the air, not directed at Abel specifically, but at the universe itself. Why had it come to this? Why did Silas have to die? Why did Abel have to be the one to end him? She knew, intellectually, that Silas had been a threat, that Abel had acted to protect her. But the raw, emotional impact of witnessing death, of seeing a life extinguished so abruptly, was overwhelming.

Abel raised his head, his eyes meeting hers with a steady, unwavering gaze. "He was a danger," he stated, his voice resonating with a quiet authority. "To you. My purpose is to ensure your safety. Silas's intent was to harm. To inflict pain. I could not allow that." "But... like this?" Truly's voice cracked. "He's... dead, Abel. Truly dead." The finality of the word settled over her, heavy and cold. "Yes," Abel conceded, his voice laced with regret. "He is dead. My intention was not to end his life, Truly. It was to stop him. To neutralize the threat he posed. But in the struggle, in his attempt to rise, my... assistance... was too much for his fragile form. He fell. And he struck his head. The outcome was unforeseen. Unintended."

He paused, letting his words sink in. The confession, though not an admission of guilt in the human sense, carried the weight of immense sorrow. He was not human, but he understood the gravity of taking a life. He understood the irreversible nature of death. "I regret that it ended this way," he continued, his gaze unwavering. "I regret that Silas's path led him to such a destructive end. But I do not regret ensuring your survival. You are alive, Truly. You are safe. And that, for me, is the only outcome that truly matters."

His words, meant to be reassuring, only amplified the internal conflict raging within Truly. She was safe. Silas was gone. Yet, she felt no sense of victory, no triumph. Only a profound emptiness, a chilling awareness of the darkness that had been unleashed and the irreversible consequences it had wrought. The cabin, once her haven, now felt like a place of haunting. The silence, once a welcome respite from Silas's torment, was now a deafening testament to his absence.

She looked at Abel again, at the immense creature who had, in a matter of moments, become both her savior and the instrument of a man's death. She saw not a monster, not a brute, but a being of ancient power, bound by a code of protection, a code that had led to this tragic, brutal conclusion. His regret was palpable, a palpable aura that emanated from him, softening the harsh edges of his immense form. "What... what do we do now?" Truly finally asked, her voice barely a whisper. The immediate danger had passed, but the weight of what had happened, the enormity of Silas's death, had created a new, daunting reality. They could not simply pretend that this had not happened. The cabin, once filled with the volatile tension of Silas's presence, was now imbued with the chilling stillness of his demise.

Taking a deep, shaky breath, Truly reached out and placed her small hand, trembling, into Abel's immense, warm palm. The contrast between their sizes, their very beings, was stark. But in that touch, a fragile connection was forged, a shared understanding of the darkness they had just navigated and the uncertain path that lay ahead. The silence of the aftermath was still heavy, still suffocating, but within it, a new resolve began to form, a quiet determination to face whatever lay beyond this moment, together. The cabin, though now a scene of tragedy, would not be their tomb. It would be the place where their shared journey, born from conflict and ending in an unintended death, would truly begin. The memory of Silas, and the brutal efficiency of his end, would forever be etched in their minds, a stark reminder of the fine line between protection and destruction, a lesson learned in the echoing silence of the aftermath.

12

THE HUNT BEGINS

The first blush of dawn was an indifferent artist, daubing the Ozark hills with pale, ethereal strokes of pink and gold. It crept over the jagged peaks, indifferent to the somber reality that had unfolded within the small, secluded cabin. The silence that greeted the new day was not the gentle hush of nature waking, but a heavy, oppressive stillness, a void where Silas's boisterous, often menacing, presence had been. His absence was a palpable thing, a phantom limb that Truly felt with every breath. The lingering scent of woodsmoke, usually a comforting aroma, now carried a faint, metallic undertone that snagged at her senses, a subtle reminder of the night's brutal conclusion. Abel, ever watchful, remained by her side, his amber eyes scanning the edges of the clearing, his massive form a silent, imposing bulwark against any lingering threats. But the true threat, the one that had loomed largest, was now reduced to a grim, silent tableau within the cabin walls.

Truly felt a tremor pass through her, a residual echo of the terror and the shock. The events of the previous night were a jumbled, horrifying mosaic in her mind, the glint of Silas, the desperate struggle, Abel's explosive, protective fury, the sickening thud, the ensuing silence. It was a nightmare she couldn't shake off, a persistent chill that seeped into her bones despite the rising sun. Abel's steady presence was a comfort, a grounding force in the swirling chaos of her emotions. He had protected her, undeniably. He had fulfilled his purpose. Yet, the cost... the cost was etched into the very fabric of her being.

As the sun climbed higher, its rays piercing the gloom within the cabin, the stark reality of Silas's demise became undeniable. The dark stain on the floorboards, so horrifyingly vivid in the dim light of the previous night, now seemed to gleam dully in the morning sun, an irremovable testament to the violence that had occurred. Truly's gaze kept drifting to the corner of the table, the unforgiving wood that had been the instrument of Silas's final, fatal impact. It was a detail so mundane, so ordinary, that its role in the night's grim finale felt almost surreal.

The creak of a wagon on the rutted track leading to their isolated cabin was a sound that usually signaled a visit from Mrs. Tate, a kindly, if somewhat gossipy, neighbor from a few miles down the valley. Today, however, the sound was an unwelcome intrusion, a harbinger of the wider world encroaching upon their private tragedy. Truly's heart leaped into her throat. She hadn't considered how her solitary existence, or Silas's sudden disappearance, would be perceived by others. With the sound of the wagon, Abels primal defenses surfaced. As the sounds drew closer Able gently expressed his commitment to Truly through a low guttural hum. Seemingly understanding, Truly's hand gently touched Abel's arm. As if in silent swiftness, Able reseeded, quietly blending into the tree line.

Mrs. Tate, a woman whose ample frame was always draped in practical, calico prints, pulled her horse to a halt outside the cabin, her weathered face etched with a mixture of curiosity and concern. "Truly, dear?" she called out, her voice carrying on the morning air, tinged with the familiar Ozark drawl. "Everything alright? Haven't seen hide nor hair of Silas since yesterday, and I was just passing by, thought I'd check in." Truly's breath caught. She glanced at the tree line which concealed Abel, a silent question in her eyes. Truly took a shaky breath, forcing herself to step away from the shadowed interior of the cabin, towards the bright, unforgiving light of the doorway. "Mrs. Tate," Truly began, her voice thinner than she intended, betraying the strain she felt. "It's... it's been a difficult night."

Mrs. Tate's keen eyes, accustomed to observing the subtle nuances of rural life, immediately registered the tremor in Truly's voice, the haunted look in her eyes, the unnatural stillness that clung to the small dwelling. "Oh, dearie," she murmured, her kindly expression clouding with apprehension. She dismounted, her movements surprisingly agile for her size, and approached the cabin, her gaze sweeping over Truly, then darting to the open doorway, as if seeking an explanation for the palpable unease.

The air inside the cabin, even with the door now open, felt heavy, laden with an unspoken horror. Mrs. Tate's eyes widened as she took in the scene. The overturned stool, the scattered wood near the hearth, and then, her gaze landed on Silas. He lay sprawled on the floor, his limbs askew, his eyes wide and unseeing, a dark, stark contrast to the familiar rough-hewn wood beneath him. The stain, so damningly obvious in the daylight, spoke a silent, brutal language.

A sharp gasp escaped Mrs. Tate's lips, a sound of pure, unadulterated shock. Her hand flew to her chest, her knuckles turning white.

"Merciful heavens!" she exclaimed, her voice trembling. "What... what happened here?" Her eyes darted between Truly, who stood pale and rigid, and the broken frame of Silas. Truly found her voice, though it was a ragged whisper. "There was... a struggle, Mrs. Tate. Silas... he was... he's gone." The words felt inadequate, a gross understatement of the brutal finality of the scene.

Mrs. Tate, a woman who had seen her share of hardship and tragedy in the isolated mountains, was nonetheless visibly shaken. The sight of Silas, dead on his own cabin floor, was a shock that went beyond the everyday tragedies of the Ozarks. The signs of a struggle were undeniable, the violence of the impact evident even to her untrained eye. Her initial horror quickly morphed into a grim, practical determination. She had always been a woman of action, and inaction was not an option when faced with such a grim discovery. "We can't leave him like this," she declared, her voice gaining a measure of its usual firmness, though still laced with disbelief. She looked at Truly, her gaze steady. "You need to stay here, dear. Don't touch anything. I'll go fetch Sheriff Brinks. He'll know what to do."

Truly nodded, her mind a numb blank. The idea of Sheriff Brinks arriving, of outsiders intruding upon this deeply personal tragedy, was almost another layer of horror to bear. But she understood. This couldn't be hidden. This couldn't be ignored. "Will he... will he understand?" Truly asked, her voice barely audible, her gaze flickering towards Abel. The sheer improbability of the situation, the presence of a creature like Abel, was something she feared might be too much for the grounded reality of the local authorities.

Mrs. Tate followed her gaze, her eyes widening further as she truly registered the hidden presence of an unknown creature, just beyond sight but who's presence was evident.   She had heard whispers, of course, local legends about strange creatures in the deeper woods, but she had always dismissed them as fanciful tales. Now, faced with the undeniable reality, a flicker of something akin to fear mingled with her shock. But her innate sense of duty, and perhaps a touch of innate bravery, overrode any apprehension. "Sheriff Brinks has seen his share of peculiar things in these hills, Truly," Mrs. Tate said, trying to sound more confident than she felt. "He's a fair man. You just... you just let him do his job. And you, dear, you stay put. Don't move." With that, Mrs. Tate turned, her sturdy boots crunching on the gravel outside. She mounted her wagon with practiced ease and, with a final, worried glance back at Truly then again to the edge of the forest. She urged her horse into a trot, disappearing down the winding track, leaving behind a silence that felt even heavier than before.

Truly remained rooted to the spot, the morning sun doing little to dispel the chill that had settled over her. She looked towards Abel, her protector, her unlikely companion, who remained a guard, watching his friend. Truly, although thankful, considered how Abel's presence, so comforting just moments ago, now felt like an additional complication in an already overwhelming situation. How would Sheriff Brody react to a man-sized creature of myth coming to her aid? Would he see Abel as a suspect? A threat?

The hours that followed stretched out, each minute a painstaking crawl. Truly sat on the porch steps, her gaze fixed on the empty track, her mind a whirl of fear and apprehension. Abel remained near the forests edge, a silent sentinel, his imposing form a stark contrast to the peaceful Ozark landscape. The birds sang their cheerful melodies, the wind rustled through the leaves, and the world outside continued its indifferent, beautiful existence, oblivious to the grim reality contained within the small clearing.

Finally, the distant sound of a wagon, growing steadily louder, announced the arrival of authority. The dusty, mud-splattered sideboards came into view, Sheriff Brinks at the reigns, his face set in a grim, professional mask. Beside him sat Deputy Martin, a younger man, his eyes wide with a mixture of professional duty and thinly veiled curiosity. Mrs. Tate was in the seat, her face a picture of concerned relief, no doubt eager to hand over the reins of this unsettling situation.

The wagon crunched to a halt, and Sheriff Brinks, a man built like an oak stump with eyes that missed nothing, surveyed the scene. His gaze, initially assessing the overall situation, quickly locked onto tree line, sensing the presence of something unseen. The deputy's frame shifted with unease as his hand instinctively hovering near his sidearm. Sheriff Brinks, however, remained remarkably calm. He had been in law enforcement for over thirty years, navigating the complexities of a rural community where strange occurrences were not entirely unheard of. He had seen things. Perhaps not *this* exactly, but enough to temper his initial surprise with a healthy dose of professional pragmatism. He met Abel's steady shadowed figure for a long moment, a silent exchange passing between them. "Mornin', Mrs. Tate," Sheriff Brinks said, his voice a deep rumble, cutting through the tension. "You said there was trouble?" His eyes then swept over Truly, taking in her pale face and the tremor that still ran through her. "And you, Truly. You alright?"

Truly found herself nodding, finding a strange solace in the sheriff's gruff, no-nonsense demeanor. He seemed to accept Abel's presence with a surprising lack of fanfare, his focus immediately shifting to the more immediate concern: Silas. "Sheriff," Mrs. Tate began, her voice still a little shaky, "it's... it's Silas. He's... he's dead. Inside." She gestured towards the cabin with a trembling hand. "I found him when I came by this morning. There'd been a struggle." Sheriff Brinks's face grew sterner. He nodded slowly. "Deputy Martin, secure the perimeter. No one in or out. Mrs. Tate, if you could wait with Truly for a moment, perhaps over there by the wagon." He then turned his attention to the cabin, his expression one of grim professionalism. As Sheriff Brinks approached the cabin, Deputy Martin, still looking warily at the tree line, cautiously began to circle the clearing, his eyes darting between the cabin and the surrounding woods. Abel remained motionless, his amber eyes fixed on the cabin entrance, a silent observer of the unfolding investigation.

Sheriff Brinks stepped inside the cabin, his boots crunching softly on the floorboards. The harsh light of day illuminated the scene with unforgiving clarity. He surveyed the overturned furniture, the scattered wood, and finally, Silas's body. He knelt down, his movements deliberate, his experienced eyes taking in the details. He noted the unnatural angle of Silas's head, the dark stain spreading from the impact point, the stillness of his form. He saw the remnants of a desperate struggle. He then looked around the cabin, his gaze sweeping over every surface, every object. He saw Truly's simple belongings, the few pieces of furniture, the hearth. Nothing seemed out of place, save for the obvious signs of violence. His gaze returned to Silas. This was not a natural death. This was the result of a violent confrontation.

After a thorough examination, Sheriff Brinks emerged from the cabin, his face etched with a grim understanding. He looked at Truly, who was sitting beside Mrs. Tate, her arms wrapped around herself as if to ward off an unseen chill. "Truly," Sheriff Brinks said, his voice low and steady. "I'm going to need you to tell me exactly what happened here last night. From the beginning. And I need you to be completely honest with me. Every detail." He glanced briefly in Abel's direction, a flicker of acknowledgment in his eyes, before returning his gaze to Truly. "And that includes... anyone else who might have been present."

Truly's heart hammered against her ribs. The moment of reckoning had arrived. The world of legend and protection had collided head-on with the mundane reality of law and order. She took a deep, steadying breath, the image of Silas falling, of Abel's immense power unleashed, flashing through her mind. She knew, with a certainty that chilled her to the bone, that the truth, however unbelievable, was the only path forward. The hunt for Silas had ended. Now, the hunt for answers, for understanding, was about to begin. And she knew, with absolute clarity, that the tale she was about to tell would redefine not only her life, but the perception of reality for more than just the quiet residents of the Ozarks. The silence of the cabin, once filled with dread, was now about to be broken by the stark, and perhaps unbelievable, truth.

The dust hadn't even settled from Sheriff Brinks's departure, yet the tendrils of Silas's abrupt and violent end were already weaving their way through the Ozark valley like insidious vines. Mrs. Tate, bless her well-meaning heart, was the first to carry the grim tidings, her hurried footsteps on the creaking floorboards of her own small cottage acting as an unofficial town crier. Her voice, usually a gentle murmur, had taken on a sharp, breathless quality as she relayed the shocking discovery to her nearest neighbors. By the time the sun had climbed to its zenith, casting long, distorted shadows across the dusty roads, Silas's demise was no longer a hushed secret but the undisputed, and deeply unsettling, topic of every conversation.

In the general store, a place usually bustling with the mundane gossip of crop prices and the latest church bake sale, the air was thick with a different kind of speculation. Men gathered around the worn counter, their faces grim, their voices low and urgent. "Dead, you say?" Jedediah, his overalls stained with the rich earth of his farm, scratched his grizzled beard. "Silas? How in the Sam Hill did that happen?" "They say there was a struggle," Martha, the storekeeper's wife, chimed in, her voice laced with a morbid fascination. She'd heard the initial report from Mrs. Tate, who, in turn, had received the details, albeit a heavily edited version, from Deputy Martin as he'd waited for Sheriff Brinks to finish his initial assessment. "Overturned furniture, signs of a fight. Nasty business."

A hush fell over the small gathering as a new thought, a darker, more primal fear, began to take root. Silas was not a well-loved man. His temper was legendary; his presence often laced with a simmering menace that kept most of the townsfolk at arm's length. But even those who disliked him couldn't quite grasp the reality of his violent end. It was too sudden, too brutal for the quiet rhythms of their lives. "But who would...?" Jedediah trailed off, his gaze drifting towards the dense, emerald wall of the surrounding forest. The Ozarks, beautiful and bountiful, also held a wildness, a primal essence that could be both awe-inspiring and terrifying. It was a place where the veil between the ordinary and the extraordinary felt thinner, where old tales and superstitions were not so easily dismissed. "Some say it was an animal," a younger man, barely more than a boy, ventured hesitantly. He wrung his hands, his eyes wide. "A bear, maybe? Or something... bigger?" The word "bigger" hung in the air, unspoken but deeply felt. The deep woods were a source of endless mystery, and in the absence of a clear explanation, the human mind had a tendency to conjure the most terrifying possibilities. They were hardy folk, accustomed to the dangers of nature, but this felt different. This felt... unnatural.

As the day wore on, the whispers began to solidify, gathering strength and shape. Truly, the reclusive woman who lived up in the isolated cabin, came into focus as a figure of suspicion. She was an outsider, a woman who kept to herself, her only companion a creature of immense size and unsettling silence that had been spotted on rare occasions at the edge of the woods. The locals, already wary of her isolation, now linked her to Silas's death. "She's always been a strange one," muttered Agnes, a woman whose needlepoint was as sharp as her tongue. "Never one for company. And that... *thing* she keeps with her. What kind of woman has a creature like that for a pet?" Her voice dropped to a conspiratorial whisper. "They say it's unnatural. Maybe she and her beast did it. Silas, he was a mean sort, but to be torn apart like that... it ain't natural."

The fear was palpable, a contagion spreading faster than any disease. The image of Silas, gruff and menacing as he was, being brutally dispatched by an unknown force was deeply unsettling. It was easier to blame a wild animal, or even Truly and her shadowy companion, than to confront the chilling reality of human violence or the unsettling possibility of something truly monstrous lurking in their midst. The whispers, at first hesitant and uncertain, began to gain volume, morphing into insistent murmurs, then into outright pronouncements. "It was a beast," the cry went up, echoing from cabin to cabin, from the general store to the small, clapboard church. "A monster from the deep woods. It took Silas." The absence of a logical culprit, coupled with the visible brutality of Silas's death, created a void that superstition and fear were all too eager to fill.

Sheriff Brinks, a man who prided himself on his grounded approach to the often-fantastical tales of the Ozarks, found himself battling more than just the evidence. He had seen the scene. He had spoken to Truly, her quiet, almost ethereal presence a stark contrast to the violence that had occurred. He had observed the shadow, inevitably a creature that defied all logical explanation, yet seemed to possess a quiet dignity and an undeniable protective aura. He knew the truth, or at least as much of it as Truly was capable of articulating in her traumatized state. But the community, fueled by fear and a deep-seated need for a tangible enemy, was not ready for the truth. "A beast," Jedediah declared, his voice ringing with conviction as he addressed a small crowd gathered outside the general store. His words, amplified by the growing hysteria, carried the weight of communal belief. "It's the only explanation. Silas wouldn't have gone down without a fight, and no man I know would do that to him. It was something from the wilderness, something that broke into his cabin and took him."

Martha nodded, her eyes wide with a manufactured terror. "And that Truly woman! Living out there, all alone, with that... that hulking shadow of hers. Who's to say she didn't unleash it? Or that it wasn't her own beast that did the deed?" The implication, though unspoken, was clear: Truly was somehow complicit, or perhaps even the mastermind behind a monstrous act. The carefully constructed narrative of a rampaging beast began to take hold, a collective delusion born of fear and a desperate desire to make sense of the senseless. The initial shock of Silas's death was quickly eclipsed by a burgeoning sense of outrage and a chilling fear of the unknown. The Ozark community, a tight-knit group bound by shared experiences and a healthy respect for the untamed wilderness, found a new target for their anxieties. "We can't let this stand," a gruff voice called out from the back of the crowd. "If there's a beast out there, a killer, we need to hunt it down. Before it comes back for more."

A murmur of agreement rippled through the assembled townsfolk. The idea of a hunt, of taking action against a tangible threat, was more comforting than the unsettling ambiguity of the situation. It offered a sense of control, a way to push back against the creeping dread. "Yup," Jedediah boomed, his eyes gleaming with a newfound purpose. "Sheriff Brinks might be after the truth, but we need to protect ourselves. We need to find this... this monster. We need to hunt it."

The whispers had indeed turned to shouts, a unified chorus of fear and determination that was about to set a dangerous hunt in motion. The rational mind of Sheriff Brinks was about to be drowned out by the collective, primal roar of a community terrified by shadows and eager to strike at anything they perceived as a threat. And Truly, the quiet woman with the impossible companion, found herself at the epicenter of a storm she had never sought, a storm that threatened to consume her and all that she held dear. The legend of the beast, once a mere whisper, was now a deafening roar, and it was coming for her.

A chorus of agreement rose from the crowd. The fear of the unknown was a potent motivator, but the prospect of a hunt, of taking decisive action against a perceived threat, offered a sense of agency. It was a way to reclaim control from the creeping dread that had begun to settle over the valley. The image of Silas, gruesomely dispatched, served as a grim reminder of what awaited them if they did nothing. "Aye," Martha chimed in, her earlier fascination now replaced by a genuine tremor of fear. "We need to form a search party. Go into the woods. Find this thing before it finds someone else."

Truly's heart hammered a frantic rhythm against her ribs, a frantic drumbeat that echoed the storm brewing outside and within the small, shadowed confines of her cabin. The scent of pine and damp earth, usually a comforting balm, now seemed suffocating, laced with the acrid tang of fear and the metallic hint of what had transpired. She knew the truth, a stark, undeniable clarity that cut through the fog of terror. Silas had been the aggressor, his drunken rage a palpable force that had breached her sanctuary, his intent clear and brutal. And Abel, her silent, steadfast guardian, had acted, as he always did, to protect her.

Her loyalty to Abel was a fierce, unyielding flame, a protective instinct born from years of shared solitude and unspoken understanding. He was not a beast, not a mindless killer. He was a gentle giant, a creature of ancient wisdom and profound loyalty, whose very existence was a testament to the hidden wonders of the world. Yet, her loyalty warred with the terrifying reality of her position. She was an outcast, a woman living on the fringes, her life intertwined with a being that the townsfolk already deemed an abomination. Her word, in the face of their collective fear and burgeoning hysteria, would be nothing more than a whisper against a gale. She was vulnerable, isolated, and the weight of their suspicion pressed down on her, heavy and suffocating.

She traced the intricate patterns on the worn wooden table, her fingers finding familiar grooves as if seeking solace in the tactile. The cabin, usually a haven of peace, now felt like a cage. Every creak of the floorboards, every rustle of leaves outside, sent a fresh wave of anxiety through her. She imagined the whispers escalating, morphing from hushed speculation into outright accusations. They would see her as complicit, as a dark sorceress who commanded a creature of destruction. The story of Silas's violent end, so easily attributed to a monstrous beast, would inevitably lead back to her, the woman who harbored such a creature.

Truly closed her eyes, the image of Abel's immense, shaggy form a comforting presence in her mind's eye, even as its reality was the source of so much dread. He had shielded her, his silent growl a warning that Silas had foolishly ignored. He had moved with a speed and power that belied his gentle nature, a primal force unleashed in defense of his charge. But the sheer brutality of it, the finality of Silas's end, was undeniable. And in the eyes of the valley, it was not an act of defense; it was an act of savagery, perpetrated by a monster.

The air in the cabin grew heavy, thick with unspoken fears and the scent of her own rising panic. She was trapped. Her silence was a condemnation, her knowledge a burden too heavy to bear. The hunt, she knew, was already beginning, fueled by the very fear she now felt in her own bones. And she, along with Abel, was at its heart, an unwitting quarry in a chase born of terror and misunderstanding. She had to protect Abel, not just from the townsfolk, but from their fear. But how could she protect them both when her own voice was so easily silenced by the roar of their collective dread? The path forward was obscured by a fog of fear, and Truly, standing at its precipice, felt utterly, terrifyingly alone.

The air crackled with a potent mix of outrage and terror, a combustible atmosphere that Sheriff Brody, a man usually grounded in pragmatism, found himself struggling to contain. The news of Silas's demise had spread through Oakhaven like wildfire, each retelling embellished with lurid details, transforming a tragic incident into a monstrous spectacle. Silas, a man known more for his bluster than his bravery, was now cast as a victim of unspeakable horror, and Truly, the reclusive woman on the edge of the woods, was undeniably linked to the "beast" responsible.

Sheriff Brinks stood on the porch of the general store, the usual morning bustle replaced by a grim congregation. Faces, usually etched with the everyday concerns of rural life, were now taut with a shared dread, their eyes darting towards the shadowed tree line as if expecting the very creature of their fear to emerge. Jedediah, his imposing frame radiating an almost palpable anger, was at the forefront of the growing assembly. His voice, a deep rumble that carried across the hushed crowd, articulated the collective sentiment. "We can't stand for this, Sheriff. Not in our valley. Not under our watch. Silas was one of our own, and whatever... *thing*... did this to him needs to be dealt with."

Jedediah's words resonated with the hushed murmurs of agreement that rippled through the townsfolk. The unspoken accusation hung heavy in the air: Truly was somehow involved, a puppet master to a monstrous entity. The legends of the Ozarks, tales of creatures lurking in the shadows, of ancient pacts and forgotten beasts, were no longer just stories whispered around campfires. They were suddenly, terrifyingly, relevant. "We need to organize," Jedediah continued, his gaze sweeping over the men gathered. "We need to form a posse. Arm ourselves. Go into those woods and find it. Before it decides to pay another visit." He gestured towards the dense, ancient forest that embraced the valley, a place that had always been both a source of sustenance and a boundary. Now, it was perceived as a den of predation.

Sheriff Brinks, despite his own unease, tried to inject a semblance of order. "Now, Jedediah, let's not get ahead of ourselves. We don't know what we're dealing with. Rushing into the woods unprepared could be... dangerous." He didn't voice his deeper concern: that the "it" they were hunting might not be a creature of pure instinct, but something far more complex, something connected to Truly, a woman he'd always found enigmatic, now undeniably entangled in this grim affair.

Agnes, the town's unofficial keeper of secrets and purveyor of gossip, clutched her shawl tighter, her sharp eyes missing nothing. "Dangerous? What's more dangerous, Sheriff, is letting this... *thing*... roam free. What if it comes back? What if it comes for our children? Truly, she lives out there, all alone. Maybe she knows something. Maybe she's been keeping it from us." Her voice, though softer than Jedediah's, carried a sting of innuendo that landed with unsettling accuracy. The seed of doubt, planted by fear, was already blossoming into suspicion.

The mention of Truly's name sent a fresh wave of unease through the crowd. They knew her. Or rather, they knew *of* her, the solitary woman who lived by the deep woods, who stayed to herself, whose silence was as profound as the forest itself. They had always viewed her with a degree of suspicion, an outcast who chose to remain apart. Now, that distance, that self-imposed isolation, was being interpreted as something far more sinister. "She's been too quiet for too long," someone in the crowd muttered, their voice barely audible, yet it echoed the sentiment of many. "Spending countless hours out there with... who knows what."

Sheriff Brinks sighed, the weight of the community's fear pressing down on him. He understood the primal instinct to protect, to confront the unknown with force. He also understood the danger of a mob, driven by fear and conjecture. "Alright," he said, his voice firm, projecting an authority he didn't entirely feel. "We'll form a search party. But we'll do it my way. We'll go in organized. With proper hunting rifles. We'll comb the area around where Silas was found. We need evidence, not a wild goose chase." He glanced at Jedediah, his expression conveying a silent plea for cooperation. "And we will not harm Truly. She is not our target. If she has information, we will seek it through proper channels." Jedediah, though his brow remained furrowed, nodded curtly. "Agreed, Sheriff. But don't expect me to trust that woman's word. Not after this." The unspoken alliance formed, a grim pact forged in the crucible of shared fear. The hunt for the creature, whatever it was, had officially begun, and it was already colored with prejudice and a deep-seated distrust of the woman who called the woods her home.

As the men dispersed, their conversations a low murmur of strategy and grim pronouncements, Sheriff Brinks felt a chill that had nothing to do with the morning air. He knew the Ozarks. He knew their vastness, their deceptive beauty, their hidden dangers. He also knew that the line between legend and reality could blur with terrifying speed in these ancient hills. The "creature" they were hunting was a mystery, but the true danger, he suspected, lay not just in its physical form, but in the fear it had unleashed within the hearts of his townsfolk. And that fear, he feared, was far more destructive than any beast.

The men began to gather their gear. Hunting rifles, their polished barrels gleaming dully in the pale sunlight, were checked and rechecked. Ammunition pouches were filled with a grim efficiency. Each man carried a certain weight, a burden of responsibility, a thirst for vengeance. They spoke in hushed tones, their words punctuated by the rustle of canvas and the clink of metal. They were farmers, loggers, trappers, men accustomed to the wilderness, to tracking game, to enduring hardship. But this was no ordinary hunt. This was a hunt born of a primal fear, a need to expunge an unknown terror from their midst.

Jedediah, his movements deliberate and precise, handed out extra rounds of ammunition. "Make every shot count," he instructed, his voice low and resonant. "We don't know what we're up against. But we know it's dangerous. It took Silas. It could take any of us." He looked around at the faces, a mixture of apprehension and grim determination. "We go in, we find it, we put an end to it. For Silas. For Oak Holler."

The dense Ozark forests, which had always been Truly's sanctuary, her refuge from the judgmental eyes of the world, were now transformed into a labyrinthine hunting ground. The familiar rustle of leaves underfoot, once a comforting sound, now carried the ominous echo of pursuit. The towering trees, their branches interlaced to form a verdant canopy, seemed to press in, their shadows deepening the sense of unease. Every snap of a twig, every distant bird call, was amplified, twisted into the sound of an approaching threat.

Sheriff Brinks, his face set in a mask of grim resolve, rode at the head of the makeshift posse. He carried a well-worn rifle, its wood smooth from years of use, but his mind was a whirlwind of conflicting thoughts. He was a lawman, tasked with protecting his community, but he was also a man who had seen the impossible, who had witnessed Truly's quiet strength, and Abel's unsettling presence. He knew, with a certainty that gnawed at him, that the story the townsfolk were telling themselves, a simple tale of a savage beast, was incomplete, perhaps even entirely wrong.

He remembered Truly's eyes, wide with a fear that went beyond the immediate horror of Silas's death. It was the fear of being mis-understood, of being ostracized, of her protector being hunted. But the evidence, the gruesome, undeniable evidence of Silas's fate, was too potent for reason to penetrate the veil of fear that had descended upon Oak Holler. "Stay alert," Brinks called out, his voice cutting through the hushed tension. "Keep your eyes sharp. This isn't like hunting deer." He knew that the creature they sought, if it was indeed a creature, was unlike anything they had ever encountered. The sheer force required to inflict such injuries on Silas was beyond the capability of any known animal in these woods.

The posse moved with a practiced rhythm, their steps synchronized, their senses honed. They were men of the land, their knowledge of the forest ingrained. They could read the subtle signs of passage, the disturbed undergrowth, the broken branches, the faint scent carried on the wind. But the woods, under the shadow of this looming hunt, seemed to hold their breath. The usual symphony of the forest, the chirping insects, the chattering squirrels, the distant call of a hawk, was muted, as if nature itself was holding its breath, anticipating the coming clash.

Jedediah, his stride long and powerful, kept pace with the Sheriff, his rifle held at the ready. His jaw was set, his gaze sweeping the dense foliage with an unnerving intensity. He was a man driven by a deep sense of justice, and in his eyes, Silas's death was an unforgivable transgression that demanded retribution. He saw the forest not as a place of beauty or solace, but as a potential hiding place for a dangerous enemy, a place that needed to be purged of its darkness. "Sheriff," Jedediah said, his voice low, barely audible above the rustling leaves. "We should split up. Cover more ground. The longer we wait, the further it gets." Brinks shook his head. "Not yet, Jedediah. We stay together for now. We need to be a cohesive unit. And we need to maintain a clear line of sight on each other. This isn't a race." He knew the dangers of splitting up a posse in unfamiliar or hostile territory. Panic could set in, and with it, mistakes. Mistakes that could be fatal.

They moved deeper into the woods, the sunlight growing dimmer, the air cooler. The trees seemed to grow older, their trunks gnarled and thick, their branches heavy with moss. This was the part of the forest that even the most seasoned woodsmen approached with a degree of caution, the territory that bordered Truly's secluded cabin. The very stillness of the place was unnerving, a profound quiet that felt less like peace and more like a held breath.

A sudden rustle in the undergrowth ahead sent a jolt of adrenaline through the group. Rifles were raised, fingers finding the triggers. The men froze, their bodies tensed, every muscle coiled. A moment later, a deer bolted from the thicket, its white tail a fleeting flash against the green. A collective sigh of relief swept through the posse, though the tension remained, a taut string that had been momentarily plucked.

"Just a deer," Jedediah grumbled, lowering his rifle, though his eyes still scanned the area where the animal had disappeared. "Could have been anything." The fear, once awakened, was not easily soothed. Every shadow seemed to harbor a threat, every sound a potential warning.

Sheriff Brinks, however, felt a different kind of unease. He knew this part of the woods. He knew the habits of the wildlife. And he knew that the silence, the unnatural stillness, was not the silence of a normal forest. It was the silence of a place holding its breath, waiting for something. Or perhaps, it was the silence of something already watching them, assessing them, knowing they were there. They continued their slow, methodical advance, their progress measured in the crunch of leaves and the rhythmic creak of their leather boots. The scent of pine and damp earth, usually so invigorating, now seemed heavy, oppressive, tinged with the metallic tang of fear and anticipation. They were hunters, yes, but they were also prey, unknowingly walking into a territory that was not entirely their own. The woods, in their immensity and mystery, were about to reveal their secrets, and the townsfolk of Oak Holler, armed with their rifles and their fear, were about to discover that some hunts were never meant to be simple.

The distant, growing clamor of Oak Holler, a sound that had once represented the comforting hum of community, now vibrated with a chilling resonance. Abel, his massive form coiled with an instinctual awareness, felt the shift. The primal dread that had settled over the valley like a shroud was no longer a subtle tremor; it was a palpable tremor of approaching violence, a storm gathering on the horizon of the familiar woods. He heard it not just with his ears, but with the very marrow of his bones, the thudding of boots, the harsh, guttural shouts of men, the unmistakable metallic glint of weapons being readied.

They were coming. And they were not coming with curiosity, but with a burning, untamed fury.

His gaze, dark and ancient as the forest itself, swept across the shadowed undergrowth. Truly. The thought was a sharp, protective pang. Her solitude, her quiet existence, had always been a fragile thing, shielded by the very wilderness that now teemed with hostile intent. He could not face them. Not like this. Not with the raw, untamed power that surged beneath his skin, a power that would only confirm their worst fears, painting him as the very monster they sought. Confrontation would be their victory, a justification for their terror. Evasion was the only path to her continued safety.

A silent understanding passed between Abel and the ancient trees that stood sentinel around him. They were his allies, his confidantes, the keepers of his secrets. He turned, his movements fluid and impossibly silent for a creature of his immense size. Each step was deliberate, each rustle of leaves a carefully orchestrated whisper. He didn't run in a panic, but flowed, a living shadow detaching itself from the dappled light. The forest floor, damp and yielding, seemed to absorb the sound of his passage, muffling his retreat. He moved deeper, not towards the known paths, but into the wilder, untamed heart of the Ozarks, a place where even the most seasoned hunters faltered.

His large hands, surprisingly deft, brushed aside low-hanging branches, his powerful frame bending and twisting with an almost impossible grace. He was a mountain of muscle and bone, yet he moved like mist, a fleeting specter against the backdrop of dense foliage. The urgency in his movements was a silent testament to the danger he perceived. He knew the men of Oak Holler; he had observed them from the periphery for years, their boisterous laughter, their easy camaraderie, their capacity for both kindness and a terrible, blind rage. And he knew, with a certainty that chilled him to the core, that their current rage was far from blind. It was focused, armed, and aimed directly at the perceived threat.

He willed himself to be invisible, to become one with the rustling leaves and the whispering wind. He visualized himself dissolving into the dappled sunlight, his form becoming indistinguishable from the gnarled bark of the ancient oaks and the moss-covered rocks. It was not a trick of magic, but a profound connection to the earth, a deep communion with the wild that allowed him to blend, to fade, to become part of the very fabric of the forest. The air itself seemed to conspire with him, carrying the scent of pine and damp earth away from the approaching mob, masking his trail.

He thought of Truly, her quiet strength, her unwavering kindness, the gentle way she tended to him when he was injured, her eyes holding a wisdom that far surpassed her years. She was his sanctuary, his reason for being. The thought of her being harmed, of her being dragged into the center of this mess, was an unbearable weight. His escape was not merely for his own survival, but for hers. To be captured, to be killed, would leave her vulnerable, exposed to the very fear and suspicion that now gripped Oak Holler. He had to be her unseen shield, her silent guardian, even from a distance.

He pushed himself further, his muscles burning with exertion, but his resolve only hardening. He knew the winding paths, the hidden ravines, the dense thickets that offered true concealment. He navigated the treacherous terrain with an innate knowledge, a lifetime of communion with the wilderness guiding his steps. He skirted the edges of familiar hunting grounds, the territories where Silas had often roamed, knowing that this was precisely where the posse would be looking. He needed to draw them away, to lead them on a chase that would exhaust their fervor and their ammunition, a chase that would ultimately yield nothing but the rustling of leaves and the mocking silence of the deep woods.

The sounds of pursuit grew fainter, the harsh shouts replaced by the less distinct murmur of a determined, but perhaps slightly disoriented, group. Abel allowed himself a moment to gauge their direction, his senses reaching out like tendrils, mapping their progress. They were heading west, towards the older growth, the part of the forest where the trees stood like ancient titans and the undergrowth was a tangled maze. Good. That was a place where they would find only frustration, where their numbers and their weapons would be less of an advantage than their ignorance of the hidden ways.

He paused at the edge of a small, babbling brook, its water crystal clear, tumbling over smooth, grey stones. He knelt, his large hands cupping the water, and drank deeply, the cool liquid a balm to his parched throat. As he drank, he scanned his surroundings. The forest here was alive with the usual sounds of nature, the chirping of unseen birds, the scuttling of small creatures in the undergrowth, the gentle sigh of the wind through the leaves. It was a stark contrast to the grim pronouncements and the fear-laden whispers of the townsfolk. This was the world he belonged to, a world of balance and quietude, a world that was now under threat.

He knew that his presence in Oak Holler, however well-intentioned, had been a catalyst. Silas's death, a tragedy he still grappled with, had ignited a powder keg of fear and superstition. He had seen the fear in the eyes of the townsfolk, the way they had recoiled from him, the whispers that had followed him. He had also seen the fear in Truly's eyes, the worry that he would be blamed, hunted, misunderstood. He carried the weight of that misunderstanding, the burden of being an anomaly in their world.

His mission now was clear: to disappear, to become a ghost in the woods, until the fury of Oak Holler had subsided, until the immediate danger had passed. He needed to create distance, not just physical distance, but a distance that would allow their fear to dissipate, their rational minds to reassert themselves. He would weave through the deepest parts of the forest, where the sunlight barely penetrated, where the air was thick with the scent of decay and ancient secrets. He would become a whisper on the wind, a ripple in the undergrowth, a presence felt but never seen.

He pushed himself to his feet, his large frame casting a long, distorted shadow in the dim light. The path ahead was unknown, fraught with the natural dangers of the wilderness, but it was a path he could navigate. He was a creature of the wild, and the wild was his ally. He moved with a renewed sense of purpose, his large, sensitive ears straining to catch any hint of pursuit, his keen eyes scanning the dense foliage for any sign of danger. He was a hunter, yes, but now, he was also the hunted. And in this ancient, whispering forest, he would use every skill, every ounce of his strength, to evade their grasp and to ensure that Truly remained safe from the storm that was brewing. The trees around him seemed to nod in understanding, their ancient branches reaching out like protective arms, welcoming him into their deep, emerald embrace. He was one with them now, a part of their silent, enduring strength.

13

PROTECTING THE PROTECTOR

The panicked shouts of the townsfolk, echoing through the ancient trees, were a stark counterpoint to the gentle rustling of leaves that had always soothed Truly's spirit. Each cry, each thud of a hurried footstep, sent a fresh wave of icy dread through her veins, but beneath the fear, something else was beginning to solidify. Abel, her gentle giant, her protector, was out there, fleeing. Fleeing from the very people he had sought to understand, from the very valley he had hoped to find peace in. And why? Because he had stood by her, because he had shown her kindness when the world had shown her only suspicion.

She pressed her hands to the rough-hewn wood of her cabin's door, her knuckles white. She could hear the growing commotion, the baying of hounds, the grim pronouncements of men fueled by fear and misunderstanding. They were hunting Abel. The thought was a visceral blow, a physical ache that settled deep within her chest. He had done nothing to deserve this. He had saved her, protected her, shown her a loyalty she had never known. And now, he was the one in peril, driven into the shadowed depths of the forest by the very people he had tried to coexist with.

A tremor ran through her, not of fear, but of burgeoning anger. Years of isolation, of being ostracized, of enduring the whispers and sidelong glances, had forged a resilience within her. She had learned to find solace in solitude, to draw strength from the quiet persistence of nature. But this... this was different. This was an injustice so profound, so blatant, that it ignited a fire within her that she hadn't known existed. Abel was not a monster. He was a guardian, a friend, a gentle soul trapped in a form that the fearful minds of Oakhaven could not comprehend.

She thought of his quiet strength, the way his large, dark eyes held a depth of understanding that surpassed any human she had ever known. She remembered the times he had appeared at the edge of the woods, a silent sentinel, his presence a reassurance even in her darkest hours. He had never intruded, never demanded, but had always been there, a silent promise of protection. And now, he was being hounded, accused, his very existence deemed a threat.

The unfairness of it all settled upon her like a heavy cloak. They were so quick to judge, so eager to embrace suspicion. They saw his size, his raw power, and their minds conjured images of beasts and destruction. They couldn't see the kindness etched in the lines of his face, the gentle cadence of his movements, the evident care he showed for the smallest creatures. They couldn't see the protector he truly was, the one who had, in his own way, guarded her from the shadows.

A quiet determination began to firm her features. She couldn't stand by and let this happen. She couldn't allow Abel, who had offered her nothing but selfless protection, to be captured or harmed. He had acted out of a deep-seated need to keep her safe, and now, the roles were reversed. It was her turn to shield him. The thought was audacious, almost terrifying, given her own precarious standing in the community, her own ingrained fear of confrontation. But the image of Abel, hunted and alone, spurred her on.

She straightened her shoulders, her gaze hardening as she listened to the receding sounds of the chase. They were heading deeper into the woods, towards the denser parts of the Ozarks, the wilder territories where even seasoned hunters rarely ventured. He was trying to lose them, to draw them away, to protect her from being caught in the crossfire. His every instinct was still focused on her well-being. It was a debt she couldn't repay with inaction.

A solemn vow, made in the quiet sanctity of her own heart, began to form. She would protect Abel. It was a promise whispered into the stillness of her cabin, a vow that resonated with the quiet strength she had cultivated over years of solitude. She might be an outcast, a recluse, feared and misunderstood, but she was not without courage. And she would find it, wherever it lay hidden within her, to stand against this tide of fear.

Her isolation had taught her self-reliance, but it had also made her keenly aware of the injustices of the world. She had seen how fear could twist perception, how suspicion could warp truth. Abel was the victim of that fear, a scapegoat for the lingering anxieties of a community clinging to old prejudices. She understood, perhaps more than anyone, what it was like to be judged by your appearance, to be branded a threat before you had even spoken a word.

The bond she shared with Abel, though unconventional, was forged in a shared sense of being misunderstood, of existing on the fringes of society. He had never judged her; he had simply accepted her. And in that acceptance, she had found a quiet strength she had never realized she possessed. Now, that strength had to be amplified, had to be brought to bear against the misguided fury of Oak Holler.

She took a deep, steadying breath, the scent of pine and damp earth filling her lungs. The woods were Abel's domain, his sanctuary. He knew them intimately, their hidden paths, their secret places. He would be hard to find. And that was good. It meant he was safe for now. But safety was a fragile thing, and the mob's determination was a potent force. She couldn't fight them directly, not with their numbers and their weapons. But she could do something else. She could be a different kind of protector.

Her mind began to race, piecing together fragments of knowledge, of whispers overheard, of the subtle shifts in the forest she had come to understand. She knew the patrol routes of the townspeople, the trails they favored. She knew where their search would likely begin and end. And she knew, with a growing certainty, that their pursuit would be driven by a blind, unthinking rage, not by logic or reason.

A flicker of an idea, bold and perhaps even foolish, began to take root. If Abel was the target, then the path of least resistance for her would be to make him harder to find. To subtly misdirect, to create confusion, to sow seeds of doubt in the minds of his pursuers. It was a dangerous game, one that could expose her, but the alternative, doing nothing, was no longer an option.

She moved to the small, cluttered table in her cabin, her hands reaching for a worn leather-bound journal and a stub of charcoal. Her fingers, usually hesitant and careful, moved with a new purpose, sketching out rough maps, noting landmarks, tracing possible routes. She wasn't planning to join the hunt, not in the traditional sense. Her role would be far more subtle, more insidious. She would be a whisper in the wind, a misdirection in the shadows.

She thought about Silas, his death a tragedy that had set this whole chain of events in motion. Abel had been there, trying to help, and had been branded the culprit. It was a cruel twist of fate, a testament to the ease with which people could be led to believe the worst. And Truly, who had witnessed the events firsthand, knew the truth. She knew that Abel's actions had been born of a desperate attempt to prevent further tragedy.

The fear that had once paralyzed her was slowly being replaced by a steely resolve. She wouldn't let them take him. She wouldn't let their ignorance and their fear dictate the fate of a creature who had shown her only gentleness. The isolation she had endured had taught her the value of alliances, of unexpected bonds. And her bond with Abel was the strongest she had ever known.

She remembered the stories her grandmother used to tell her, tales of forest spirits and hidden pathways, of ancient guardians who protected the wild. She had always dismissed them as fanciful folklore, but now, looking out at the dense, whispering woods, she felt a connection to those ancient legends. Perhaps, in her own quiet way, she could become one of those guardians. Her plan was still in its infant stages, a tangle of brave intentions and practical challenges. She didn't have the strength of Abel, nor the cunning of a seasoned hunter. But she had something else: an intimate knowledge of the surrounding terrain, an understanding of the forest's subtle language, and a fierce, burning desire to protect her friend.

She began to gather supplies: a sturdy cloak, a pouch of dried berries and nuts, a waterskin, and a small, sharp knife she kept for foraging. She would need to move quickly and silently, staying out of sight, observing, and subtly influencing the direction of the search. It was a daunting task, fraught with peril, but the image of Abel's troubled eyes, his solitary flight into the unknown, fueled her determination.

She closed her eyes for a brief moment, picturing Abel's silhouette against the fading light, his massive form moving with a silent grace through the trees. He was strong, resilient, but he was also alone. And in that moment of profound vulnerability, Truly found a fierce protector within herself, a guardian spirit born of injustice and unwavering loyalty. She would be his unseen shield, his silent advocate, and she would not rest until the storm had passed, and he was safe once more. The fear was still there, a cold knot in her stomach, but it was overshadowed by a burgeoning sense of purpose, a fierce resolve that burned brighter than any fear. She was no longer just the reclusive girl in the woods; she was Truly, and she was ready to fight for her friend.

Truly emerged from her cabin, not with the hesitant steps of a woman accustomed to avoiding notice, but with a newfound stride, purposeful and silent. The familiar, dense undergrowth of the Ozarks, a place she'd always considered her sanctuary, now felt charged with an almost palpable sense of urgency. The sounds of the chase, though fading, still echoed in her mind, the panicked shouts, the baying of hounds, the determined stride of men driven by fear and accusation. Abel was out there, a creature of immense gentleness, being hunted like a beast.

Her intimate knowledge of this wilderness was her only weapon, a stark contrast to the crude tools of the Oak Holler folk. She knew the Ozarks like the back of her hand, not just the well-trodden paths leading in and out of the valley, but the hidden arteries of the land: the narrow deer trails that wound through the thickest briar patches, the secret caves tucked away behind weeping willows, the treacherous ravines that could swallow an unwary traveler whole. These were not mere geographical features to her; they were allies, extensions of her own being. She moved with a fluidity born of years spent traversing this terrain, her steps light, her presence a mere whisper amongst the rustling leaves. The hunters, focused on Abel's massive form, would be looking for a creature crashing through the underbrush, a trail of destruction in its wake. They wouldn't be looking for a phantom, a woman who had learned to move with the grace of a shadow.

Her first objective was not to find Abel, but to understand where the hunt was leading them. She skirted the edge of the woods, her keen eyes scanning the tree line, her ears attuned to the faintest sounds. She could discern the difference between the frantic rush of a frightened animal and the more deliberate, if still panicked, movement of men with a purpose. The direction of the shouts, the cadence of the dogs, all told a story of their pursuit. They were heading northwest, deeper into the wilder, less explored regions of the Ozarks, towards the Whispering Falls, a place known for its treacherous terrain and disorienting echoes. A smart beast, she thought, would try to use the environment to its advantage. Abel, with his innate understanding of the wild, would undoubtedly do just that.

She made her way towards a series of ancient, moss-covered boulders, a landmark she often used when navigating by feel rather than sight. From here, she could gain a vantage point, observing the distant movement of the hunters without revealing herself. She found a thicket of wild rhododendron, its broad leaves offering perfect concealment, and settled in to watch. Soon, the sounds became clearer. She saw them then, a scattered line of men, their faces grim, their movements less coordinated than they would have liked. They were relying on the dogs, their primary guides. Truly knew these hounds, or at least their breed; they were bred for tracking, relentless and determined, but also easily confused by subtle shifts in scent and terrain. She knew Abel would be trying to break their scent trail, to utilize the wind and the water. He would likely head towards the creek that fed into Whispering Falls, where the running water would further obscure his passage. This was a critical juncture. If they reached the creek, and the dogs picked up his scent again, their pursuit would be renewed with ferocity.

Truly began to move, not towards the creek, but parallel to it, downstream. She knew of a small, hidden spring that fed into a series of underground channels, eventually emerging in a completely different part of the woods, miles away from the falls. It was a difficult passage, one that required scrambling over slick, moss-covered rocks and navigating through tight, vine-choked crevices. It was a path no human hunter would readily follow, especially not in a hurry.

She reached the spring, a place of cool, clear water bubbling from the earth. She didn't drink, though her throat was dry. Her purpose was to influence, not to rest. She began to subtly alter the area. She disturbed the loose earth around the spring, creating what looked like fresh tracks leading away from the creek, towards a denser, more forbidding section of the forest. She carefully arranged a few fallen branches to create the illusion of a struggle, a momentary entanglement. Then, she used a patch of particularly pungent wild mint she'd gathered earlier, crushing its leaves and scattering them near the "tracks." The strong scent, when mixed with the damp earth, might create a confusing olfactory mirage for the hounds.

Her actions were a silent, intricate dance, a series of subtle manipulations of the natural landscape. She was not fighting the hunters directly; she was fighting their perception, their reliance on the simplistic logic of the hunt. She was introducing doubt, misdirection, into their path. She moved on, her internal compass guiding her through the increasingly wild terrain. She knew Abel would be acutely aware of his pursuers; his senses honed to a razor's edge. He would be looking for signs, for anything that might indicate where they were headed, or more importantly, where they *weren't* headed. She needed to leave him a breadcrumb, a subtle signal that would assure him he was not alone, that someone was working to protect him.

She reached a towering ancient oak, its branches spread wide like the arms of a benevolent giant. This was a place she often sat, a vantage point from which she could survey the surrounding canopy. She had noticed that the hunters, in their haste, were veering away from the general direction of this tree, perhaps deeming it too dense to harbor any prey. This was good. It meant they were being drawn further west, away from Abel's likely intended escape route.

She took a handful of dried blueberries from her pouch, crushing them slightly to release their scent. Then, she carefully placed them on a prominent, low-hanging branch of the oak, arranging them in a small, deliberate cluster. It was a simple marker, one that Abel would recognize. She had shown him this very tree once, pointing out the unusual clusters of berries that grew there, a sign of its unique microclimate. It was a message: *I'm here. I'm watching. Keep moving east, away from them.* She knew Abel would understand. He was not merely an animal; he possessed an intelligence that transcended words, a deep connection to the natural world that mirrored her own. He would see the berries, recognize the significance of the tree, and understand that the hunters were not coming this way. It was a small gesture, but in the chaos of the hunt, small reassurances could make all the difference.

As she moved, she actively considered the hunters' likely path. They were moving towards the treacherous terrain near Whispering Falls. She knew that area intimately. There were hidden sinkholes disguised by thick layers of fallen leaves, and sheer, slippery rock faces that offered no handholds. If they weren't careful, the terrain itself would become their greatest adversary. She began to nudge them in that direction, but not directly. She used the landscape itself as a subtle guide. She'd subtly clear certain paths that led towards the falls, while at the same time making other, seemingly easier routes appear more convoluted or blocked. She knew the hunters would likely stick to paths that offered the illusion of speed and directness, even if those paths were ultimately more dangerous.

She came across a place where a large oak had fallen, blocking a well-worn game trail. The hunters, if they followed this path, would have to detour around it, a delay that would benefit Abel. But the detour itself would lead them closer to a series of narrow, winding ravines. Truly, knowing Abel's ability to move silently through even the most difficult terrain, made sure to reinforce the impression that the game trail was the most viable route. She even nudged a few loose rocks near the fallen oak, creating a slight disturbance that might catch the eye of the lead hunters, suggesting a recent passage. She paused, listening intently. The sounds of the chase were growing fainter, the baying of the hounds more distant. They were indeed heading towards the falls, and Abel was likely well ahead, using the dense forest to his advantage. Her heart ached for him, for the fear he must be experiencing, but a grim satisfaction settled within her. She was doing something. She was not helpless.

She knew that Abel, even with her subtle aid, would be relying on his own instincts and knowledge. He would be seeking out the most obscure and difficult routes, places where the scent would be lost, where the terrain would slow his pursuers. She thought of the old smugglers' caves, hidden deep within the limestone cliffs overlooking the river. They were a network of winding tunnels, a labyrinth that had once been used to move illicit goods in and out of the valley. Abel, with his quiet strength and his uncanny ability to navigate even in the darkest of conditions, might find refuge there.

To further encourage the hunters' misdirection, Truly decided to create a false trail that would lead them away from the direct path to the caves, but towards a more open, treacherous area known for its dense fog banks, especially in the late afternoon. She found a patch of disturbed earth, clearly marked by a few large, heavy footprints –

not Abel's, but perhaps from a deer that had passed through earlier. She carefully added to the disturbance, using her boot to mimic the impression of a large, clumsy foot, then smeared some mud from a nearby stagnant pool onto the leaves, giving it the appearance of a hasty, uncertain passage. She then took a piece of dried, mossy bark and rubbed it vigorously against the base of several trees in the general direction she wanted them to go, leaving a faint, earthy scent that might, just might, be interpreted as a scent trail by the dogs, leading them astray.

Her movements were precise, economical. Every action was calculated to achieve a specific outcome. She wasn't trying to make them give up; that would be too much to ask of their fear-driven minds. She was trying to slow them down, to make them doubt, to buy Abel time. Time to escape, time to find a truly safe haven, time to simply survive this ordeal. She found a small, natural hollow, shielded by an overhang of rock and thick ferns. It was a place she had discovered years ago, a place of quiet solitude. She settled there, catching her breath, her muscles beginning to ache from the sustained effort. She pulled out her waterskin, taking a long, cool drink. The water tasted of the earth, of the ancient rocks through which it had filtered.

From her vantage point, she could still hear the faint, intermittent shouts of the hunters. They were indeed heading towards the fog-laden region she had subtly directed them towards. The dense fog, coupled with the treacherous ground, would likely cause them considerable trouble, slowing their progress and potentially leading to injuries. It was a gamble, but a calculated one. She thought about Abel's immense strength, his capacity for endurance. He would be moving with a purpose, driven by the instinct for survival. Her role was to be the unseen hand, the subtle whisper that guided him, that protected him from the blind fury of the mob. She was his terrestrial guide, his silent guardian in the realm of the familiar, yet suddenly perilous, woods.

She knew that once the initial pursuit waned, once the hunters became exhausted or disoriented, Abel would need a place to rest, to regroup. She had a few more routes in mind, a series of hidden clearings and abandoned game shelters that only she knew about. She would continue to move, to observe, to be his unseen protector. Her knowledge of the Ozarks was not just about knowing trails and caves; it was about understanding the subtle shifts in the ecosystem, the language of the wind, the mood of the weather. She knew that as dusk approached, the temperature would drop, and the mist would thicken around the river valleys. This would further aid Abel, masking his movements and disorienting his pursuers.

She began to trace a path that would lead her towards a known crossing point of the main creek, a place where the water ran shallow and wide. It was a route that Abel might choose to cross, a place where he could leave the immediate vicinity of the falls and move further afield. Here, she would leave another marker, a subtle sign that would indicate a safe passage, a direction to follow if he needed it. She reached the creek, the water cool against her bare ankles as she waded across. On the opposite bank, near a cluster of smooth, grey stones, she found a patch of loose soil. With her small knife, she carefully etched a symbol into the dirt, a simple, looping line, reminiscent of a flowing river, a mark she often used in her private sketches to denote a passage or a journey. It was a sign of safe passage, a subtle beacon in the encroaching twilight.

She knew this was a dangerous game she was playing. If she was discovered, if the Oak Holler folk realized she was aiding Abel, her own ostracization would be complete. She would be branded a traitor, an accomplice to whatever they imagined Abel to be. But the thought of Abel, hunted and alone, was a far greater deterrent to inaction than any fear of her own future. Her isolation had taught her the value of observation, of understanding motivations, of predicting behavior. She knew that the Oak Holler townsfolk, driven by fear and superstition, would likely exhaust themselves, their initial fury giving way to frustration and exhaustion as the terrain and the fading light worked against them. They would eventually retreat, perhaps to regroup, perhaps to simply admit defeat for the day.

Abel, on the other hand, would be conserving his energy, moving with a quiet efficiency. He would be looking for signs of respite, for a place where he could disappear until the immediate danger had passed. The markers she left were not just for him, but for the possibility of his return, for the chance that he might need a safe haven in the coming days. She continued her silent patrol, her senses alive to every rustle, every snap of a twig. She was a phantom in her own land, a guardian operating in the shadows. The Ozarks, her lifelong companion, were now a battlefield, and she was fighting a war of misdirection, of subtle manipulation, of unwavering loyalty. The image of Abel's gentle eyes, clouded with fear and confusion, propelled her forward. She was Truly, the recluse, the outcast, but in this moment, she was also a protector, a strategist, and the silent, steadfast guardian of the gentle giant. The hunt was on, and she was playing a game of her own, a game of shadows and whispers, a game for survival.

She continued her deliberate disruption, moving further into the more challenging terrain. She knew that the hunters, in their haste, would be looking for an easier path, a more direct route. Abel, on the other hand, would be seeking out the most difficult, the most convoluted. She needed to make her false trail appear to lead towards the latter, while subtly guiding the hunters towards a dead end, or at least a significant delay. She came across a dense thicket of briars, a tangled, formidable barrier that would slow any pursuer. She began to push through it, deliberately tearing her cloak and scratching her skin, making sure to leave a visible trail of ripped fabric snagged on the thorns, and even a few drops of her own blood. The scent of her blood, a stark contrast to Abel's earthy aroma, would be a powerful, albeit misleading, lure.

She emerged on the other side, breathless and a little shaky, but with a grim sense of accomplishment. The hunters would be drawn to the blood, to the sign of a struggle, a clear indication that something had passed this way. And the briars, a formidable obstacle, would suggest that their quarry was either desperate or perhaps injured, further fueling their predatory instincts. She knew the path beyond the briars led to a small, secluded clearing, a place that looked promising at first glance but ultimately offered no clear escape route, a natural trap.

As she moved towards the clearing, she heard the renewed baying of the hounds, closer now, more insistent. They had picked up the scent, or rather, the scent she had so carefully manufactured. A wave of nausea washed over her, a mixture of fear and a strange, nascent excitement. She was playing with fire, directly confronting the very fear that had kept her in isolation for so long, but the thought of

Abel, his gentle nature so cruelly misunderstood, gave her a courage she hadn't known she possessed.

She entered the clearing, a small patch of open ground surrounded by dense trees. She knew this place. It was where she had once found a nest of newborn fawns, their mother nowhere in sight. She had sat with them for hours, a silent sentinel, until the doe had finally returned. It was a place of quiet solitude; a place Abel might have sought for refuge if he had been less of a target. Now, it was to be her stage. She began to make noise, not the frantic snapping of twigs, but a more deliberate, sustained sound. She struck two smooth stones together repeatedly, the sharp clacking echoing through the clearing. She whistled a tune, a mournful, simple melody that carried on the wind. She stomped her feet, creating a rhythmic thudding that mimicked the movement of a large creature trying to break free. She was a beacon, a clear signal that something, or someone, was here.

She could hear the hunters now, their voices rough with exertion and anticipation, closer than ever. She saw the glint of metal, the dark shapes of men pushing through the trees at the edge of the clearing. They were closing in. Her heart leaped into her throat, but she held her ground, her eyes fixed on the point of their entry. Then, she did something that sent a tremor of pure terror through her. She picked up a handful of dried leaves and scattered them upwards, into the air, a visual disturbance designed to catch the eye, to suggest a sudden, frantic movement. It was a desperate measure, a final, bold stroke. She even let out a small, choked gasp, a sound of feigned surprise and fear.

The hunters burst into the clearing, their faces a mixture of grim determination and a savage kind of triumph. They saw her, a solitary figure amidst the trees, the source of the disturbance. Their eyes widened, a flicker of confusion crossing their features. She was not the hulking beast they expected. "Who are you?" one of them, a burly man with a weathered face and a cruel glint in his eye, shouted, his voice hoarse.

Truly didn't answer. She couldn't. Her voice had seized in her throat. Instead, she took a hesitant step back, her eyes wide with a practiced fear, then turned and bolted, not in the direction Abel had gone, but deeper into the woods, towards a part of the forest she knew was dense and impassable, a place where a lone woman could easily become lost and disoriented. She ran, her breath coming in ragged gasps, her lungs burning. Behind her, she could hear the shouts of the hunters, the excited barks of the hounds. They were following her. They had taken the bait. The gamble had paid off, at least for now. She risked a glance over her shoulder. The burly man, and a few others, were in pursuit, their focus entirely on her. The hounds, their instincts honed and their scent trail clear, were also locked onto her. Abel, she prayed, was safe, slipping away into the vastness of the Ozarks, his path clear.

She led them on a chase, a desperate flight through tangled undergrowth and across treacherous, hidden ravines. She deliberately chose paths that would slow them, paths that would lead them further away from Abel's intended escape route. She stumbled, she fell, she scraped her knees and hands, all to enhance the illusion of a panicked, less capable quarry. She navigated through a dense stand of hemlock, the thick, fragrant needles creating a disorienting, almost suffocating atmosphere. She knew that the scent of Abel would be lost here, but the scent of her own fear, her own blood, would be a clear and undeniable signal to the pursuing hounds.

She reached a section of the forest where the ground sloped steeply towards a hidden gorge. She knew of a narrow, almost invisible deer trail that wound its way down the side, a treacherous descent that would be difficult for armed men to navigate, especially in their haste. She scrambled down it, her body moving with a desperate agility born of adrenaline. She could hear them behind her, their progress hindered by the terrain, their curses echoing up from below.

At the bottom of the gorge, a small, swift-flowing creek cut through the rocks. She splashed into the icy water, letting it swirl around her ankles, washing away some of the scent of her passage. She knew that further downstream, the creek widened, and the water became turbulent, creating a natural barrier for the hounds. She waded across, her movements as quick and silent as she could manage, and then scrambled up the opposite bank, her gaze fixed on the dense woods ahead.

She paused, listening. The sounds of pursuit were growing fainter, more distant. The creek, the difficult terrain, the disorienting hemlock grove, they were all working to her advantage. They were slowing the hunters, creating distance. She knew that eventually, they would realize their quarry was not the hulking creature they had expected, but a desperate young woman. The confusion would be immense. They might even believe she was Abel's accomplice, trying to lead them astray. The thought was terrifying, but it was also her only hope.

She pressed on, her body aching, her lungs burning, but her resolve unwavering. She had to keep moving, had to continue to draw their attention. She found a small, rocky outcrop overlooking a particularly dense section of forest, a place from which she could be seen if they were looking. She stood there for a moment, a solitary figure silhouetted against the darkening sky, then turned and disappeared into the trees, her movements now deliberately less frantic, more measured. She was no longer just running; she was leading them on a calculated path, a labyrinth of her own design.

She knew that Abel, with his keen senses, would be aware of her actions. He would understand that she was creating a diversion, sacrificing her own safety for his. The thought brought a lump to her throat, a mixture of gratitude and profound sorrow for the predicament they both found themselves in. She had to ensure that her diversion was convincing, that it held their attention long enough for him to truly escape, to find a safe haven, to disappear into the vastness of the Ozarks until the immediate danger had passed.

She continued to create disturbances, to make herself visible, audible. She found a hollow log and began to bang on it with a rock, the resonant boom echoing through the twilight. She climbed a tall, old oak, carefully selecting a branch that would be clearly visible from a distance, and shouted out, a single, piercing cry that was designed to sound like a startled animal or a person in distress. Each action was a calculated risk, a deliberate placement of herself in harm's way to protect him. She was the distraction, the decoy, a willing sacrifice in the hope that Abel, her silent protector, would find his freedom. The pursuit was still there, a tangible threat, but now, it was focused on her, and in that focus, she found a strange, grim satisfaction. Her own fear, though still present, was tempered by the knowledge that she was actively fighting for Abel's survival, using the very wilderness that had once been her prison to become his unlikely savior.

The adrenaline that had fueled Truly's desperate flight began to ebb, leaving behind a gnawing weariness and the lingering chill of fear. She had led them on a chase, a convoluted path through the whispering pines and across treacherous ravines, all to create a buffer for Abel. The hounds' baying had faded to a distant echo, the shouts of the hunters a muffled murmur against the vastness of the Ozarks. She knew she couldn't simply melt back into the shadows. The immediate threat had been averted, but the deeper problem remained. The town, blinded by fear and manipulated by Silas, saw Abel as a monster. They needed to see the truth, a truth she was now uniquely positioned to share.

Hiding Abel, even with her diversion, was a temporary solution. His exile was a testament to the town's ignorance, an ignorance that protected Silas and endangered everyone. She needed to plant seeds of doubt, fragments of her own understanding, in the very soil of their collective fear. It was a dangerous gamble, a whisper against a hurricane of prejudice, but it was the only path forward. She began to move with a newfound purpose, her steps no longer those of a frightened fugitive, but of a messenger.

Her plan began to take shape, an intricate blanket woven from whispers and half-truths, designed to unravel the tightly held narrative of Silas's innocence and Abel's guilt. She knew the townsfolk, like sheep, followed the shepherd's call without question. The townsfolk's pronouncements, amplified by fear, had painted Abel as a primal threat, a creature of the wild who had lashed out in malice. But Truly had seen the raw terror in Abel's eyes, the desperate defense, the unmistakable signs of a prolonged and brutal struggle. She had also seen Silas's manipulative whispers, his calculated cruelty that had festered in the shadows of their community.

She remembered the old fishing shack, a dilapidated structure nestled beside a quiet bend in the creek, a place frequented by the younger folk of the town, a place where secrets were often exchanged amidst the scent of brine and drying nets. It was a perfect canvas for her message. Under the cloak of twilight, she approached the shack, her heart a steady drumbeat of resolve. She carried with her a piece of charcoal, scavenged from a recent campfire, and a scrap of parchment, saved from a discarded grocery list.

With swift, practiced strokes, she began to write. She didn't write a manifesto, nor a detailed account of Silas's transgressions. Such a direct accusation would be dismissed as the ramblings of a disturbed girl, or worse, a fabricated tale by someone in league with the "monster." Instead, she opted for ambiguity, for questions that would gnaw at their conscience, for hints that would bloom into suspicion. Her first message was simple, etched onto the weathered wood of the shack's interior wall: "Was the pain always his? Or was it put upon him?" She let the words hang in the air, heavy with unspoken implication. It was a question designed to make them look at Abel not as a perpetrator, but as a victim, a creature who had endured something terrible. She then added, in smaller letters beneath: "The strong do not always bleed. Sometimes, they bear scars that cannot be seen."

She moved to another part of the shack, near where the fishing lines were stored, and left another fragmented message, this time on the parchment, tucked carefully into a crevice: "He protected. That is what the wild ones do. They protect their own. Even from those who claim to care." This was a direct counterpoint to the town's narrative, a subtle redefinition of Abel's actions, framing them not as an attack, but as a defense. As she exited the shack, her eyes caught the shadow of a form she knew well, Abel.

14

SANCTUARY AND SACRIFICE

The canopy overhead was a tapestry of emerald and jade, so thick that only slivers of sunlight managed to pierce through, dappling the forest floor in shifting patterns of light and shadow. Truly moved with a practiced, almost silent grace, her boots barely disturbing the carpet of fallen leaves and moss. Behind her, Abel followed, his massive frame surprisingly adept at navigating the dense undergrowth. His keen senses, usually a source of anxiety in the proximity of human settlements, were now his greatest allies, allowing him to anticipate the subtle shifts in the terrain and the rustle of unseen creatures.

They were venturing into the heart of the Ozarks, a region Truly knew intimately, having spent countless hours exploring its hidden corners since childhood. These were not the well-trodden paths near the edge of town, but the deep, untamed wilderness, where ancient trees with gnarled roots clutched the earth like skeletal fingers and the air hung thick with the scent of damp soil and decaying leaves. This was a place that swallowed sounds, a sanctuary woven from remoteness and the sheer indifference of nature to the affairs of men. "We need to keep moving," Truly murmured, her voice a low whisper that seemed to blend seamlessly with the murmurs of the forest. She pointed towards a narrow, almost imperceptible game trail that snaked its way between two colossal boulders, their surfaces slick with emerald moss. "This way. It leads to a series of ravines. They'll be harder for them to follow, especially with Abel."

Truly pushed aside a curtain of thick ivy, revealing a dark, gaping maw in the hillside. "This is the entrance to the Outlaw Caves," she explained, her voice barely audible above the sigh of the wind through the pines. "They're a labyrinth, and most of the passages are too narrow for anyone but me. And for Abel... well, he'd be safer outside, but we can find a spot for him where he'll be protected." She paused, looking back at him, her eyes reflecting the moonlight that now began to filter through the thinning canopy as dusk deepened. "Are you ready, Abel? This is the deepest we can go. It's going to be difficult, and we'll be completely alone." He met her gaze, his large, intelligent eyes conveying a depth of understanding that transcended words. He was ready. His loyalty to Truly was a bedrock, an immutable force that had guided his actions for years. He had always been her shadow, her silent protector, and now, more than ever, he felt that purpose settle upon him. He nudged her gently with his snout, a silent reassurance.

Together, they descended into the cool, damp air of the caves. The entrance was deceptively small, but as Truly had promised, it opened into a vast network of tunnels and chambers, carved by years of water erosion. The air grew heavy, carrying the mineral scent of ancient rock and the faint, earthy aroma of bat guano. Truly moved with a headlamp, its beam cutting a stark white path through the darkness, illuminating glistening stalactites and stalagmites that formed eerie, silent sentinels.

They navigated the winding passages, Truly's steps sure and steady, her knowledge of the cave system uncanny. She pointed out formations, shared snippets of local lore she'd learned from her grandfather, her voice echoing softly in the subterranean silence. "These are the Echoing Chambers," she'd say, her beam sweeping across vast caverns where the slightest sound would reverberate and multiply. "If anyone followed us, they'd be announcing their arrival long before they saw us." Abel found himself surprisingly at ease in the darkness. His nocturnal vision, already superior to any human's, was enhanced here. He could discern the subtle shifts in the texture of the rock, the faintest currents of air that indicated a passage yet unexplored. He kept a careful watch, his ears swiveling, his nose sampling the air for any scent that didn't belong, the metallic tang of human sweat, the acrid smell of fear.

They found a large, relatively dry chamber, its ceiling studded with glittering crystals that caught the headlamp's beam, casting a soft, ethereal glow. It was here that Truly decided they would make their temporary sanctuary. She checked for signs of recent habitation, for anything that might indicate human intrusion, and found none. The air was still, ancient, undisturbed. "This will do," she announced, her voice filled with a weariness that Truly tried to mask. She settled down against a smooth, cool rock face, her body language betraying the exhaustion she felt. The journey had been arduous, pushing both her physical and mental limits, but the knowledge that Abel was safe, that they had momentarily outrun the hounds, brought a flicker of relief.

Abel, sensing her fatigue, settled down beside her, his massive form a comforting presence. He lowered his head, resting it on his paws, but his eyes remained open, scanning the entrance to their chamber. He was the sentinel, the guardian, and even in this supposed sanctuary, his instincts remained sharp. Truly produced a small, worn pouch from her satchel. Inside were dried berries, nuts, and a hunk of hard bread, provisions she had carefully gathered, anticipating the need for a prolonged stay in the wilderness. She offered some to Abel, who accepted them with a gentle nudge. He ate slowly, deliberately, his large teeth grinding the food with an almost comical delicacy. "They won't find us here, Abel," Truly whispered, her voice laced with a mixture of hope and uncertainty. "Not easily, anyway. The terrain is too difficult, and these caves... they're a maze even for me. But hunters know the mountains. They know how to track." She shuddered, the thought of the townspeople with their cunning, relentless pursuit, a cold knot in her stomach. They were men who harbored deep-seated malice, and their hatred for Abel, and by extension, for her, was a potent fuel. Abel let out a low growl, a sound of pure, unadulterated protection. He shifted closer, his warmth a tangible shield against the chill of the cave. He understood the threat the men posed, not just as hunters, but as perceived protectors. And he knew, with an absolute certainty, that Truly's continued safety was paramount.

Days blurred into a cycle of cautious movement and watchful stillness. Truly would venture out periodically, always under the cover of deepest night or the thickest fog, to scout their surroundings, to check for any signs of pursuit. She moved like a phantom, her knowledge of the wilderness her shield, her senses her guide. She knew which plants were edible, which streams flowed with the purest water, and how to move without leaving a trace. She would often leave Abel with a small, carved bird, a silent promise of her return. He would remain in the caves, a hidden beast of burden, his presence a secret that only she could keep.

During these solitary excursions, Truly felt a profound sense of connection to the wild. The village, with its clamor and its judgment, seemed a distant, alien world. Here, in the embrace of the ancient woods, she felt a sense of belonging, of peace. The rustling leaves whispered secrets, the flowing streams sang ancient songs, and the silent majesty of the mountains offered solace. She was no longer merely a young woman running from a threat; she was a part of something larger, something ancient and enduring.

Abel, left to his own devices in the labyrinthine caves, found a strange sort of comfort in the isolation. The darkness was not a void, but a familiar embrace. He could hear the subtle symphony of the earth, the drip of water, the scuttling of unseen insects, the low hum of the planet's energy. He was an outsider in the human world, a creature of myth and misunderstanding, but here, in the deep wilderness, he was simply a being of instinct and power, a part of the natural order. He would often lie by the cave entrance, his senses attuned to the slightest tremor in the earth, the faintest disturbance in the air, always vigilant, always waiting for Truly's return. He would watch the slivers of moonlight paint shifting patterns on the cave floor, and in those moments, he would recall the warmth of Truly's hand on his fur, the quiet trust in her eyes, and he would know that this was where he belonged, protecting her, and through her, protecting the fragile truth they both held dear.

The hours spent in the caves were not merely a waiting game; they were a period of reflection for Truly. She thought of her grandfather, of his stories of the wilderness, of his deep respect for the natural world and the creatures that inhabited it. He had taught her to observe, to listen, to understand the intricate balance of life. He had also taught her about courage, about standing up for what was right, even when it was difficult. The towns pursuit was a direct challenge to everything her grandfather had stood for, a betrayal of the harmony he had so cherished. One evening, as Truly returned from a scouting mission, her face grim, Abel sensed a shift in her demeanor. She approached him, her usual steady gait faltering, her eyes troubled. "They're getting closer, Abel," she said, her voice tight. "I saw signs... men, dogs. They're systematic. They won't stop until they find us." She sank down beside him, her breath coming in ragged gasps. "We can't stay here forever."

Abel nudged her hand, a low, comforting rumble in his chest. He could feel her fear, the weight of responsibility that bore down on her small shoulders. But he also sensed her resolve, the unyielding spirit that Silas had underestimated. He licked her hand, a gesture of pure, unadulterated devotion. "I know," Truly whispered, leaning her forehead against his warm fur. "I know you'll protect me. But we need a plan. A better plan than just hiding." She pulled away, her eyes gaining a spark of their former fire. "There are places deeper still, Abel. Places that are truly untouched. Places where even the hunters trained eyes might falter."

She began to sketch in the dirt with a stick, her brow furrowed in concentration. "There's a ridge, known as the Devils Backbone. It's treacherous, barely passable. And beyond that, there's a valley that's been isolated for centuries. Legends say it's a place where time itself slows down, protected by its own natural magic." She looked at him, her gaze earnest. "It's a long shot, I know. But it might be our only chance." Abel watched her, his large eyes filled with unwavering trust. He had followed her into the heart of this wilderness, and he would follow her to the ends of the earth if need be. Her determination was his anchor, her courage his inspiration. He let out a soft huff, a silent agreement. Wherever Truly went, he would go.

The journey to the Devil's Backbone was the most arduous yet. The terrain grew steeper, the paths narrower, and the vegetation denser. Truly moved with a renewed urgency, her senses heightened, her awareness of their pursuers a constant, gnawing presence. Abel, though still immensely powerful, had to tread with extreme caution, his immense weight a liability on the crumbling edges of precipices. Truly would often scout ahead, clearing pathways, testing the sturdiness of roots and rocks before signaling for him to follow.

They climbed through ancient forests where trees, impossibly tall and draped in moss, formed an almost impenetrable ceiling. The air grew thinner, cooler, and the sounds of the forest began to change, replaced by the mournful cry of the wind and the distant, echoing calls of unseen birds of prey. Truly's knowledge of the mountains was their lifeline, guiding them through a labyrinth of sheer drops and narrow ledges. One particularly challenging ascent involved a sheer rock face, its surface slick with a fine mist that seemed to emanate from the very stone. Truly, with surprising agility, scaled it using a series of almost invisible handholds and precarious footholds. Abel watched, his massive limbs scrabbling for purchase on the less sheer sections, his powerful muscles straining. He knew Truly wouldn't leave him, that she would find a way. And she did. She called down instructions, pointing out larger fissures, guiding his powerful frame with her voice, her unwavering confidence a tangible force that bolstered his own.

When they finally crested the Devil's Backbone, the view was breath-taking, and terrifying. Below them stretched a vast, uncharted valley, shrouded in a perpetual mist that softened its edges and gave it an almost otherworldly appearance. The slopes leading down were steep, covered in a dense, untamed growth of ancient ferns and gnarled, twisted trees. It was a place that seemed to have been forgotten by time, a true wilderness. "This is it," Truly whispered, her voice filled with awe and a touch of trepidation. "The Valley. My grandfather told me stories about this place. He said it was protected, a sanctuary from the outside world." She looked at Abel, her eyes shining with a mixture of hope and determination. "We'll be safe here, Abel. For a while, at least. They won't follow us down there."

The descent was slow and painstaking. They moved as a single unit, Truly leading the way, her small form a beacon of unwavering courage, Abel following close behind, his presence a powerful assurance. The mist swirled around them, dampening sounds, muffling their movements, creating an ethereal cloak that seemed to swallow them whole. The air grew heavy, laden with the scent of unknown blossoms and the rich, earthy perfume of a world undisturbed. It was a sanctuary unlike any they had known, a place where the wild held sway, and where, for the first time in a long time, a fragile sense of peace began to settle upon Truly. Abel, sensing the shift, let out a soft sigh, the rumble in his chest a deep, contented sound. They had found their haven, deep within the untamed heart of the Ozarks.

The mist that clung to the Valley like a shroud seemed to hold a particular quietude, a muffling balm to the raw edges of their flight. Truly sank down onto a bed of impossibly soft moss, the dampness seeping through her worn trousers, a welcome sensation against her overheated skin. The frantic pounding of her heart had begun to subside, replaced by a dull ache of exhaustion that settled deep in her bones. Beside her, Abel settled with a soft groan, his massive body a solid, comforting anchor in the alien landscape. The sheer, unrelenting pressure of being hunted, the constant awareness of the villages shadow, had finally receded, leaving a vast, unsettling stillness in its wake.

She looked at Abel, truly looked at him, in the muted, diffused light of the valley. His fur, usually a rich, dark hue, seemed to absorb the dimness, making him appear even more formidable, more ancient. His great head was lowered, his intelligent eyes, dark and deep as forest pools, fixed on her. There was no need for words. In that shared gaze, Truly saw a mirrored understanding, a profound acknowledgment of the journey they had undertaken. The adrenaline, the sheer force of will that had propelled them through treacherous terrain and relentless pursuit, had finally ebbed, leaving behind a quiet melancholy, a somber realization of the cost of their sanctuary.

"We made it," Truly whispered, the words barely disturbing the pervasive hush. She reached out, her hand trembling slightly, and rested it on Abel's enormous, calloused palm. His fur was thick and coarse, a familiar texture that usually brought her immediate comfort. Today, however, there was a new resonance to his touch, a palpable sense of shared hardship, of trials overcome. His skin, beneath the thick fur, felt warm, alive, and incredibly steady. She traced the prominent veins that ran beneath the surface, each one a testament to the strength that had carried them here, that had protected her when her own strength faltered. His fingers, thick as tree branches, instinctively closed around hers, a gentle, possessive grip that spoke volumes of his unwavering devotion. It was a bond forged in the fires of fear and desperation, tempered by shared resilience, and now, in this secluded valley, it felt as immutable as the ancient mountains surrounding them.

He rumbled, a low vibration that resonated through their clasped hands and up Truly's arm, a sound of reassurance that seemed to carry the weight of all the unspoken fears and anxieties they had both endured. It was a sound that said,

We are together. We are safe. For now. Truly squeezed his hand, a silent response, her gaze drifting over his broad, powerful shoulders, the sheer physicality of his form a stark contrast to her own slender frame. He was a creature of immense power, a being designed for the wild, and yet, he had chosen to stand by her, a fragile human, against forces that sought to exploit and destroy him. The sacrifices, she knew, had been immense. He had given up the relative peace of his solitary existence, his hidden life, to become a fugitive, a target, all for her. And she, in turn, had left behind any semblance of normalcy, the familiar comfort of her home, the quiet routines of her life, to embark on this perilous path. The weight of those choices settled upon her, heavy and profound.

"It wasn't easy, was it?" she murmured, her voice thick with unshed tears, her thumb stroking the rough skin of his hand. She remembered the desperate scramble up the sheer rock face, Abel's powerful muscles straining, his immense weight a terrifying liability on the crumbling ledge. She recalled her own terror, the dizzying height, the gnawing fear of falling, and the even greater fear of him falling with her. But his trust in her, her calm instructions, had carried them both through. And the sheer force of his presence had been a constant, unwavering bulwark against the encroaching despair. He had followed her, blind faith in his large, dark eyes, through the labyrinthine caves, through the dense, whispering forests, through the treacherous ascent of the Devil's Backbone. He had been her shadow, her protector, her silent guardian.

Abel nudged her hand with his snout, a gentle, insistent pressure that drew her attention back to him. His eyes held a depth of understanding that went beyond mere comprehension. He had felt the terror, the desperation, the sheer physical strain as acutely as she had. He had felt the sting of the townsmen pursuit, the acrid scent of their fear and their hatred. Yet, he had never faltered. His loyalty was an instinct, a primal force as deeply ingrained as his need to hunt or to protect his territory. But with Truly, it had become something more, something honed by shared experience, by a mutual respect that transcended their disparate natures. He knew the fear that had gripped her, the gnawing doubt that must have plagued her in the darkest hours of their flight. And he also knew the unyielding strength that lay beneath her surface vulnerability.

"You didn't have to," Truly continued, her voice barely audible. "You could have... stayed hidden. Gone your own way. But you stayed. You fought for me." She swallowed, the lump in her throat making it difficult to speak. "I owe you everything." The words felt inadequate, a pale imitation of the gratitude that surged through her. She felt a profound, almost overwhelming sense of responsibility for his current predicament, for the life he was now living, a life of constant vigilance and fear, all because of her.

He made a soft, guttural sound, a low rumble that seemed to vibrate through the very earth beneath them. He shifted his weight, bringing his massive head closer, and nudged her shoulder, a gesture of comfort that was both simple and profound. His fur was warm against her cheek, and for a moment, Truly closed her eyes, leaning into his presence, drawing strength from the sheer, unwavering solidity of him. He was more than just a creature of immense power; he was her confidante, her protector, the silent witness to her journey. He was the one being in the world who saw her not as a pawn or a prize, but as an equal, a partner in their shared struggle.

"I've been thinking," Truly said, her voice regaining a measure of its usual clarity, though still tinged with weariness. She looked at Abel, her eyes seeking his understanding. "And you, Abel... you represent everything Silas feared. You're wild, untamed, and you possess a strength that he can't comprehend, let alone replicate." Abel remained still, his gaze steady, his keen senses taking in the sounds and smells of their new surroundings. He understood the nature of fear, the corrosive power it held. He had seen it in the eyes of the villagers, in the frantic movements of the men who had sought to hunt him. Silas's fear, however, was different. It was a cold, calculated thing, born not of immediate danger, but of a profound insecurity. He craved dominance, and Abel, with his innate power and his connection to the wild, was a living embodiment of everything that threatened Silas's carefully constructed world. She met his gaze, her own eyes filled with a quiet resolve. "We may have lost much, Abel, but we haven't lost ourselves. We haven't lost what makes us... us." She tightened her grip on his hand, feeling the steady thrum of his pulse beneath her fingers. "This sanctuary, it's not just a place. It's a testament to our refusal to be broken."

He responded with a low, resonant sigh, the sound carrying a profound sense of acceptance. He nudged her again, a gentle insistence, and Truly understood. The past was a weight they carried, a shadow that followed them, but their present, their shared existence in this secluded valley, was a breath of fresh air, a moment of respite. They were not simply fugitives anymore; they were survivors, standing together against the encroaching darkness. The sacrifices had been great, the cost immeasurable, but in the quiet strength of Abel's presence, in the unwavering bond that now held them inextricably linked, Truly found a solace that transcended any loss. They had found their sanctuary, not just in the physical isolation of the Whispering Valley, but in each other. The reflection in Abel's dark eyes was not just of the chase, but of a future, uncertain and perilous, yet one they would face, side by side.

The air in the Valley had become a familiar embrace, no longer solely the scent of damp earth and ancient moss, but the very breath of their new existence. Truly found herself breathing deeper, her lungs filling with the wild perfume of their sanctuary. It was a life irrevocably intertwined with Abel's, a delicate dance between the human and the wild, a rhythm she was slowly, but surely, learning to follow. The uncertainty that had once gnawed at her, a constant companion to their flight, had not vanished, but it had softened, morphing into a quiet acceptance. Their future, a path forged in secrecy and mutual reliance, stretched out before them, not as a vast, intimidating emptiness, but as a territory to be explored, understood, and, in their own way, protected.

Abel, his presence a constant, grounding force beside her, was the compass by which she navigated this new world. His movements, once a source of awe and a little fear, were now a language she was beginning to decipher. The flick of his ears, the subtle shift of his weight, the low rumble that emanated from his chest – all spoke volumes, conveying warnings, insights, and a profound connection to the environment that cradled them. He was no longer just her protector, but her teacher, his ancient wisdom a vast reservoir from which she drew her understanding of the wilderness. He taught her the names of the herbs that healed, the roots that sustained, and the subtle signs that foretold the changing moods of the forest. He showed her how to read the sky, to anticipate the rain, and to find shelter before the storm broke.

Their days were woven with threads of necessity and discovery. Mornings began with the soft light filtering through the canopy, a gentle awakening that banished the lingering shadows of their former lives. Abel would often lead Truly to a hidden stream, its water so pure it tasted of melted snow and starlight. There, he would patiently demonstrate how to coax sustenance from the earth, the plumpness of certain berries, the starchy heart of specific roots, the delicate art of setting simple snares for small game. Truly, though initially clumsy, found a surprising aptitude for these tasks. Her hands, once accustomed to turning the delicate pages of ancient texts, now learned to gather, to prepare, and to respect the offerings of the forest.

It was a life of stark contrasts. The beauty of a dew-kissed spiderweb, spun between ancient branches, existed alongside the raw reality of Abel's hunt, a swift, decisive act that provided their evening meal. There were moments of profound peace, sitting by their carefully concealed fire, the flames dancing like captured stars, sharing the silence with Abel, a silence that was not empty but brimming with unspoken understanding. And then there were the moments of acute awareness, the heightened senses that Truly had cultivated, her ears straining for the faintest snap of a twig, her eyes scanning the perimeter for any sign of intrusion.

The isolation was profound, a ocean of solitude that stretched in every direction. They were a world unto themselves, their existence hidden from the bustling villages, the fortified towns, and the grasping influence of Silas. This separation, while a necessary shield, also brought a quiet ache. Truly missed the simple camaraderie of shared meals, the comfort of a familiar face, the easy laughter that had once punctuated her days. But these were sacrifices she had willingly embraced, traded for the freedom to live authentically, to stand by Abel's side, unwavering.

Their bond, she realized, was more than just friendship or loyalty. It was a pact, an unspoken agreement forged in the crucible of shared adversity. Abel had saved her life, and she, in turn, had offered him sanctuary, a haven from a world that would hunt him to extinction. This mutual dependence had blossomed into a profound connection, a love that defied the boundaries of species and the fear that permeated the human world. It was a love that was patient, understanding, and fiercely protective, a silent legend whispered on the wind, a testament to their enduring friendship.

Truly began to see herself not just as a fugitive, but as a guardian. Alongside Abel, she was becoming a protector of the wild, a silent sentinel in the Whispering Valley. They were not merely surviving; they were living in harmony with the wilderness, their presence a subtle but significant force. Abel, with his innate understanding of the forest's delicate balance, guided their actions. They never overhunted, never took more than they needed, always leaving a respectful offering to the spirit of the wild. Truly, armed with her newfound knowledge and an innate sense of empathy, became the voice of caution, ensuring their actions did not disrupt the natural order.

One evening, as they sat near a moonlit clearing, Abel nudged a cluster of luminous fungi with his snout. He then looked at Truly, his dark eyes conveying a clear message: these were not for consumption, but for a different purpose. He led her deeper into the woods, to a gnarled, ancient oak, its branches reaching towards the heavens like supplicating arms. There, he showed her how to collect the spores of the luminous fungi, a task requiring a delicate touch and absolute precision. Truly understood. These were not for their sustenance, but for the forest itself, their soft glow a balm to the shadows, a beacon for nocturnal creatures. "We are not just living here, are we, Abel?" Truly murmured, her voice soft, reverent. "We are... part of it. We are tending to it."

Abel let out a low chuff, a sound of deep contentment. He nudged her hand, his rough tongue briefly touching her skin, a gesture of affection that always sent a warmth through her. He understood that their role extended beyond mere survival. They were becoming woven into the fabric of the Whispering Valley, their lives intertwined with its growth, its seasons, its very essence.

The hardship was undeniable. There were days when the rain seemed to fall without end, chilling them to the bone and making the simplest tasks a struggle. There were nights when the sounds of the forest, magnified by the darkness, could be unnerving, the cries of unseen predators a stark reminder of their vulnerability. Truly sometimes found herself dreaming of warm hearths and soft beds, of the easy comforts she had so readily abandoned. But these dreams were fleeting, quickly dispelled by the stark reality of their shared existence, a reality that, despite its challenges, held a beauty and a purpose all its own.

She learned to embrace the discomfort, to find resilience in the face of adversity. The calluses on her hands were a badge of honor, a testament to her growing strength. The keenness of her senses, once a source of anxiety, now felt like a gift, allowing her to perceive the subtle nuances of their environment. She discovered a deep well of inner fortitude she never knew she possessed, a strength born not of brute force, but of quiet determination and an unwavering commitment to their shared path.

One day, while exploring a less-traveled part of the valley, they stumbled upon a hidden waterfall, its cascade a curtain of silver against the verdant rock face. Behind the shimmering veil of water, Truly discovered a small, secluded cave, its entrance almost completely concealed by moss and ferns. It was dry, sheltered, and offered a new level of privacy, a place where they could truly be unseen. Abel seemed to approve, his tail giving a slow, deliberate sweep as he surveyed the small cavern. "This is good," Truly said, her voice echoing slightly in the enclosed space. "A new sanctuary within our sanctuary. A place to... regroup, when we need it."

Abel dipped his head in agreement. He then nudged a collection of smooth, dark stones towards her. Truly recognized them; they were often found near sources of potent, earthbound magic. He was showing her something more, a deeper connection to the land they protected. He conveyed, through a series of gestures and low vocalizations, that these stones held a unique resonance, a subtle energy that could be amplified when placed together in a specific pattern. He demonstrated the pattern, his massive paws moving with surprising dexterity, arranging the stones in a swirling, intricate design on the cave floor.

As he completed the arrangement, a faint hum began to emanate from the stones, a soft vibration that Truly could feel in her very bones. The air in the cave seemed to shimmer, growing warmer and more potent. It wasn't a tangible magic, not the flashy displays of power seen in tales of sorcery, but a deeper, more primal energy, a connection to the very life force of the valley. Abel looked at her, his gaze steady, conveying a sense of ancient knowledge, of secrets held within the earth. "You are showing me the heart of this place," Truly whispered, awestruck. "The energy that sustains it. You are teaching me to feel it, not just to see it." This discovery marked a turning point in her understanding. They were not just guardians of a physical space; they were becoming caretakers of its energetic essence. Abel, with his innate connection to the natural world, was the conduit, and Truly, through her growing attunement and willingness to learn, was becoming a co-conspirator in this sacred stewardship.

As the seasons turned, Truly's understanding of Abel deepened. She learned the subtle nuances of his moods, the quiet expressions of his joy, the rare moments of melancholy that would pass across his noble features. He, in turn, continued to guide her, to protect her, and to love her with a devotion that transcended any earthly barrier. Their shared silence became a language of its own, a comfortable communion that needed no words.

The legend of the girl who ran with the beast was a story for the human world, a cautionary tale spun from fear and ignorance. But in the Valley, they were not a legend, but a reality. They were Truly and Abel, guardians of a sacred space, their enduring friendship a quiet symphony played out against the backdrop of the ancient forest, a testament to an unwavering love that had found its truest sanctuary. Their future remained unwritten, a path veiled in the mists of the unknown, but they would face it together, two souls united, their bond a silent promise whispered on the wind, a beacon of hope in a world often consumed by darkness.

The relentless pursuit had finally waned, its feverish intensity bleeding out into the vast indifference of the wilderness. The whispers of the manhunt, once a chilling chorus that haunted Truly's every step, now receded, becoming faint echoes against the ancient, stoic silence of the Ozarks. It was a silence that had become their sanctuary, a palpable presence that enveloped them, shielding them from the clamor of a world that had sought to tear them apart. The immediate danger, a shadow that had stretched long and menacing across their lives, had finally receded, leaving behind a fragile peace, a quiet hum of survival that vibrated in the very air they breathed.

In the heart of this wild embrace, their sanctuary was not a place marked on any map, but a shared existence, a profound understanding that had taken root between Truly and Abel. Their extraordinary friendship, once a whispered secret, a clandestine promise exchanged in hushed tones, had unfurled itself like a hardy vine, its tendrils reaching deep, becoming a powerful testament. It spoke of courage in the face of overwhelming odds, of an unwavering loyalty that transcended the boundaries of species, and of the audacious possibility of love blooming in the most barren and unlikely of circumstances. They had walked through the deepest darkness, traversed treacherous landscapes both external and internal, and in doing so, had emerged, not unscathed, but irrevocably transformed. They were forever bound by the heavy weight of the sacrifices they had willingly made, and by the enduring, unshakeable strength of their unique connection. Theirs was a love story, not of grand declarations and whispered vows, but one etched into the very soul of the wild, a saga written in the rustle of leaves, the flow of unseen currents, and the deep, resonant beat of two hearts that had learned to beat as one.

Their shared meals were no longer hurried affairs, snatched in the shadow of constant vigilance. Now, they could savor the bounty of the land, prepared with a newfound respect and understanding. Truly had become adept at foraging, her fingers, once accustomed to the delicate turn of pages, now expertly identifying edible roots, succulent berries, and fragrant herbs. Abel, with his keen senses, would often guide her, nudging a particular cluster of mushrooms with his snout, or indicating the presence of plump, unsuspecting game that had strayed too close to their unseen encampment. There was no cruelty in their sustenance, only necessity, a profound acknowledgment of the cycle of life and death that sustained them both. Truly had witnessed Abel's hunts, and while the raw power of it could still stir a primal tremor within her, it was tempered by an understanding of his grace, his efficiency, and the quiet dignity with which he took a life to preserve their own.

One evening, as they sat by the soft glow of a carefully concealed fire, the flames casting dancing shadows against the ancient trees, Truly found herself reflecting on the journey that had brought them to this precarious peace. The world outside the Whispering Valley, the world of Silas and his insatiable hunger for power, seemed a distant, almost unreal memory. The fear that had once been a constant companion, a cold knot in her stomach, had begun to loosen its grip. It hadn't vanished entirely, for the scars of their past were too deep for that, but it had been transmuted into a healthy caution, a heightened awareness that served them well in their secluded existence. She looked at Abel, his great head resting on his paws, his dark eyes, pools of ancient wisdom, reflecting the firelight. There was a profound sense of calm that emanated from him, a steady presence that grounded her, reminding her that in the vast, untamed wilderness, they were not alone. "Do you ever miss it, Abel?" she asked softly, her voice barely disturbing the tranquil air. "The world before?"

He shifted slightly, his hand giving a slow, deliberate sweep across the mossy ground. He didn't answer in words, of course, but his gaze met hers, and in its depths, she saw a flicker of understanding, a shared acknowledgment of the lives they had left behind, the people they had been. He then nudged a smooth, river-worn stone towards her with his finger. Truly picked it up, its coolness a comforting sensation in her palm. It was a simple gesture, but it spoke volumes. *This is our world now,* it seemed to say. *And it is enough.*

As the sun dipped below the jagged peaks of the Ozarks, casting long, ethereal shadows across the valley, Truly found herself gazing at Abel, his silhouette a majestic testament against the twilight sky. He was more than a companion; he was a part of her. And she, she realized, was a part of him, and a part of this wild, beautiful place they now called home. The manhunt had faded, but their story, the enduring epic of their friendship, their courage, and their extraordinary love, was just beginning, a legend whispered not by fear, but by the very heart of the wild itself. Their sanctuary was not merely a haven from the world, but a testament to the possibility of finding wholeness in another, a story of truth etched into the soul of the wild, a promise of enduring connection against the vast, silent expanse of forever. Their bond, once a fragile seedling nurtured in fear, had grown into a mighty oak, its roots deeply entwined with the earth, its branches reaching towards the heavens, a symbol of their enduring strength and unwavering devotion. The world might never understand, but in the quiet sanctuary of their shared existence, it was all that mattered. They had found their haven, not in a place, but in each other, a story written in the language of loyalty, sacrifice, and the wild, untamed heart of their shared destiny.

BACK MATTER

Sanctuary: In the context of this narrative, "sanctuary" transcends a mere physical location. It represents a state of being, a shared existence built upon trust, mutual protection, and understanding between Truly and Abel, offering refuge not only from external threats but also from the isolation of their pasts.

Valley: A metaphorical and potentially literal secluded area within the Ozarks, characterized by its profound silence and the subtle dissemination of sounds, serving as the primary refuge for Truly and Abel.

Ozarks: A physiographic region in the Central United States, characterized by mountainous terrain, dense forests, and a rich natural environment, forming the expansive and untamed setting for their survival.

ABOUT THE AUTHOR

Retired County Sheriff, Richard Stephens has spent a lifetime serving the people of the communities he lives and works within. Not known for shying away from challenges, Richard has filled numerous roles throughout his thirty-year career in Law Enforcement including Detentions Officer, Shift Supervisor, Patrol, Investigations, Swat commander, Training. Mayor, Program Director, County Sheriff, Consultant, Academy Instructor, and Liaison.

Richard obtained his master's degree in management and leadership in 2012 from Liberty University out of Lynchburg Virginia and has lead teams of men and woman through a wide variety of incidents including: The Columbine High School Shooting aftermath, Multiple natural disasters including floods, Ice storms, and tornados. Additionally, Richard has led multiple major search efforts and managed major crime scenes, Officer involved shooting scenes, critical incident management scenes as well as event and special celebrity event management.

Feeling a deep desire to ensure our men and women wearing the badge receive not only the tools required for carrying out their job effectively but the resources to do so. Richard has spent over twenty-five years instructing groups both large and small. Upon retiring from active enforcement, he has taken on the role of Criminal Justice Liaison within the behavioral health industry. This role has allowed him to introduce the behavioral health industry to the mind of the Law Enforcement Officer and how we work, feel, and derive motivation. While simultaneously ensuring that the resources necessary for ensuring Officer wellness and resiliency are afforded to every officer and first responder.

Richard, desiring to help others tell their story and heal, embarked upon a journey of obtaining a second master's degree. With an emphasis on clinical mental health counseling, Richard remains posed to impact his community, regardless of the situation.

Discovering a love for writing, Richard has not only found purpose in sharing his story as a public servant with others struggling through the battles, they so often face he has also found solace in the process. Authoring multiple books, this vivid storyteller strives to take his readers on a journey of discovery through the pages of his offerings.

www.ingramcontent.com/pod-product-compliance
Lightning Source LLC
Chambersburg PA
CBHW070555120726
47909CB00007B/2345